PENGUIN CRIME FICTION

THE GRAIL TREE

Jonathan Gash's novels include *The Very Last Gambado*, *Jade Woman*, *Moonspender*, *The Tartan Sell*, *Pearlhanger*, and *The Great California Game*. He lives in England.

THE
GRAIL TREE
JONATHAN GASH

PENGUIN BOOKS

PENGUIN BOOKS
Published by the Penguin Group
Penguin Books USA Inc., 375 Hudson Street,
New York, New York 10014, U.S.A.
Penguin Books Ltd, 27 Wrights Lane, London W8 5TZ, England
Penguin Books Australia Ltd, Ringwood,
Victoria, Australia
Penguin Books Canada Ltd, 10 Alcorn Avenue,
Toronto, Ontario, Canada M4V 3B2
Penguin Books (N.Z.) Ltd, 182–190 Wairau Road,
Auckland 10, New Zealand

Penguin Books Ltd, Registered Offices: Harmondsworth,
Middlesex, England

First published in the United States of America by
Harper & Row, Publishers, Inc., 1979
Reprinted by arrangement with Harper & Row, Publishers, Inc.
Published in Penguin Books 1988

3   5   7   9   10   8   6   4   2

LIBRARY OF CONGRESS CATALOGING IN PUBLICATION DATA
Gash, Jonathan.
The Grail tree.
Reprint.   Originally published: New York
Harper & Row, c1979.
I. Title.
PR6057.A728G7   1988   823'.914   87-25719
ISBN 0 14 02.3015 7

Printed in the United States of America
Set in Garamond

I

ntiques, women and survival are my only interests. It sounds simple, but you just try putting them in the right order.

I was in this tent when somebody hissed my name. It was Tinker, unshaven and shabby as ever. Betty dived with a muted shriek behind a trestle table, clutching at her blouse. I couldn't blame her. I'd too thought it was her husband for a second. Tinker wormed his way under the tent flap. I almost went berserk. Trust Tinker to interrupt the one chance Betty and I had, even if it was in the middle of our village's annual fair.

"Can't you leave me alone when I'm—?"

"Quick! Come and see for Gawd's sake!" He looked stupid, his head craned upward in the grass.

"No," I said. "Get out." My heart was thumping. It's typical of Tinker. Always around when you don't want him. I could hear the band and nearby chattering voices outside.

"There's an *antique* out here."

I was just going after Betty again when the magic word cleared the love fog from my mind and made me stop dead. It has to. I'm an antique dealer keen on survival.

"Eh?"

"Antique." Tinker started to wriggle backward, his job done. "One of the kids in the pageant's got it."

"Who was that horrible little tramp?" Betty was ashen. She started tidying herself mechanically.

"Tinker Dill," I said, thinking hard. "My barker. He finds antiques for me." I didn't add that he gets paid a fortune in commissions from every antique I buy or sell. When I'm not broke, that is.

"He won't tell on us, darling?"

I hoped not. Her husband's built like a shire horse.

"No. Er, look, love." I began to edge away.

"But we haven't got long—" She came to me smiling, but I pushed her aside and made for the flap. The huge marquee was full of tables laden with food and jugs of orange. A million villagers would descend on it at four o'clock and clear the lot. Betty was in charge of the arrangements. Hence the solitude, if a love tryst in a cathedral-sized tent in the middle of a village pageant can be called solitude.

"You're not *going?*" She pulled at my arm, angry and disbelieving.

"Let go." I got enough of the flap undone.

"Of all the—" Betty tried a furious swipe at my head, but I clouted her before her hand landed. She tumbled over a table and a trifle splashed nastily.

"See you Friday?" I thought she'd be pleased at that, but it only seemed to make her more mad.

"You swine! I'll—" She recovered and came for me again, but I was through the flap and off. Safe and sound among the strolling hundreds, nodding and smiling as I went.

Sometimes women really nark me. No sense of priorities. Ever noticed that?

Things hadn't been too good for me recently. Antiques tend to come in droves or not at all. The few I'd seen lately were either rubbish or so highly priced it was heartbreaking. One gem had lit my life for an instant, a luscious porcelain Ting bowl from Hopei Province, about A.D. 1150. Some maniac had removed the bronze rim, but the dazzling magnolia ivory color had moved me to tears when I saw it. A friend of mine, Michelle, had bought cleverly at one of the local auction sales. She deals mostly in furniture and natural history prints and wanted the earth for the bowl. We're supposed to be close, but you can't help hating somebody who has what you want, can you? You'll have guessed by now I'm a full-time dedicated antique dealer. Don't get annoyed just because I make money out of lovely things. I admit dealers are mostly wanderers, lustful, greedy, savage, crude and vulgar. In fact, just like you. The difference is that I'll bet I'm a lot more honest about me than you are about you. And if you don't believe me, you're a bigger rogue than I am. Where was I?

"Lovejoy." A shout among the crowd. Tinker was waving across the field near the medieval pageant. I started over through the press of people. I'm owner of Lovejoy Antiques, Inc. In fact I'm the firm as well, the sole proprietor and its one miraculous asset. I add the "Inc." bit to make me sound a bit more like a huge American firm than otherwise might seem the case. Anything to help with the thousand-year mortgage on my cottage.

Pushing between rows of open-air stalls on our village's fete days is like running the gauntlet. I'd only got a yard before a gushing voice cooed out.

"Lovejoy! You *naughty* man!" The vicar's wife playfully wagged a finger at me from the bottle stall. "I've caught you at it! Red-handed!"

"Eh? Er . . ." I dithered. Mrs. Woking's a nice old dear in tweeds.

"Scrumping those cream cakes before teatime!" she trilled.

"Oh. Well . . ." I broke into a sweat of relief. Of course. The nosh was crammed into Betty's marquee. The old dear thought I'd been after her meringues. Some hopes. I've still got my own teeth.

"Such an *appetite!*" The ladies with her tittered. Women love appetites, any old appetites.

3

"I thought nobody noticed." I shrugged with mock resignation.

"You're becoming known for it, Lovejoy." Jean Evans gazed innocently at me as she put the barb in. Our village schoolmistress, addicted to young gentry with fast cars. She was running the bingo today. Nine hundred people here, and it was just my luck for her to be nice and handy. I grinned weakly and pushed on toward the silver band. I'd have to sort Jean Evans out sooner or later. Too cool by far. I hurried on. You can't help becoming excited at the sniff of an antique.

A good crowd had turned up at the pageant. Constable Jilks was in his element at the gate, flagging down the occasional car and pointing the way in to families walking over from our one crossroads.

"Hey, George," I called as I trotted past. "They all know the way to the village green. It's not shifted for three thousand years."

His pompous smile faded as he blotted under his helmet. "What are *you* doing here, Lovejoy?" he asked suspiciously.

That left me the choice of admitting I'd come to snog with his dahlia-growing friend's wife or telling a lie. I settled instantly for falsehood, the way one does.

"Just enjoying the fresh country smog, George." I gave him my blandest beam and left him to his useless job. Why people are so suspicious of me I honestly don't know.

"Here, Lovejoy." Tinker was hopping about eagerly by the display field. People along the ropes had left a space around him, perhaps because he stinks of stale beer. He's not really completely horrible, as barkers go. But he usually looks disheveled and half-sloshed, partly because he is and partly because of his tatty greatcoat. He's not taken it off since he was demobbed, and he goes around shod in old pit-clogs. Somebody once grafted him into worn corduroy trousers and there he's stayed. I suppose the fashion might come back.

"You're always after the birds, Lovejoy," he criticized piously.

"I was only helping her," I said lamely. "Where is it?"

"Aye," he said, disbelieving old clown. Not even my own

4

barker believes me. No trust these days. "See that little kid dressed like Caesar?"

Tinker meant a little blond lad in tin. The Romans had dusted our local Iceni tribesmen over as soon as the pageant opened. They were now changing noisily behind the plywood castle façade while our band played manfully on and parents and teachers ran about rounding up stray infants. Bunting and flags, banners and coats of arms were everywhere. It was bedlam. What the hell we do it for God alone knows. I'd been knackered from helping Jean's assorted nine-year-old psychopaths build a chariot in her school. I'd been really proud of it. It took me three days. Then they'd ridden it into the Boadicea scene for a couple of seconds and that was it. You can't help getting peeved. I'd have the bloody blisters for months. I tell you, never again.

"Behind him, Lovejoy." Tinker had more sense than to point.

"The two serfs?"

"Between them." Two little servants were carrying a long wooden board with something on it. Rising on tiptoe didn't help me see. I glanced at a neighbor's program. They were probably up to King Arthur. A score of children, suddenly pious, were in procession across the grass toward a cardboard Camelot. Our village band played a noble march slightly out of gear. They'd be sloshed by half time. They'd already got through a fortifying crate of brown ale. The tin lad clanked inexpertly past, followed by a straggle of attenders.

"See the sword, Lovejoy?" I edged away from the acrid fumes of Tinker's alcoholic breath and gazed.

The child was struggling, but he managed to lift it above his head. A fanfare sounded. A dozen tinfoil knights on Shetland ponies trotted out of the painted castle's doors to welcome the new king. Applause rippled round. Suddenly I couldn't move. My breath froze and the world halted on its axis.

"Yes," I croaked.

"Lovejoy." Tinker was holding me back. I'd inadvertently started to climb the rope onto the field. I guessed Norman or late English. I broke into a sweat. A real find.

"Come on, Tinker." I backed out of the press of spectators.

"Is it genuine, Lovejoy?" He trotted beside me as I started round toward the changing areas.

"Maybe."

"Where'd the little basket get it?" The eternal wail of the barker.

"Where does anybody get anything?" I said—the eternal wail of the antique dealer.

You can't help being bitter. Any collector will tell you why. You can spend your life searching for a particular antique and never get within a light-year of the bloody thing. Then somebody will fall over it. Or buy it for a quid in a junk shop. Or decide to replace an old mantelpiece, and it's eureka for somebody all over again. Like the South London lad who broke his drum and found its parchment skin was the lost priceless medieval manuscript deeds to a ruined abbey's entire lands. And the massive priceless fourth-century silver treasure from that innocent-looking field in Mildenhall.

It happens a lot hereabouts. To everyone else, that is. It really hurts.

In the past five years I've seen valuable flintlock dueling pistols in old beam crannies. I've seen a Celtic gold torque hoed up by a farm laborer and brought in as a funny old bent horseshoe. I've seen a collector's Venetian veneered cabinet used as a mechanic's tool bench in a garage. I've seen an early Chinese black-ink jade cup used for tiddlywinks. And a beautifully preserved genuine 1751 Chelsea dish stuck under a penny plant pot out in a garden. It breaks your heart. Precious finds happen daily—to damned near everybody but me.

I tried not to run, Tinker Dill shambling alongside. The end of the green was roped off. A wooden scaffolding held a line of rickety façades in place. Various porchways were labeled to show where each group of children was to enter. Needless to say, many bits had blown off or been pinched by the little fiends.

"What are you doing here, Lovejoy?" That's all people ever say to me, I thought furiously.

"Get back to your bingo," I replied without looking at Jean. "I've as much right on the village green as everybody else. I've

6

got blisters to prove it." That was a mean one.

"Shouldn't you be back in the tea tent?" she said sweetly, shooing a cluster of wandering Druids back.

"That big sword." I couldn't be sidetracked, not so near a precious find. "Whose is it?"

"Why not ask Betty Marsham?" That sugary voice again. "Perhaps she can . . . satisfy you."

I gave her the bent eye and waited.

"Well," she said defiantly. There was a pause while Cromwell and a little squad of Ironsides clanked tinnily past on ponies. Now two tiny Anglo-Saxons had got among the Druids.

"Are these in any sort of order?" I couldn't help asking. The milling children were giving me a headache. Jean laughed and shook her head.

"Supposed to be," she said a bit helplessly. "Actually, you'll have to see Mrs. Cookson. She brought the sword." She stared about. "Over there. Flowered hat."

I glanced from the plump elderly lady to Tinker Dill and back. The cultural shock would be too great for one of them. I gave Tinker a note.

"Meet me in the pub, Tinker," I told him.

"Ta, Lovejoy." He burned off through the crowd.

The Arthurian children were already streaming out one of the gaps to scattered applause. I tried to cut past. King Arthur was flushed with triumph at having got his duty over with. He and one of his serfs were lugging the luscious sword along, trailing it on the grass because of its weight. Jean found time to shoot a venomous glance in my direction, but what had I done? I'd only been supporting her pageant in my own little way.

I reached the plump woman. "Excuse me, please."

"Yes?" She was pleasant, smiling, wide-eyed. "Are you with the morris dancers?"

I repressed a shudder at the thought of all that energy. "Well, not exactly." I drew breath. "My name's Lovejoy. I, er, helped Miss Evans with the chariot. It's the sword."

A curious gleam of amusement flared for a split second. Then, oddly, when she spoke again it had gone and she was calmly

7

shepherding children into the right pens. Some private joke, no doubt. "Oh. Are you interested?" she said absently. Her accent was faintly transatlantic. "It's very rare, I believe. Early English."

"Is it yours?"

"A friend's," she explained. "Do examine it, if you wish." King Arthur and his mob arrived. I practically fell on the sword, as politely as I could. The children thronged about explaining and accusing what they'd done right or wrong. I gently brushed aside the two serfs and laid it reverently down on the grass. I could hardly breathe at first. Then I calmed and rose.

"Yes, well." I stretched and cleared my throat, trying not to let my disappointment show.

"I don't suppose you've seen another antique like it?"

"No." I couldn't bring myself to tell Mrs. Cookson outright it was a forgery. A clever one, but a forgery. I fumed inwardly. There's only one really good metalwork forgery artist in our area. Bannon. I've a standing agreement with him to show me everything he makes before selling it. I decided to pop across and cripple him, in the interests of fair play.

"You don't sound very enthusiastic." The gleam in her eye was one of genuine interest now.

"Er, no." I moved off. There were signs Napoleon was on the move. I hadn't time to get conscripted into the Peninsular War.

"Wait a moment, please," she called after me, but I was off.

I'd brought my car, a tiny derelict Austin Ruby. A black packing case with an engine. It stood near the hedge ready for a fast getaway. I only found it because I'd remembered where I'd left it in the tall grass. It no longer had its pram top. Open air. I switched its ignition and stirred the insides vigorously with the handle. It'd win nothing at Silverstone, but it will see the century out.

"I'll give you a lift, Lovejoy." That familiar voice, so dear to all our hearts. He was sitting on one of the trestle tables. Two admiring women fawned nearby. The only person alive to wear an astrakhan coat on a bright summer's day, the goon.

"Get stuffed, Honkie." Honkworth's as gruesome as his name. He's another antique dealer, Edwardian furniture, late

8

Georgian domestic silver and ignorant. Like most antique dealers Honkie couldn't tell the Wartski collection of Fabergé jewels from frogspawn.

"You can put your toy car in my boot," he said cheerfully enough to give offence. He has a shop in Clacton for tourists. Some people you can trust. Some, like Honkie, you daren't even ask the time.

My engine fired. I dashed round and flung myself behind the wheel.

"This is ground control," Honkie boomed into cupped hands. "We have lift-off." His adorers laughed adoringly. I clattered the Ruby across the grass and out onto the road. Tinker Dill waved from the beer tent as I passed. He hadn't even made it to the White Hart. I could understand that. It's almost two hundred yards further on, and heat's so tiring.

Bannon was in his forge whistling happily until I pinned him by the throat.

"Now, Bannon," I said. "This sword."

"For God's sake, Lovejoy."

I stood off and let him rub his neck. His forge's furnace was fading because of our scuffle. I'd kicked the foot bellows aside to reach him faster.

Blacksmiths are on the way back. Bannon does fancy metalwork now for East Anglia in general and the odd forgery for me —er, I mean for some unscrupulous local antique dealers. Once he actually used to shoe horses. Now he couldn't tell Hyperion from a double bass. I examined the scrap of metal cold on the anvil.

"A Victorian interior balustrade decoration?"

"Torch holder." He coughed. "What the hell's up, Lovejoy? I ain't done nothink." He's a migrant Cockney.

"You've made a forgery of a late Saxon long sword, lad," I explained gently. "And before I break your two index fingers, explain why you didn't tell me."

"Long sword?" He seemed honestly puzzled. Scared but genuine. "I never."

9

"Bannon," I said warningly. He tried to back through the wall.

"Honest, Lovejoy," he said desperately. "I don't know *how* to forge till you draw the bloody things for me and tell me what to do, do I?"

"Tea for you and Lovejoy?" his wife called cheerily from nearby. He lives in a cottage next to the forge.

"Yes, please, Mrs. Bannon," I called back merrily, a real bit of Merrie England.

"Two minutes then," she trilled.

"I can prove it," Bannon urged in a low frantic voice, still keeping out of reach. "Just ask whoever has it."

I paused. He had a point. "Fair enough, Bannon. Know of any others besides yourself?"

"None any good." He thought a bit more. "That Southend geezer two years ago." He'd been clinked by the magistrates and was still doing porridge. No remission. Served him right. He'd used Britannia metal of 1897 vintage to solder a forgery of an eighteenth-century Florentine small sword. Forgers have to be really professional expert craftsmen or pay the penalty, so it served the Southend goon right. I'm all for upholding law and order, I told myself piously. I'd have to find out from Mrs. Cookson. She'd said a friend owned it.

I stepped away, nodding. "See you, Bannon."

"See you, Lovejoy," he called thankfully.

"Tell your missus I had an emergency."

Luckily the Ruby's engine hadn't cut. I clattered around the pond in an erratic circle and headed for the pub half a mile away. The wind was behind me so I'd make it before dark. It's all downhill. Two kids overtook me on their bikes, pedaling and jeering like mad. If I'd had the power I'd have caught them up and given them a thick ear.

So there was another expert forger living locally. But who the hell was he and why hadn't I heard of him? I was extremely peeved. The antique game is difficult enough. If he was useless, like so many forgers of antiques, it wouldn't have mattered. But

I'd seen the sword. It was good—too good by far.

The pub was crammed. I signaled ahead and Ted the barman waved acknowledgment. The crowd was mainly refugees from the pageant's shambles, plus the usual sprinkling of antique dealers. Saturday evening is assembly night. We gather in pubs all over England and lie about how great things are in the antique business. The knack is to sob silently into your drink while spreading an impression of having urgent business with a millionaire collector you've left waiting on your doorstep. It's not an easy impression to create.

Tinker was with a group of barkers near the fireplace chatting lightheartedly of happier and cheaper times, the way they do. During the fight through the saloon I had a word with Angela, a tiny flirtatious piece full of ceramics and pre-Victorian tapestries. She'd married a local landowner a year ago and ran her antique business on the proceeds of hubby's colossal income. Every little helps, I always say.

"Bill's got a de Wint watercolor," she told me.

"He says," I shot back.

"And you still owe me for that Keppel."

Today's tip: buy the best-condition first editions of the early scientific geographers you can lay hands on. Like Keppel, Cook, Darwin. Don't delay or you'll be sobbing into your beer too. My great fault is I don't let a little thing like my abject poverty get in the way of buying. It's a handicap. It's also why I'm always in debt, mainly to people like Angela.

"Ah," I said. "Er, will tomorrow do?"

"We might come to some arrangement," Angela said, looking cool and straight at me. My eyes wavered first. You never know exactly what women mean, do you?

"I'll bring the money round," I promised.

"Do," she said precisely. "Fancy a set of Windsor wheelbacks?" She was with John Laxton, her barker. He's a senile sour-faced rum drinker with a flair for porcelain. Not as good as Tinker Dill at sniffing antiques out but more knowledgeable.

"Thanks, love," I said. "But my warehouse is full."

There was laughter at that. Ownership of a huge warehouse

is the antique dealer's favorite myth. Saying it's full is our slang for being broke.

"Tinker." I got to the bar and Ted had it ready. He was going to exchange a word but saw my face. No chitchat.

"Here, Lovejoy," Tinker began nervously. "Don't blame me."

I rounded on him. "A bloody *forgery,* you stupid burke."

"I wasn't to know, was I?" He slurped his beer fast to encourage me into buying another. Dealers have to provide their barkers with beer, and on very rare occasions food as well. "Even old Sowerby said it was real." Sowerby's been the village schoolmaster since Adam dressed. I wasn't mollified. Betty would be raging at me for days now, women being notoriously unreasonable. We might not get another chance to meet till the next Open Championship. Her husband's a golfer.

"Next time . . ." I let the threat hang. Of course both of us were smiling affably, just being a dealer and his barker chatting in the pub. You don't advertise arguments in our game.

"I didn't know it was naughty," he said defensively.

Naughty is also dealers' slang. Old pewterers' marks, if forged, were called "naughty" hundreds of years ago. Now it means crooked, fake, wrong, in the sense of being deliberately falsified.

"Never mind," I said, hoping some kind recording angel would note my forgiveness and somehow persuade Betty to say the same to me. "What'll you have?"

"Ta, Lovejoy." Tinker was relieved. "Here." He pulled out of the depths of his filthy old overcoat a piece of paper. "That fat lady gave me this." He meant Mrs. Cookson.

I took it gingerly. A group of helpers gusted in from the pageant calling greetings and orders. It had to be about finished. They had a lorry outside the pub's garden, laden with wood and scaffolding, obviously thirsty work.

Her letter asked me to call on her at my earliest convenience. An elegant little scribble on a page torn from a notebook, obviously done hurriedly on the spur of the moment. The address was in Buresford, a larger village about seven miles north.

"What the hell's she want?" I grumbled.

"You must have made an impression," Tinker leered, nudging me suggestively.

"Shut your teeth."

"It, er, looks a good tickle, Lovejoy," he urged. I eyed him suspiciously.

You can always tell when a barker doesn't come clean. Barkers are a curious mob. They're never precisely honest on principle. This doesn't mean they're treacherous. On the contrary, it requires a very durable kind of morality to be a barker—you'll see why later on. Difficulties only happen when people lie all the time. Then it isn't so much a question of spotting the truth but one of actually sorting out their lies in order of size, a much more dicey business.

I decided I'd better go, even if it only turned out a commission job for a quid.

"Look, Tinker," I spoke fast, "when Lardie comes, tell him I'll have that Gujerat silver brooch, but his Whiff-Waff's too dear. Okay?" Lardie's a wealthy po-faced lanky dealer from Norfolk, in love with antique jewelry, old West African ethnology, a rich Clacton widow and himself, in reverse order. To him that hath shall be given.

"His what?"

"Whiff-Waff. Table tennis was called that years ago." The cased sets aren't worth much even now, but they add color to any antique shop which displays one. Our trade admires touches like this.

I pushed to the exit, waving to Angela. Honkworth barged into me at the door, arriving with sundry crawlers. There are only two kinds of people who can't go about without an entourage. One kind's the real leader of men, like your actual Napoleon. The other kind's the born duckegg. Guess which category Honkworth's in.

"Why, it's Lovejoy!" he boomed. "Let's see him off!"

They trailed me outside. We all park our cars end-on toward the old inn's forecourt. Honkie had cleverly placed his massive Rolls-Bentley tourer blocking my little Ruby in, a typical touch of light humor. He made a noisy exhibition of shifting it, revving and backing. I just waited while this pantomime was going on, leaning on the wall and saying nothing. A few people emerged from the public bar to cheer him on. Honkworth attracts sightseers, but so did Attila the Hun.

He had three adorers with him. One was a bleak unsmiling man, young and tall with a waistcoat like a flag day. Hair slicked down, thin mustache, early Gable. I'd seen him before somewhere, a property agent if ever I saw one. Even when he smiled it came out as a faint sneer. You know the sort. The two women were sharp contrasts. The younger was looking slightly uncomfortable at all this malarkey, bonny and light. Good bones. I don't know quite what it means when people say that, because all bones are good, aren't they? But it sounded exactly right when I looked at her. Somebody had chosen the wrong earrings for her, pendants too long with a casual dress. The older woman was blond, florid and bouncy, given to sudden shrill bursts of laughter through teeth like a gold graveyard. She darted excitedly malicious glances at me with every one of Honkie's noisy witticisms.

"Milord, the carriage awaits," Honkworth yelled. Only Honkie can misquote a sentence that short.

I swung the handle. Naturally it didn't fire till third go, to ironical cheers of all. By then I was red-faced and looking at the ground.

"Remember the speed limit, Lovejoy," Honkie yelled. "Everybody pray for rain!"

And they say wit is dead.

I climbed in and clattered off. As the diminutive Ruby began to move I got in a wink at Honkworth's young blonde, just to set folks wondering. Passing between Honkie's massive tourer and the laden lorry made me feel I was pedaling a walnut. The swine reached out and patted me on the head as I passed.

I had to skirt the scene of the pageant to reach the main Buresford road, so I stopped to see if Betty was still about. The field was emptying now. Bunting was being rolled. A few stray colored papers were blowing across the grass in the early evening breeze. Some village children called, "Hello, Lovejoy," chasing rubbish into plastic bags. I waved. All the trestle tables were gone. Most of the stalls were dismantled. Some blokes from our victorious tug-o'-war team were getting the marquee down, Betty's husband with them. No sign of her. I've heard women take it out on their husbands when they're mad. I wonder if it's true. He'd soon find out.

No sign of Mrs. Cookson either, so there was nothing for it. Throttle down to get the right feeble spluttering sound, and kerzoom. Off. I'd worked it out by the time I reached the road. Open country, seven miles. Say an hour, with a following wind.

II

The house was enormous, snootishly set back from the river Stour just in case any riverborne peasants disturbed the affluent class by nocturnal carousings. Some democratically minded leveler had parked a derelict old barge right against the private river-walk. Even warped it to the balustrade with short ropes, I saw with amusement. A great mooring hawser was twined clumsily round an otherwise graceful weeping willow. A drive curved among yews and beech. There was a stylish ornamental pond and a fountain. Thank heaven she'd avoided plastic gnomes. The mansion itself was beautiful. Even the door furniture looked original. As I puttered up the gravel I examined the house. Definitely Queen Anne, though some maniac had mucked about with the gables. You always get some nutter wanting to gild the gingerbread. The Ruby made it up the slight slope, though it was touch and go.

"Lovejoy!" She was on the doorstep, smiling. "How good of you to come so soon."

"I'll just point this downhill." I coaxed one last effort from the half-pint engine and turned the car around the fountain. It wheezed thankfully into silence.

"So you got my message." She hesitated. "Hadn't you better cover your motor up? It looks like rain."

"I want air to get to it." I don't like admitting it's not got all its bits.

The hallway had its original panels, promising elegance and style right through the house. To realize how grim modern architecture is you have to visit a dwelling like this. Once you're plonked down in a Sheraton chair gazing out through hand-leaded windows set in a balanced oak-paneled room you become aware what grotty hutches builders chuck up nowadays. Even the walls had feelings in this house. Beautiful.

She went ahead and we were welcomed by the drawing room. I'd have given my teeth for an engraved lead-glass cordial glass, its luscious baluster stem done in the form of a solid acorn. It stood, throbbing life, in a corner cabinet among some Silesian-stemmed glasses and managed to convey the appearance of having been there since it was made in 1700. The cabinet and its contents were three times as valuable as my cottage, with my tatty furniture chucked in. I dragged my eyes away and paid attention.

"Do sit down."

"Er . . ." There was only the Sheraton. It was like being told to sit on a kneeling bishop. I sank my bum reverently onto it, trying hard to contract my muscles and minimize the weight.

"You were very definite about the sword, Lovejoy," she began.

I hoped she wasn't the sulky kind. Some of the honest old public—a right swarm of barracudas—become very funny when their dreams are shattered.

"You obviously think it's a forgery."

"A good one," I said, anxious to please. "Very good, in fact."

"But still a forgery?" she said with careful insistence.

"Er, well." There was no way out. "Yes. A good guess."

"I think not," she said. We sat in silence digesting this.

She sat opposite, definitely in possession. Bright, too. A really resilient character who'd seen a few upheavals in her time. I began to wonder where all her wealth had come from. We were both being quite pleasant but wary with it.

"The point is, Lovejoy," she resumed, "the sword has deceived the most expert authorities in its time."

"That means you know the faker." I tried to turn it into a question at the last minute but didn't quite manage it.

"Yes." More pause, with me wondering how to ask straight out. "Your friend," she continued. "He told me you're one of those special people who just . . . know."

Friend? She must mean Tinker Dill. Good old blabbermouth. "He means well," I said lamely.

"A . . . a divvie?" The word was unused to her.

Silence.

"Are you one, Lovejoy?" She seemed fascinated, full of interest. "If there's a fee for revealing this . . ."

I drew in that lovely luscious aroma of money.

"All right. I'll tell you. No." I stopped her reaching for her handbag. "I only charge for work done." I swallowed, nervous as a cat. "Yes, I'm a divvie."

She examined me as one does a specimen, head tilted, eyes everywhere. I felt uncomfortable. My shirt cuffs are always a bit frayed. If I'd known I was visiting posh I'd have hurried back to the cottage and pressed my one good pair of trousers.

"I'd heard there were such people but never expected to meet one. What actually happens?"

"I don't know. Honest." I'm always nervous talking about myself. "Saying you've a gift sounds like bragging, because it's so special. A divvie just . . . well, knows."

"How?"

"I don't understand it myself." I struggled to explain. "Think of a woman who just knows when the colors in a redecorated room are exactly right. That's a sort of gift, too."

"It's also common sense, Lovejoy." A reprimand.

"No it isn't," I countered. "It's a gift. Some have a gift for handling dogs, for designing clothes. Or take to the piano like . . . like Franz Liszt. Some have it for finding water with a bit of twisted stick—"

"Water diviner!" she exclaimed. "Divvie. I see."

"Everybody's a divvie," I added. "Nobody's left absolutely

without some special gift. For *knowing* the feel of a true diamond. For knowing straightaway which horse will run fastest, which boat will balance right. There are divvies everywhere, for everything. For knowing next year's weather. Which bushes will grow. What musical notes will hold the imagination of millions. Even for knowing what'll happen." I didn't mean to become so enthusiastic, but it's true. Nobody's left out. You as well, dear reader. You might be the world's greatest living divvie for antique Sumerian gold. Find out quickly what your special gift is, for heaven's sake, or you're being thrown to waste.

"And you're an *antiques* divvie."

"Yes." I wondered how to explain. "It's like a bell. In my chest."

She pointed to a picture, a small watercolor. It hung over a Pembroke table. "Try that sketch."

I crossed to look. A few dashes of the brush for a wash, a demented scar of Prussian blue, three fast smudges in Vandyke brown. All on a torn page. That was all. But it screamed of Dedham's church on a blustery autumnal evening, with the sea wind gusting up the Stour for all it was worth. Bells clamored and rang. Beautiful, beautiful.

I could hardly manage the words. "Original. Constable?"

"Good." She'd followed me to watch. "We have the provenance."

Nowadays, with so many forgers about, provenance is vital. Innocent buyers should demand written proof of a painting's progress, right from the artist's lily-whites into your very own. That means evidence of the original sale, bills of purchase, auction dates and invoices. Don't say I didn't warn you. If you're going to become a regular collector you should make a secret list of the painters of whom forgers are especially fond. Just for a bonus I'll start you off with the first three. The brilliant David Cox. The elusive Samuel Palmer. The magic John Constable. Good luck.

"Even," Mrs. Cookson was saying, "even the frame's original. Constable framed it himself."

"Balls," I said. "Er, I mean, impossible." I closed my eyes, touching the frame. No bell. No life. Phony. I borrowed a tissue and rubbed gently. The frame gave up a light russet stain. "Look, love. It'll stain a wet tissue for years yet. Modern crap."

"But . . . it can't be."

"Somebody's knocked it up recently." You have to be patient. Women can be very possessive, worse than any bloke. I showed her the bright glistening creases, always a dead giveaway. "Easily done. Fresh beechwood. Varnish. Then sandpaper a spare piece of beechwood over the dried wood stain and rub it in with your finger. It'll age a hundred years in about ten minutes."

"How dare you!" She rounded on me furiously.

I was halfway to the door in a flash. "I'll not stay for tea, love." You get too many of these scenes in the antique trade to waste time. Another end to a beautiful friendship. The trouble is that people love their illusions.

"He's right, Martha."

I almost barged into the speaker. A thin wisp of a man blocked my way. Well, hardly blocked. A featherweight sixtyish. He looked as if he'd actually been born that tiny shape, slightly balding, in his waistcoat. And he hadn't grown much. If I hadn't spotted him in time I'd have stepped on him and driven him in like a tent peg.

"Henry!" Martha Cookson twisted anguished hands. "Not you again!" *Again?*

"I'm afraid so." He wore his cleric's dog collar like a slipped halo.

"Er, excuse me please, Reverend." I edged past. It was beginning to look like somebody's big scene. Rather private, but undoubtedly big.

"Don't go, Lovejoy." I dithered uneasily. "I apologize for having disbelieved you," she added to me, wrenching the words out before lashing back at her frail old pal. "But *why,* Henry?"

He shuffled like a caught child. "Those wretched Council rates, Martha." He tried to appeal to me, but I wasn't having any. Definitely neutral, I began examining the Pembroke table's hinges. "So tiresome," he cried. "Always more taxes, more charges."

"You promised to ask me, Henry," she said sternly, "before making any more things." My ears pricked. I'd found the forger, the cunning old devil. "You *promised.*"

Hey-ho. The good old sexual standoff. Woman versus man again. They said their lines a few more times while I moved gently to one side. Pembroke tables are among the most copied items of furniture on earth. Both of the natty little folding flaps must have three hinges. Each flap lifts up and rests on fly runners or rails. This luscious Pembroke was serpentined, double fly rails both sides. Glancing at Henry and Martha to check they were still at it I stood on tiptoe and peered downward. The inner aspects of the slender legs tapered elegantly, so maybe 1790. Definitely eighteenth-century, anyhow.

I came to, smiling. Henry and Martha were watching me. Silence.

"Oh, er . . ." I cleared my throat and looked innocent. "You rang?" Not a flicker of a smile from either. "Er, just looking."

"Henry. May I introduce Lovejoy." We bowed. That's what a lovely old house like this does for you, puts back your manners a couple of hundred years. "Lovejoy, may I introduce the Reverend Henry Swan." We bowed again. No wonder people do nothing but slouch and yawn and scratch nowadays. There's no point in bothering with things like manners if everything all around you's crummy plastic junk, is there? I even pulled out one of my cards and presented it with a flourish.

"Lovejoy Antiques, Inc.," he read through lowered steel-rimmed specs. "Sotheby's Authorized Expert, London."

Christ. I'd given him the wrong card. A quick improvisation was called for. "Ah," I said casually, "I'm no longer with, er, Sotheby's. Not right now." You can have too much elegance. It'd made me forget which pocket held my legitimate cards.

"Were you ever, Lovejoy?" Martha Cookson was smiling now.

"Well, not really." I shrugged at her, but I was blazing inside. Women get me really narked. They always guess more than is good for them. No wonder they get under your skin.

"Ahem." Swan's eyes twinkled. "A . . . free-lance," he brought out proudly.

"Yes," I replied. And broke, but I didn't say that.

"Is this the young man of whom you have spoken, Martha?"

Of whom you have spoken, I thought. Dear God. I'd even have to get my tenses right. It was becoming one of those days.

"Yes, Henry."

"Then why did he need to inspect the Pembroke?" he asked. A shrewd old nut.

"To find out *what* it was," I explained. "My bell only tells me *if*."

They glanced at each other, signaling with looks. I watched with sudden interest. You can always tell when people are more than just good friends.

"Very well, Lovejoy." Martha Cookson came to a decision. Henry nodded agreement as she spoke. "We wish to commission you, Lovejoy, if that's the right expression."

I sweated with relief. If things improved this quickly I'd be eating again soon. Maybe I'd forgotten how.

"Fine by me."

We all waited, some more patiently than others.

"Oh!" Henry Swan came to, a dusty little creased beam lighting his countenance. "Oh. Quite, Lovejoy. We . . . *dig,* don't we, Martha?"

"Dig, dear?" She was lost.

"Yes," he exclaimed impatiently. "You know, Martha. To understand, comprehend, appreciate." He gave a crumpled grin, unexpectedly toothy. "We might live in deepest East Anglia, Lovejoy, but we do move with the times. The retainer, dear. Deposit."

"Oh, the fee." She did the handbag bit. I felt the blessed ecstasy of notes in my digits. After listening to Henry's dated slang I deserved every penny.

Suddenly though there was something wrong. They glanced at each other shiftily. We were waiting too long.

"Good, good," Reverend Henry said, clearing his throat. "Ahem." He actually pronounced it A . . . *hem.* "Good heavens! Is that the time?"

"Are you free for lunch tomorrow?" Martha Cookson asked affably.

"I'll be here." Another nasty wait. "Look," I said at last. "Sooner or later you'll have to tell me what you've commissioned me *for*." I was beginning to lose patience. "Or do I have to guess?"

"Goodness me," old Henry said. "How careless of us, Martha."

"You'd better explain, Henry."

"No. You, Martha."

"Both together," I suggested. A sudden thought. "It isn't something you've half inched?" They seemed quite blank. I translated. "Pinched. Stolen."

"Certainly not." They were indignant enough to be truthful.

"Sorry. Well, funnier things have happened." I tried to help. "You want me to find some particular antique?" This is the commonest thing.

"Oh no," said Henry earnestly. "We already have it, you see."

"And you want it examined? Dated?"

There were three Imari plates in the cabinet. The lovely precious colors were exactly right, but nowadays dealers will call any porcelain "Imari ware" if it's got those delectable royal blues and mandarin reds even vaguely approximated. I'd known since I'd arrived they weren't legitimate. Oh, genuine antiques. But Dutch copies of the true Japanese. No Nippon potter ever drew bamboos in layers with a ruler like that. It's the really wooden feeling of the artistry that gives these copies away every time, so beware. I came back to earth.

"Your porcelains?" I nodded at the Imaris.

"Er, no."

"But you want something authenticated?"

"That's correct." More glances. I felt part of one of those music-hall melodramas.

"Is it here?"

"Er, no. I'll bring it. We must explain about it first."

"What is it?" I demanded. "I might have to bring documents, references."

23

Martha took a quick breath. "It's . . ." She smiled at me with something approaching defiance. "It's . . . it's the Grail."

"Grail?" For a moment the penny didn't drop.

"Yes." They stood together, gazing at me.

"I only know of one Grail," I jibed pleasantly, still stupid. "And that's . . ." I looked from Henry to Martha. Then back. Then from Henry to Martha again.

"Exactly, Lovejoy." Henry was letting me in on it gently. "I have it."

I gaped back at the two lunatics for a second. Then turned on my heel and walked out, blazing.

I'd cripple Tinker. That was why he'd been evasive in the pub, the great Neanderthal buffoon. He's always doing this. Bloody barkers are all at it, hoping something will turn up without doing any proper bloody legwork. Supplying me with duds when I was on my uppers for proper worthwhile collectors. No wonder I'm always starving.

I swung the Ruby's starting handle viciously. It knows me too well to push its luck when I'm wild. An obedient first-time start.

"Lovejoy."

Martha Cookson had followed me. As I clunked the hand brake down I saw old Henry peering anxiously from the door-step behind her.

"You won't forget lunch tomorrow?" she said, rather pale. "And he really has got it, you know, Lovejoy."

"Missus," I gave back like ice, "you had Excalibur till this afternoon."

She said something more, but I was too upset to listen. I coaxed all ten ccs into throbbing power and spluttered the Ruby down the gravel drive. What a waste of a whole bloody day. First Betty. Then Jean Evans getting mad at me. Then Martha Cookson and her tame nutter. Tinker had better not be around for a day or two, that's all.

You get times when everything goes wrong all at once. And it's always women at the back of them, every blinking time. Ever noticed that?

III

___

I stormed angrily homeward down the Buresford road,
notching an aggressive twenty miles an hour down the slope past
Saint Margaret's Well. The Ruby's G force even made me blink
once or twice. Who the hell makes up all these tales of Grails and
tombs I don't know. Only I wish they'd pack it in.

Dusk fell when I still had about four miles more to go. I
needed to borrow some matches so I called in at an antique shop
in Dragonsdale, a giant metropolis of seventeen houses, three
shops, two pubs and a twelfth-century church. That's modern
hereabouts. Liz Sandwell was just closing up. She came out to
watch me do the twin oil lamps on the Ruby. Well, you can't
have everything. Liz is basically oil paintings and Georgian inci-
dental household furnishings. She has a lovely set of pole screens
and swing dressing mirrors.

"I love your little noddy car, Lovejoy." She's a great leg-
puller. Twenty-five, shiny dun hair and style. She wears floral
frocks. I know it sounds old-fashioned, but Liz never looks it
somehow. "Finished," she asked blandly, "your inspection?"

"Oh. Yes." I must have been looking at her too hard and too

long. I wiped the lamp glasses and set about trimming the wicks.

"Hard day at the pageant, I hear," she said. She accepted my quick glance blithely, all sweet innocence.

"Not too bad." I was very preoccupied.

"They say Betty Marsham's gunning for somebody."

I said carefully, "That's women all over, isn't it? No patience."

She was laughing as I got both front lamps alight. The domes slid on with a comforting click.

"One day you'll get in real trouble, Lovejoy." Her hand paused, taking her matches back.

"Who, me?" I gave her my best angelic face.

"Time to come in for a sherry?"

The memory of her bloke floated across my mind. He's the one they wind the rope around at the back of our tug-o'-war line. Our anchor man on account of his size, muscle and weight.

"Er, another time, Liz. Thanks all the same." I hesitated. "Here, love. One thing." I asked her about Martha Cookson and her tame priest.

"Henry Swan? Yes, I know him." A couple of modern cars swished grandly past, their head lamps illuminating the houses and trees. "He's a manorial lord, one of those ancient titles. Poor as a church mouse."

"Poor? In a house like that?" I began describing the mansion, but Liz gave one of those short laughs which show you've missed the point.

"It's hers. Not his. Not any more."

"You mean . . . ?" I remembered their simultaneous glances.

"They've lived together for years. His family went broke. Mrs. Cookson bought it." She shrugged prettily. "It was a terrific scandal years ago." Her antique dealer's antennae alerted. "Why, Lovejoy? Are you buying from them?"

"Just wondering. Social call, really," I lied easily. "Look. Are they . . . well, reliable?"

"Never heard anyone ask that about them before, Lovejoy." She paused. "Pots of money, if that's what you're worried about."

I nodded thanks, but I was getting one of those feelings.

26

Maybe it was standing about in the evening cold after such a burning hot day. She told me about a couple of Jacobean pewters she'd salted away for me to see and said to come inside because it wouldn't take a minute. "I've three lovely pieces of Irish cut glass as well, Lovejoy." I wavered, sorely tempted, but that tough anchor man would be back soon and I was in enough trouble.

"Tomorrow, if I can make it," I promised, cranking away.

"I hope those lamps hold out, Lovejoy," Liz called as the Ruby creaked into a rather drifting acceleration. "Remember what happened to the Foolish Virgins and *their* lamps."

"Promises, promises," I yelled over my shoulder, but she'd gone in.

It was full dark by the time I reached home. This cottage where I live, occasionally without assistance, lies in a small village a few miles north of our nearest big town. It's one of those villages which people call sleepy, no street lights. Sleepy in East Anglia's moribund anywhere else. We only have two streets, a church as old as the hills and a few straggly lanes leading off into rather spooky low-lying mist-filled valleys. A fine evening drizzle began. Welcome home, Lovejoy.

"Good kid." I patted the Ruby's stone-pocked radiator and blew its lamps out.

The door seemed intact. I always check because antique dealers are forever being burgled. I found the key and switched off the key alarm to save old George Jilks having another infarct in his police hut. He's always on at me for being careless with it. That's our modern police for you. No dedication.

I washed and put the kettle on. There isn't much space in the cottage. It's one of those old thatched wattle-and-daub dwellings. You can't get a proper bank loan on them because they're judged to be dicey, having stood all weathers for only four centuries or so. A minuscule hallway leads into the one main living room. This divan I now have extends into a double bed. I've enlarged the kitchen alcove and put a curtain across.

I made my tea—two pasties and beetroot, a pint of tea, five

slices of bread and marge. You can get some of that sweet pickle, but it costs the earth. I'd left some mushrooms soaking in dark honey, copying the Roman Apicius' recipe for truffles. The trouble is that Apicius didn't specify what sort of honey you have to use, but that very pale honey we get in East Anglia after a dry hot summer just will not do. I grill them on skewers. Really great, as long as you're not a mushroom.

I cleared the table of books and notepaper scraps for my meal.

Normally I turn on the telly to watch the politicians for a laugh. This evening I couldn't settle. You know the feeling. Books you'd normally leap at seem suddenly too familiar and the notes you desperately want to bring up to date are too irksome. I had a pile of old photographs, some of them on glass, which I keep meaning to catalogue. Twice I picked them up and put them down again. You feel guilty, too, not even getting the pleasure of being bone idle.

A few tickles had come in, letters replying to my newspaper adverts—I place two a week. My most successful gambit is always the innocent widow (as if there ever was such a thing) struggling to make an odd groat from the sale of her pathetic belongings. This week I'd put:

> FOR SALE: PR. V. OLD & LARGE JAPANESE VASES, COLORFUL EMBOSSED FIGURES; BLACK BESS FLINTLOCK RIFLE; OLD SILVER TEA SERVICE WITH HALLMARK; BOX OF OLD STAMPED ENVELOPES. LATE HUSBAND'S EFFECTS. PLEASE WRITE WITH OFFERS. RECENTLY BEREAVED WIDOW.

We call it breading, as in loaf. Just as anglers chuck bread into a river, so we dealers "bread" the public pool. I'd no such articles, naturally, and of course I'd used terms just wrong enough to be convincing. Seven replies, five naturally from dealers taken in by my deceptive innocence. I read their ingenious scribbles with dry amusement, then chucked them away. The other two replies were from collectors. You can tell them a mile off. One, a stamps addict, babbled incoherent enthusiasm, but the scent of money was missing. I chucked that letter away too, because penniless enthusiasts are ten a penny, aren't we? The second was a genuine collector, who wrote gravely that my Japanese vases sounded Satsuma ware. We call them "Second" Satsumas, in the trade, these gross and horrible pots decorated with too many colors and white-slip outlines. People go daft over the ugly great things. Japanese made them in the nineteenth century to cater for the crazy European idea of current Japanese elegance. European collectors and Japanese potters finished up equally bemused in a lunatic situation, the former collecting the wrong stuff and the latter turning out hideous stuff they didn't like. Folk go on collecting it, thank heaven. "First" Satsuma's beautiful delicate small stuff. I've yet to see a single real nonphony piece anywhere in Europe, so beware. The collector, a Sunderland geezer, went on to ask did I not mean Brown rather than Black Bess? The former is the famous Land Pattern Musket, possession of which is the indelible mark of the flintlock collector. Black Bess, on the other hand, is a highwayman's horse. According to legend it carried Dick Turpin on his fantastic escape to York. Well, it would have done, except that brilliant ride was performed by the obscure but dashing highwayman Ned Tarleton. Poor Dick was in deep trouble with a lusty widow further south. The collector offered to have my items priced by independent valuers at his own expense and even offered a deposit to guarantee his good faith. He would supply personal references from banks, et cetera. I filed his name and address reverently. I love a real collector.

Now, I thought, where the hell do I get a pair of Second Satsuma vases and a Land Pattern from?

Believe it or not, that was the high spot of my evening. I fidgeted some more.

I was worried. The point is that tales like the Holy Grail happen every day around here. They're all as daft, not even sensible myths. Crackpot myths. I hear thirty a week. No, honestly. King John's lost treasure in the Wash up the road gets itself found every few minutes. Constable's mythical royal portraits.

29

Wellington's private autobiography—the original ten-volume manuscript, of course. Cymbeline's buried treasure house. Claudius Caesar's secret golden temple. Good Queen Bess's secret diary. And last but by no means least, of course, the poor tired Holy Grail which nobody will let rest in peace. A mere sniff of good old King Arthur's enough to set millions daydreaming and digging in back yards from one end of these islands to the other. It's no joke. To a dealer whose next meal comes through finding real antiques these legends are a drag, an absolute pest.

I played a record of a Mozart flute piece. He hated composing for that instrument and used to write home to his dad moaning about it, but he'd get no sympathy from me tonight. I finally spent the rest of the evening ringing round my mates arranging things for the next day.

Angela was first, seeing I owed her a fortune. I swore an oath that I'd bring her bloody money in first thing. May I be forgiven. Jim Fleet, who is Japanese militaria and prints, came next. I promised to see him at the next antiques auction about a Kitagawa Utamaro print of 1800 or so which he said was original. "Well, Jim, what else is new," I told him nastily. Then I left a message at the White Hart with Ted the barman for Tinker Dill. I omitted the Yours Sincerely bit, seeing I sincerely intended to sincerely cripple him.

I gave in at last, got the divan ready and switched the light off. Outside it sounded as if it had started to rain quite hard. And I'd forgotten to cover the Ruby up with that ex-army tarpaulin. Great. Just my luck if it was flooded in the morning. The trouble with my cottage is that you can only see the lights of two other houses. Some nights it feels forlorn. That's the word. Forlorn. At times like this when I'm a bit down I really wish I lived in a town. At least there are other people about. Living at one end of a remote village isn't exactly a gay social whirl.

I found myself listening for sounds. The odd bat, the odd grunt from a pink-footed hedgehog which is given to nocturnal meddling in the garden. Nothing else. I don't care for countryside. There's too much of it knocking about by far. Anything could happen to me down in this crummy hollow and nobody would know for days except a robin and a hedgehog. Great.

The phone rang, making me leap a mile. Betty, apoplectic.

"Lovejoy! You absolute *pig,*" she blazed.

This is what I like, I thought bitterly. Compassionate understanding.

"Hello, Betty, love."

"Don't you Betty, love me, Lovejoy." She began wailing. "How do you think I felt? I'm such a fool. I've had to say I'm going round to my mother's to come out and phone you."

"Sorry, love. There was a chance of picking up an antique."

"*Oh!* So you think more of an *antique* than you do of me, do you?" All frost.

I thought hard.

"Well, yes," I admitted. "It's antiques I'm always short of."

"You absolute . . ."

"Swine," I filled in for her and rang off. That's women. Very self-centered. I don't think they'll ever become like us, fair minded and well adjusted. I spotted years ago that they've no justice.

I was right when I said it looked like becoming one of those days. I climbed back into bed again, determined to erase the entire wasted day from my mind. Sleep didn't come immediately though. I tossed and turned.

Holy Grail indeed.

IV

I'm not one of these people who let themselves be affected by the weather. Rain, sun, snow and gales are all the same to me. As long as there's an antique shop or two around we could be in another stellar constellation for all I care, because then I'm as happy as a pig in muck. But next day dawned with a brilliance which dazzled the soul. The scores of our local artists, from Constable and Wilson on down, must have stirred in their graves with the feeling of this dawn's invigoration and excitement. I just knew in my bones it would be a good day, full of profit and luscious antiques.

Mind you, you don't have to *like* all antiques. They're just like people. You get all sorts. Some can bring ecstasy the minute you clap your eyes on them. Others put the fear of God into you. I mean, you'd need nerves of steel to buy one of those goat gods from Ur in Babylonia. Admittedly they are old, 2500 B.C. or so. And costly—the gold and lapis lazuli would tell you that anyway. But imagine waking up with those horrible eyes and that hunched shell-cased body lurking away on your sideboard. I tell you, you wouldn't trust some antiques with the kitten.

My breakfast was a barley cake made by my own lily-white hands, a couple of apples and a glass of milk, my attempt to copy a Roman's breakfast. Of course, you need a pair of Campanian bronze *pateral* vessels in which our people and the Roman legions hereabouts used to heat breakfasts in the first and second centuries. They warmed their wines and food in them rather like the Lancastrians used fire hobs right up to modern times. I believe you have to cook simple or sad, so to speak, to get anywhere near the historical man's grub.

Singing loudly I locked up, fending off a strong temptation to make my bed and stoutly resisting the urge to wash up my breakfast things. Handling this sort of temptation's my strong suit. The Ruby was practically pawing the ground to be surging off. "No nonsense from you," I told it pleasantly. The inside had mostly dried from last night's rain. I mopped the seat to get that extra mileage. Luckily the floor has more holes than a colander so drainage is adequate. I was full of beans, pretending to percuss its chest and chuckling. "How's your middle lobe?" I asked it, leaping in. "A bit chesty?" Wit. I throttled off down the drive singing that hard tenor bit from *Rigoletto.*

Stupid, innocent Lovejoy.

The biggest town hereabouts is on a hill above a curving river. It's only a handful of miles to the open sea. I always halt the Ruby at the middle bridge for a moment because that point was the limit of navigation for the Roman galleys arriving from Gaul. Our town council, a gaggle of real cackhanders, has tried ten billion river improvement schemes since Claudius limped off his Imperial trireme onto our wharf, with the result that boats can't even get this far nowadays. Politicians call it progress, but I do wish they'd stop trying. A huge shape purred alongside.

"Hi, Lovejoy!" Good old Honkworth with his admirers. The blonde bird again, that smarmy creep, and Diamond Lil doing her lipstick thing.

"Wotcher, Honkie." I had to crane my neck to the vertical.

"Daydreaming? Race you up the North Hill." A roar of laughter at this witticism. He leaned over me, patting my head

33

again while the traffic behind hooted us to get going. "Has your Bugatti Special recovered? It's got epilepsy, you know," he confided loudly to his mob. Two of them laughed.

"So had Alexander the Great," I said.

"Who?"

"Before your time, Honkie," I told him, clacking the hand brake free. You just have to be kind.

His giant motor wafted ahead in a second. From my lowly position his nearside exhaust looked like the Mersey Tunnel as his mobile castle dwindled grandly up the hill. Now what was he doing out so early?

I'd head for the Arcade. Our local antique dealers, a merry band of siblings, have this covered alleyway with stalls and booths. Our town planners stuck their oar in, so the architecture's neo-Gothic catastrophic with a smattering of postcard mosque. There's a café with its own popular brand of travelers' enteric.

I parked the Ruby between two Fords and chatted up the traffic warden, Brenda. She and I know each other from the trainee snogging days of our shared golden youth.

"Have you noticed," I asked her carefully, "that my horseless carriage is illegally parked?"

Brenda examined the yellow lines and the parking meters. "No, Lovejoy. In fact," she said, just as carefully but smiling, "I doubt if I ever would."

I hesitated, but antiques called from nearby along the narrow streets. She'd have to wait.

"One thing," I said. "Is your engagement ring illegally parked too?" It's best to be certain.

"Get on with you," she scolded, still smiling. Women have all sorts of knacks we don't have, like two-way smiles. Smiles should mean yes or no. Not both.

Temporarily immune from the laws of the highway I sprinted off, pleased. Well, the mayor parks free. In the café Woody was in action, ash from his cigarette busily spraying the edibles he'd carefully flung on the counter to filter his coughed droplets.

"Wotcher, Woody."

He swirled a couple of stale plaice into the frying pan. I looked away.

"Watch your women, lads," he croaked. "Lovejoy's here."

A muted chorus of jeers and greetings rose like an audible fog from the hunched dealers scattered thinly among the tables. It's not a sight for the squeamish. A plate of Woody's fried breakfast is enough to turn the strongest stomach. Imagine four charred sausages set in a solid congealed mass of clotted lard, with bacon slices checkered into pale raw and black cinder next to a wobbling egg's uncooked eye staring at you all reproachful from shame at its plight. You get the general idea: unappetizing. He bakes in the afternoons. I tell Woody I don't mind where he exports his gangrenous cream cakes to as long as the inhabitants aren't on our side. He thinks I'm joking. I waved to his survivors and called for tea. Every antique dealer in East Anglia comes through Woody's sooner or later. One or two, like Nick Maldon, came in for egg and chips the day Woody opened and haven't budged since. More deals are done in Woody's than on Wall Street and the Stock Exchange put together. Not all are carefully recorded for the Lord Chancellor's tax accountants, however. Imagine how annoyed he must be, one sometimes thinks to oneself—sympathetically of course.

"Fry-up as well, Lovejoy?" Lisa's the only waitress in the known world with a Ph.D. in ancient history, between archeological digs.

"And I call you friend," I said theatrically. She slipped into the chair opposite and lit a cigarette. This always fascinates me. Women can flick a match and hold a cigarette and have you goggling at their elegance. "Who's been in so far?"

"Too early yet." Her gaze ranged the other tables through Woody's lowering smoke. "Most don't come till elevenish."

I already knew that. "Tinker?"

"No."

I checked the tables as far as the bloodshot eye could see, about two yards. Fearless Fred was slogging his way through chips, sardines and toast. He earns his nickname every Tuesday from his bids at the local auction. He's silver tableware, Sheffield

35

plate and a diehard gambler on the horses. He gave me a nod to say good morning and a wink to say I'd struck lucky with Lisa. Jimmo was there, another threadbare soul like me, though he still had a place across the way in the Arcade. He was going through a bad patch, and rumor was he'd have to sell up soon, poor bloke. He was even doing part-time barman at the Grapes and Olive on East Hill. I waved and we both beamed a beam of derelict joviality to show how well off we were. That done, I cast around for more profitable contacts.

"Hey, Lovejoy." Cask has one of those remarkable baby faces which never looks as if it needed a shave. He's always full of corny jokes. He'd be a good barker if only he'd stick to barking, but his delusions of grandeur make him deal in early scientific and navigational instruments. His long-suffering wife Has Faith In Him, which only makes his predicament worse because Cask can't tell a Persian astrolabe from a football.

"How do, Caskie," I called. I like him, from sympathy.

"Lovejoy. Heard this one?" He fell about in his chair, spraying noshed egg as he laughed. "Two savage man-eating lions in town shopping, and one says, 'I thought you said it was crowded on Saturdays?' Get it?"

"Great, great, Caskie." I laughed along to give him heart.

Marion laughed too, she of the aggressive manner and un-plumbed appetite, delicately spooning yogurt opposite her temporary escort, Jed Radcliffe, at an adjacent table. He's a quiet smart man like all print dealers. Curious how a prints man managed to pair up with a Regency furniture specialist like Marion. Perhaps he puts his engravings in her chest of drawers. Well, I chuckled to myself, ideas save space, don't they? A trio of barkers were in, one already moderately tipsy. They'd be clocking up commission for their wallies—a wallie's the dealer the barker finds antiques for—as soon as they could stand. Two flintlock pistol specialists were huddled over gruesome porridge, nodding and talking prices quite openly the way no other antique dealers ever do. Why weapon people are like this I don't know. The shorter chap, Eric, has two wives. Everybody knows except them and the law, but one final day he'll need every loaded weapon he possesses, plus ten yards' start. I wondered idly if he'd been at yesterday's pageant and seen the sword. Eric's good at his weaponry. But good enough?

"Lovejoy." Lisa brought me back. "Going to the fireworks?"

"Maybe," I said cautiously. I'm sick of fetes, fairs, pageants, displays. We have an epidemic of them every summer. Makes me wonder how we find time for anything else.

"Take me."

We looked at each other. I don't quite understand how they do it, but women always seem to be one plot ahead.

"It's in Castle Park. Saturday night."

Middle of the town. That meant I wouldn't have to work out how to fold Lisa's impressive length into the Ruby. Even I have to adopt the fetal position to get behind the wheel.

"Well, er . . ."

"I'm not a tart, Lovejoy," Lisa said evenly. "And too many of those crummy popsies you choose to go about with *are.*"

Since when does a man have any choice?

"Well," I relented, "I like fireworks." When you think of it, they're the only explosions you can make and not get shelled at. Lisa smiled. Suddenly I realized I'd never seen her smile before. It was this morning's sunrise all over again.

"That's good," she said. "See you outside the Arcade. Dusk."

"Er . . ."

Margaret has a shop in the Arcade. Lisa swiftly understood.

"No," I said suddenly. "The castle doorway." It's a common meeting place with no prying lights after dark. She rose at Woody's emphysematous shout for her to get a move on. I slurped my tea as a penance. Rising to go I crossed to Marion and Jed.

"German dolls?" I offered hopefully. We aren't ones for formal greetings in the trade. Jed drew an eager breath, but Marion said no, too sharply.

"A Wellington chest, Lovejoy?" she countered. "London, 1830?"

I sighed, saying no. If only I had the money.

"I need Irish glass," she said after a think. "And jade."

37

My spirits soared. Irish glass? Liz Sandwell had offered me some. Obviously the promised luck had just arrived.

"I've got two good buyers down from the North," Marion added.

"See you tonight at the pub," I said. Well, if I had a chance of earning a quid or two from Liz's cut glass, I could pop in for a free nosh as well at Ma Cookson's and pick up the Holy Grail. It should be worth a few pence, I thought nastily, after all these years. And she had asked me to lunch.

Mercifully I escaped without remembering to pay. Lisa once said that my trouble is I always forget but sometimes remember, instead of it being the other way around. I hope I don't know what she means.

V

Liz Sandwell's three pieces of Irish cut glass were nearly what she'd told me. We agreed on prices, and by ten to twelve the Ruby was tottering up Martha Cookson's drive, obviously beginning to feel it had done its bit for the day. Naturally I hadn't the money to pay Liz, but a day or two's no problem in the antiques world. People who pay on the nail are regarded as imbeciles or eccentric.

Liz had been proudest of a "real bluish antique Waterford flat-cut glass, Lovejoy." That mysterious bluish tinge which is supposed to be characteristic of all Waterford glass is a myth. Hand on my heart. Antique Waterford glass is no more blue than you or I. Look at an authentic piece in a museum and see. If it *is* blue, it's a fake, manufactured by the skillful for the incredulous. Dutch imitators had flat-cut Liz's bluish polygonal glass bottle, using bluish-tinted glass. There's a lot of them about. I'm all for copying as long as I know what actually goes on. The Excise Acts from 1745 on messed about with English glassmaking, so the free trade Ireland got after 1780 boomed Irish glass production, sales and reputation—you don't need to delve too far back in history to find our politicians making a balls-up. Hence the developments of the sophisticated three-piece mold system for blown glass in America and Ireland before 1825 or so. Why the Yanks aren't proud as peacocks over their lovely glass beats me. Liz had one, a lovely barreled spirit bottle complete with stopper (remember the stopper—its presence doubles the price you pay. And if it's missing start some hard bargaining). The last piece was a Cork Glass Company decanter, quite attractive, but beware. "Bainbridge," I explained to Liz, "says they made modern ones from the original molds, and I think he's right." Hers was genuinely old, though I didn't tell her that my bell was clamoring its lovely chime, so she said okay let's price it as modern. I didn't disagree. Well, all's fair in love, war and antiques.

So there I was, the Ruby crawling spluttering up Martha Cookson's drive. An ancient gnarled gardener rose from among some bushes to stare. I gave him a royal wave. He resumed work, shaking his head and grinning.

The river was running higher than last night from the rain we'd had. The old longboat seemed immovable, not rocking at its ropes like boats are supposed to do. Maybe it was stuck on the bottom by eons of silt. If it wasn't, that thick hawser would keep it from accidentally winning any races. A thin wisp of smoke rose from its black chimney. It was a fifty-footer, no longer neat but still embellished with carvings and painted floral and scenic decorations of the traditional bargee style. Curious how those gross reds, greens, yellows and light blues seem to have caught on with our itinerant workers, bargees, caravan dwellers, tinkers and gypsies alike.

"I'm so very glad you came, Lovejoy." I was brought back to earth. Martha Cookson came to say hello, both hands outstretched. I found her hands in mine. She was suddenly likable, but I suppressed the fond feeling. I had to find a way to return the money she'd given me. "Have you quite forgiven us?"

"Hello. Forgiven?"

"For offending you yesterday. Weren't we awful?" She drew

me into the hall the way they do. I started to explain why I'd rushed off with such ill grace, but she would have none of it. "We quite understand. We're appropriately ashamed of our clumsiness, Lovejoy. Now, first names immediately. Absolutely the minimum of fuss." She led the way into the same living room. Sherry was ready on an occasional table. As we entered this bird turned to inspect us, smiling economically. Last seen this morning with Honkworth. This was all going to be rather a drag, her sour expression announced, so everybody keep illusions out of it and no hang-ups, okay? "You must hear all sorts of ridiculous stories in your occupation, Lovejoy," Martha Cookson said. "We can't blame you in the least."

"Er, well, Martha, I actually came to, er, say . . ." I started a stumbling explanation that I wanted out.

"This is my niece, Dolly," Martha Cookson introduced brightly. "I made her come along in case you were still angry with us. Dolly, Lovejoy."

"Er, I think we've met." I gave Dolly a nod.

"So we have." No change out of me, Lovejoy, her tone said loudly. She turned and poured sherry for us all.

"Really?" Martha was all agog. "When and where?"

"He's a . . . friend of Alvin's," Dolly said. She held out a glass distantly, avoiding actually seeing me. I had to plod across a few million leagues of carpet to reach it. I felt like a passing pilgrim thrown a crumb. Alvin? Was poor old Honkworth actually called that?

"Not a friend," I said. Let there be no fobbery, my tone said back. I saw Martha's quick glance, but I don't go for all this coy stuff.

"You're both antiques experts," Dolly said, innocent.

"No. *I* am." I moved across to a de Wint watercolor, drawn by my clanging bell. Genuine, the boat reflected and the moonlight just right. I did my infallible watercolor trick. Always half close your eyes and step back a few inches more than seems necessary. Then do the same from a yard to its right. Then ditto left. Do this and you're halfway to spotting the valuable genuine old master. It works even for painters as late as Braque. You need not know anything about the art itself. Forgeries and modern dross look unbalanced by this trick, full of uneven colors and displeasing lines. It's as simple as that. Dolly was still bent on battle, woman all over.

"If you're an expert," she was demanding sweetly, "what does that make Alvin?"

I sighed. There's no hinting to some people. "I'm an antique dealer, love," I told Dolly kindly. "I'm the best I've ever seen, heard of or come across. Alvin Honkworth is a nerk. Even other nerks think he's a nerk."

"I'll tell him your opinion," she threatened sweetly.

"Woe is me," I said politely. I moved aside. The Imari plates called. Dutch copies, as I'd thought. Lots of pretty famous porcelain is really artistically poor. Among the poorest (and somewhat "overpriced" at provincial auctions nowadays), I rank these continental Imaris, plus soft-paste Lowestoft, the enamel-painted hard-paste Bristol porcelain figures of 1775 vintage, and much of the underglaze-blue transfer-printed hard-paste porcelain garbage from Staffordshire's New Hall China Manufactory of the mid-1780s. Seriously underpriced, though, if you can currently believe that of anything, is the eerily glowing mother-of-pearl Belleek porcelain from Fermanagh, though it's more modern. (Incidentally, the mark "Ireland" was only added to the harp and Irish hound mark after the McKinley Tariff Act took effect in America, 1890, so look before you leap.)

"Stop mauling Aunt Martha's porcelains," Dolly snapped. I replaced the lovely Belleek jug with a wrench. "Are you always so rude, Lovejoy?" Dolly was still bristling as old Henry entered our merry scene, floating discreetly in like a dandelion seed.

"Yes," I answered to shut her up. "Hello, Henry."

"Ah, Lovejoy!" he beamed. "The inherent benevolence of Man triumphs again over the onslaughts of the insensitive!"

"Before we begin," Martha interposed firmly, "let's be seated. Conversation over lunch is so much more preferable than all this hovering with empty glasses."

We hadn't been exactly stuck for words, but clearly she was expert at scuppering Henry's theological chat. We trooped into the dining room. I never know what to do with my glass. Other people usually manage to get rid of theirs somehow. Breeding, I suppose.

The meal was pleasant, served by two friendly women. I tried not to eat like a horse, but you can't help being a born opportunist. Finally I threw elegance to the wind and ate anything they put in front of me. Old Henry and Martha spun their grub out to keep me company, talking of incidentals. Dolly sat determinedly trying to disconcert me, elbows on the table and pointedly glancing at her watch. I'd made a hit there, I thought. Henry prattled about his undergraduate days at Cambridge and Martha prompted him if he tended to ramble. I tried to feel along underneath the tablecloth's hem without anyone noticing what I was doing. It was obviously a two-pedestal table, but a genuine eighteenth-century pedestal-based dining table will have no inlays. Also, simply count the number of pedestals the table's got. Subtract one. That gives you the number of leaves the genuine table ought to have. I was quivering with eagerness to get underneath and see if the legs were reeded. I ate, pressed hard against the table. If the table rim is reeded its four slender legs must be reeded. My bell was donging desperately, but the polite natter would have faltered if I'd dived underneath and fondled all available legs, so I plowed on through the meal, secretly lusting after the table.

"Your visitor's a pleasure to feed," Martha's principal serf said, all fond.

"Marvelous," the other serf chipped in. "Instead of your two wee appetites."

"We do our best," Henry said, pulling a face.

This really puzzles me. Why aren't women wild because all their work in making grub's gone up in smoke? I'd cleared the lot. Logically, you'd think they'd be annoyed.

"We shall have to make your visit a regular occasion," Henry beamed. He looked like a happy pipe cleaner. He'd only had a mouthful or two, without enthusiasm. No wonder he never filled out.

"Of course we shall," Martha said. "It's a standing invitation and you must insure that it's frequently accepted, Lovejoy. See to it. But to work. I have a plan," she announced. "Henry and Lovejoy shall discuss our, er, business walking in the garden. Dolly and I shall keep out of your way."

"How ridiculous!" Dolly snapped. "That's . . . antiquated."

"It's perfectly sensible, dear," Martha corrected blandly. "Seeing that I made a perfect mess of last night's discussion, and that you take after me on your mother's side. Besides," she added, rising, "you're always in such a temper these days. A quiet think will do you good."

"Aunt Martha!"

"This is our signal," Henry confided to me in a whisper, as if Martha had given the obliquest of hints. "I'll show you my barge."

"Is that thing yours?"

"Yes." He sounded so proud of it. "Come down."

We strolled down toward the river. A few serious anglers were spaced along the opposite riverbank. Some sort of fishing competition, judging by the white wooden stakes driven into the bank to show limits. In the distance a pub and a bridge with a few Tudor houses and a thatched cottage or two. You've never seen such moribund boredom. Henry seemed amused at my reaction.

We reached the barge by balancing across a plank. Henry led down to the single long cabin. He had it arranged quite neatly, a folding bed, and a small galley stove barely lit. He lit a candle stub, apologizing.

"I keep meaning to get one of those gas bottles," he told me, "but they keep needing filling. We must celebrate first." He poured a drink for us in enormous tumblers, rum and orange. "Martha understands my need for solitude." We sat opposite each other and listened to the river sounds entering the cabin. I glanced out at the anglers, but none had moved. They sat there like troglodytes, watching their strings and the still water, a real ball. Riveting.

"Er, look, Henry," I began. Somebody had to get it over and done with. "This Grail thing." Now for my bad news, I thought. I launched into a summary of the endless rumors, the wasted searches, the endless time expended on red herrings. "It isn't just the Grail," I finished. "It's a million other precious things."

"I know all that, Lovejoy," he said. He refilled our tumblers. "And I'm grateful for your frankness."

Funny, but the old chap didn't seem abashed.

"The chances of anybody ever finding an object like the Grail are . . ."

"About the same," he put in, smiling, "as finding the Cross?"

"Well, Saint Helena rather pushed her luck," I said. That gave him one more grin.

"I know what you must be thinking, Lovejoy." He leaned back reflectively. "That age or mental instability has deranged me. But I do have it. The Grail, I mean. It *is* real. Actual. Material."

"Oh for God's sake, Henry!" I rose and paced the narrow cabin. "This relic game's overdone. All right—I give you there must have been some object, a pottery cup or glass—"

"Pewter," Henry corrected gravely. "It looks like pewter."

"Right. Pewter, then." I rounded on him. "Whatever. But relics were an industry. Do you know how many places have been founded on the faintest hints of hearsay? Even—"

"I know, Lovejoy." He sat watching me and sipping his rum. "Everything from Christ's milk teeth to hair and foreskin. The Centurion's spear, Magdalen's linen cloth, Peter's sandals—"

"Do you know," I said rudely, "that owning a relic—real or otherwise—was such an attraction that . . . that when Francis was dying at Assisi they even had to put an armed guard on the poor bugger so he wasn't torn to pieces of premature relic? It was a game, Henry," I ended wearily. "A sad demented game." My glass was empty. "And nowadays the game's over."

He filled my glass to the brim, chirpy as ever. "I've been looking for somebody like you for some years, merely to inspect the object. Confirm what it is."

I thought about that. "And if I say it's junk?"

"Supposing," he said, "an object, worthless in itself, was the focus of veneration for millions of people. Would that be—indeed, *could* it be merely junk? Ever?" He shook his head with

45

certainty. "There is such a thing as sanctification by use, by belief. Loving," he added, "is the practice of love. Love is loving. There are no half measures, no staging posts to love. It's not a noun, Lovejoy. It's an active participle."

"Henry," I said resignedly. "You're beginning to sound like me. All right, I surrender. Where's your crummy old tin cup?"

He insisted on pouring still more for us both. I was having a hard time keeping up with the old blighter. "I'll show you. Not today, but I promise." He jerked his Adam's apple up and down under the tilted bottle.

I don't remember how long we stayed there. I vaguely recall some angler banging on the cabin roof shouting we were ruining the fishing match, but both Henry and I were sloshed and singing by then. We only yelled abuse back. Eventually we ran out of rum.

"The swine have sold us an empty bottle," the Reverend Henry accused. "Let's report them."

We fell about at this witticism and reeled back up the lawn to the house. Everything seemed hilarious. Martha had tea ready on the terrace. Such elegance. Two new visitors were there.

"Have you been hiding that foul concoction down in that dreadful boat?" she blazed. This made us laugh so much I had to pick Henry up.

"Shhh," we both told her simultaneously.

"This is Lovejoy," Martha was saying, which was odd because I already knew I was Lovejoy. I roared with laughter.

"I already know I'm Lovejoy," I said. Henry fell about at this, because he knew it too.

"How do you do?" this woman said. "I'm Sarah Devonish." I noticed the specs, amber beads and aggressive handshake full of rings. "Hello, Henry."

"Ah, Sarah, my dear." Henry gave an elegant bow and tumbled over.

"Have you been tippling again, Henry?" It sounded a threat the way she said it.

"Certainly not," Henry said with dignity from the paving.

"That will do." Sarah yanked him to his feet, full of anger and

46

hating me, why I don't know. "Thomas, give me a hand."

Thomas turned out to be a pleasant bloke about Henry's age, a bumbler. He made a mess of trying to introduce himself while struggling to prop old Henry into a chair. Somebody—Martha, probably—called him Dr. Haverro, but he's the sort who falls over your feet every second breath and never gets to his verbs.

"Wait!" our sloshed hero cried. "I want to tell Lovejoy—"

"You've probably said far too much," Sarah said severely. "Martha. Try to sober him up somehow. Thomas and I don't want a totally wasted journey."

It was interesting to see Martha subdued in the presence of this formidable younger woman. I tried to tell her that her amber beads, all opaque and really neffie, badly needed cleaning. It's a fearsome risk to dip them in solvents or cleaning agents.

"Most people use rectified turps and alcohol," I explained cheerfully. "But for heaven's sake see that you *feed* amber afterward. The beads will come lovely and deep, transparent as ever like a beautiful deep gold sea. Use dammar. Be careful to see that your beeswax—"

"*Please!*" Sarah snapped, so I shut up while they tried to bring Henry down through the superstrata. He crooned a light air from *The Mikado.* I could see she was a tough nut. Her amber beads deserved better.

"So sorry about this," Thomas said to me apologetically in an undertone. "First acquaintance and all that."

"Not at all," I said, thinking how reasonable he seemed compared to the bossy Sarah. She was an attractive middle age, but if you're savage and utterly merciless about amber, you can be as bad about people, can't you?

"Don't mind Thomas," Henry said. "We three are guardians of the most precious—"

"Do shut up, you old fool," Sarah said furiously. Henry chuckled.

"Come, come, people," Martha admonished. "Let's all keep calm. It's just as well Dolly's companions came for her," she went on reprovingly, "or she would have disapproved even more than I about this, Henry."

47

Henry and I sang a song about Dolly while they helped me into the Ruby. The gardener swung the starting handle, still grinning and shaking his head.

"I did my courting in one of these," he told me. "Before you were born."

"Will you be all right, Lovejoy?" Martha asked anxiously. "Perhaps it isn't really very wise for you to . . ."

"It knows the way," I answered. Henry and I rolled in the aisles at that. His laugh sounded like a scratchy pen nib. "Chocks away, mate."

They stood aside as I rolled down the road. I thought I drove quite well. In fact I was still thinking that when I reached the outskirts of our village. Then George, our ever vigilant bobby, caught me up on his trusty bike and booked me for drunken driving.

I went in the tavern for a drink. Driving's thirsty work.

VI

I woke up in a foul mood with a headache. My usual health-giving breakfast seemed even lousier than usual so I abandoned it and fried everything I could lay hands on. Tomatoes, celery chunks, carrots, cheese and two eggs. It was a grisly business, but after that I tottered to the phone. The mental image of old Doc Lancaster wringing his hands at my gluttony was a bonus.

I had to get to town and catch Jed and Marion during this morning's summit conference in Woody's. If I couldn't unload Liz Sandwell's antique glass I'd be selling matches by the week-end. But now no car, thanks to Henry's rum.

Margaret was frosty. I tried to put a cheerful grin in my voice. "We must introduce ourselves sometime," she said.

"Er, look, love," I croaked. "Any chance of seeing you?"

"You haven't seen me for days, Lovejoy. And not a word of explanation."

"Well, love, it was like this—"

"I know for a fact you were in the Arcade yesterday." She has the middle booth there. I tried to cut in, but she wouldn't let me. "What do you want this time, Lovejoy?"

That really hurt. As if I'd only ring a fellow dealer—with whom I am on very friendly terms, I might add—when I wanted something.

"Er, any chance of a lift?"

"If you think I'm going to leave my shop just to cart you about after the way you've ignored me lately—"

"But, sweetheart—"

Click. Burr. Another social triumph. There's a typical woman for you. Unreliable and angry. Why they can't be calm and friendly all the time I just don't know. I phoned Marion's number, then everybody else I could think of. Jean Evans was in but just on her way to the day institute to teach sculpture. She sweetly suggested I ring Betty—"You could, shall we say, *ride* together, Lovejoy"—before banging the phone down. I even toyed with the idea of ringing Honkworth, but there's a limit. I was stuck, marooned. And I'd used up all my chances of rescue.

I stood up and shook the tablecloth for the robin. He cackled angrily for some cheese so I went and got the bit I'd saved. A right dogsbody.

"Don't you start," I told him bitterly. "That old couple really had me yesterday."

The trouble is I'm too soft. If I'd just told Martha to get lost and kept her money as a deposit I'd have not got sloshed with old Henry in his crummy barge.

Nothing for it. I kicked the Ruby's tires and went in. I dialed miserably.

"Well, well, *well!*" Sandy shrilled. "Do I detect Lovejoy's dulcet tones?"

"Cut it, Sandy. Can you give me a lift today?"

"For you, dear," Sandy gushed, "no. Unless," he added firmly. We listened to the silence. I gave in.

"Unless?"

"Wait, cherub." His receiver clattered noisily. I heard Sandy call in the distance. Mel must be upstairs. They have an open-floored barn behind their house, which stands back from the road at the other end of our village. Mel is modern art, glass and porcelain as far forward as Art Deco. Sandy is Eastern items and continental household ware up to Edwardian days. They share Victoriana because Sandy says they have to meet somewhere. Despite their oddity they're a formidable pair of antique dealers.

"Mel, dear. It's that hunk, Lovejoy, positively *squirming* with embarrassment."

"What's he want?" Mel's voice.

"A lift. What shall we do?"

"Exploit him to the uttermost." There was some low-voiced —well, high-voiced—muttering.

"Hello, Lovejoy dear?" Sandy cooed. "Mel says he's all for charity, but it will cost you. Your peculiar little knack with some of the rubbish we've got here."

Typical. Sandy and Mel were saying they'd reached their limit of knowledge with their supposed antiques and wanted me to divvie their stuff.

"No," I told him. I get sick of wasting my time working for others.

"Then goodbye, sweetie."

Click. Burr. I counted ten and milled about the garden a minute or two. I locked the cottage and strolled casually up the lane to the chapel. Maybe our supervigilant constable had forgotten.

"Morning, George."

"Morning, Lovejoy." As I'd guessed he was standing by the crossroads waiting for me to appear in the Ruby. "Just let me see you in that old crate, Lovejoy, that's all." He gets depressed if I smile, so I smiled like a politician and strolled back, fuming. I rang Sandy again.

"I'll scan for you, Sandy, after you give me a lift."

"You darling boy," he gushed. "Where to?"

"To Marion's. Then maybe Liz Sandwell's."

"Oh, pus and spit." He sounded even more resigned than I did. "As long as you don't expect me to come in too and positively gape at La Sandwell's ghastly wallpaper." I said I didn't. "And no offering that whore Marion lifts in our beautiful motor. If she comes with us she comes running behind *chained* to the mudguard." He tittered. "Mel just can't stand her stinky perfumes." I said okay. "Promise," he demanded. "Say cross my heart." I promised wearily. Even a phone call's a right panto-mime with Mel and Sandy.

They couldn't come for me until five that afternoon, which was later than I wanted to be, but they were my only chance. I spent the day reading about Glastonbury and the various Grail legends. It was a wasted day. The whole story was as mystic and remote as ever. I was depressed by the numbers of experts who had broken their hearts trying to find the answer.

By the time they arrived I'd decided Henry was deranged. Their Rover had started out royal blue saloon. It was now cov-ered in a dazzling array of painted flowers, stripes, zigzags and twining greenery. A silver fringe fibrillated all the way around the outside, above the windows. It was a mess. You can see why I'd left them till last.

Mel was sulking in the passenger seat.

"Mel's in a mood, Lovejoy," Sandy called, reversing in. *"Ca-veat emptor.* But don't worry, dear. I can sulk better than him."

"Hello, Sandy. Mel." I got in the back. It felt like a hovercraft after mine.

"I'd shake hands but I'm not to be trusted." Sandy gave me a roguish wink.

"Marion's, please."

"Mel and I had the most fearsome row," Sandy said. We revved into the lane and took off.

"And for once, Lovejoy, it was *not* my fault." Mel rounded in his seat. "I've got this lovely clock by Tompion, *honestly* quite superbly divine I *mean.* And this . . . this naughty little rascal here—"

"Oh, *language!"* from Sandy.

"—enters it into the next sale up in the Smoke. Honestly."

"Well," I said nervously. Some of their fights last weeks.

"Don't you dare agree with either of us, Lovejoy!" Sandy cried, "or I'll smack your wrist. This conflict is only *apparently* about a clock. It's actually about sepia upholstery. We aren't speaking."

"Like me and George," I said. We halted at the chapel, Sandy happily grinding the gears.

"Yes, we heard all about your drunken el butcho spree." He drew alongside George. "Hello, sweetie pie."

"Any of that and I'll do you—" George tried threatening.

"Not here, love, surely?" Sandy reached out a languid hand. George backed away. "Prosecute Lovejoy and I'll park outside your house all night."

"And your mascara's just wrong, George." Mel came alive long enough to add to George's discomfiture.

"Drive on, or I'll book you for obstruction."

"No, George. Be serious." Sandy fluttered his eyelids. "Would *you* change our motor's fringe back to gold? Isn't silver on cerise and blue a *fearful* risk?"

George eyed the car with hatred. "It's a bloody disgrace."

"Fasten your flies, George—no advertising, dear." Sandy adjusted the driving mirror to see himself better and accelerated away across the front of the arriving post van, causing an ugly squeal of rubber.

"Marion'll wear one of those maddening brown waistcoats that positively *drain* colors from every possible wall, Lovejoy," Sandy predicted. "The cow really is too much . . ."

I closed my eyes and leaned back, thinking this bloody antiques game. I sometimes wish I had a dull, easy job, somewhere peaceful like on an oil rig out in the North Sea.

Marion's place is past the castle along South Hill. When she's absorbed all that Jed can teach her about prints he'll be shown the door. So far she's become quite expert in about eight branches of antiques.

"Isn't it the female tarantula which eats its mate?" Sandy was saying innocently as we pulled in. "Mel, dear," Sandy crooned, "do we stay out here in the noisy, smelly traffic, or encounter dearest Marion?" Mel glowered silently. "No contest, Lovejoy," Sandy concluded.

I shrugged and went inside. Marion was pricing two vinaigrettes, one a Willmore silver gilt fob-watch shape and the other an Empire-style gold oval of about 1810. Joseph Willmore loved the fob-watch style. Life in the good old days being sordid, dirty and full of the most obvious of human stenches, people wanted to disguise the terrible pongs of the cities. So you carried a bottle of perfumed vinegar, hence the name. Men carried them as well as women up to about 1840. You get them all shapes, even as "vinegar sticks," where the container is cleverly made into the handle of a sword or walking stick. Women tended to have them as lockets or on chatelaines. The commonest you find nowadays is a box shape.

I told Marion why I was late. We fenced quite casually, drawing blood over every groat the way friends will. The purchaser has, of course, only a few quid in hand and ten thousand starving children to support. The vendor's paid a fortune and wants at least a groat or two profit. You know the sort of thing. I listened patiently to how Marion's buyers were being driven into the workhouse, the price of rare collectable historic glass being what it is. We settled finally, when our heartstrings could vibrate no more.

"I'll drop the stuff in tomorrow afternoon, Marion."

"Great. Oh, Lovejoy. That creep Leyde was asking around after you this morning. Dealing with him nowadays?"

Bill Leyde. Of course. Honkworth's pal, the sleek sourface who traveled about with Dolly and the blousy blonde in Honkworth's car. I looked blank.

"At Woody's. Got quite agitated." She eyed me evenly. "Jed and me got the feeling he was waiting for you."

And me late into town because of George, the burke.

"Did he say why?"

"No. Jed had to shoot off to Gennell's." Our local auction warehouse near Saint Jude's derelict church.

"Thanks, love," I said casually.

She waved to me from the doorway as I stepped into Sandy's car. I'd been over an hour.

"Marion, dearie," Sandy called in syrupy tones. "Don't stand about in the street. *Do* go inside. People are *so* quick to misunderstand."

He drove off with a squeal of tires into the traffic before she could reply.

"Did you see that absolutely fearful russet bolero she was *welded* into, the stupid hag?" Mel hissed malevolently.

"Couldn't look past those crocodile shoes, dearie," Sandy said blithely. "If only she had some friends willing to tell her, poor cow."

"I thought she looked nice," I offered.

"Lovejoy," Mel said over his shoulder with feeling, "you were so *brave.*"

"Liz Sandwell's, please, lads," I said.

"That purulent green wallpaper!" Sandy shrieked.

They both groaned.

I had a lot to think about during the journey. Martha said Dolly had gone with "her friends" when old Henry and I had tottered up the garden yesterday, sloshed on his vitriolic rum. Presumably that included Leyde. Now here he was practically champing on his reins wanting to see me.

"Marion said Leyde was zipping about," I said, too casually.

"A real el butcho," Mel said. "Consorts with your buddy Honkworth." They tittered, knowing we didn't get on.

"Gelt man," Sandy added. He gave a serene regal wave to a demented gatekeeper at the level crossing toward the by-pass. I opened my eyes as the Norwich express thundered past inches from me. Sandy sounded his horn at it, irritated. "Pestered the life out of us for some lovely Belgian niello and gold pendants, didn't he, Mel?"

I scraped my memory for details of Leyde but could find very little. He seemed to deal mostly with dealers in London and the Midlands.

By the time we reached Liz Sandwell's place I was so uneasy I wasn't able to keep up with Sandy's racy comments on his side of the trade. Mel pretended I was lovelorn. Great jokes at my expense. The pubs were open as we pulled up to the curb at Liz's shop.

"You will forgive us, Lovejoy," Sandy said. "But we need

something to settle our little tummies. We'll come back for you elevenish."

"She asked us to have a bite with her," I said, but knowing they sometimes go to this tavern for supper in Dragonsdale. They tittered, nudging.

"Bouillabaisse," Sandy warned me. "It's all she can do, poor cow. *Wrong* seasoning."

"Do take care, dear boy," Mel said. "Avoid her horsehair sofa at all costs. Gallant lads have been known never to return."

They blew extravagant kisses at Liz's window as they pulled away.

"They send their apologies," I said apologetically to Liz.

She laughed. "I quite understand, Lovejoy."

"Leyde," I found myself saying as we went inside. "Any news of him lately?"

"Bill Leyde?" Liz sounded surprised. "The geltie? Not for weeks. He got a gold-mounted George the Second scent flask from Margaret in the Arcade last I heard. Why?"

"Nothing." That sort of small purchase is a typical purchase for the dedicated geltie. "May be a deal on, that's all."

It lingered in my mind, but I chatted about this and that. It was bouillabaisse, Liz told me, whatever that is. I said fine and did the wine. I'm all thumbs at things like that, but Liz only laughed at the floating cork bits. She said we could spoon them out. We spent some, er, moments on her horsehair sofa after supper.

It was a chance remark she made that connected oddly in my mind and fetched me back to earth.

"You've torn my blouse again, Lovejoy."

"Oh, er, sorry."

She smiled and said not to worry, rubbed her forehead on my face. The clock said eleven. "Everything you touch gets changed, doesn't it?" she said, still smiling but looking into me. I pulled my eyes away and went for the antiques.

We settled faster than I should have done. Unease was descending on me. The air seemed thicker. For some inexplicable reason the Irish glass seemed suddenly of secondary importance. By the end of our deal I was almost hurrying and trying not to.

Eventually it was half past and the pair not back yet.

"I've suddenly remembered something, Liz."

"Lovejoy." She was looking at me. "Are you all right?"

"Sure, sure." I found myself at the door. "I'll ring you about collecting the stuff, right?"

"Any time." She followed me anxiously onto the step. A cold wet wind was blowing. "See you at the White Hart tomorrow?"

"Sure."

We waited, talking in brittle sentences, neither knowing quite what to say. Liz asked if it was something she'd said. I told her of course not.

They came at midnight, talking simultaneously, neither listening to each other's inane prattle. Beats me how they communicate. They had full glasses of wine.

"Goodness!" Sandy squeaked, pointing as I rushed in and slammed the door. "What *did* she do to you, dear boy? You're so *pale.*"

"Er, could we go now, please?" I felt choked. "Buresford," I said.

"At *this* time?" Mel decided to sulk again. "Sodding *hell.*" He gave me his glass to hold while he took the wheel.

There was some bickering, but they did as I said. I was in an ugly sweat by now. Maybe I was sickening for something, but I didn't think so.

"This is like going to London via Cape Horn, Lovejoy." Even the tolerant Sandy was narked at me now. Great.

I began to wish I'd never heard of old Reverend Henry Swan and Martha and their faked bloody sword. I didn't even wave to Liz.

Approaching Buresford a police car overtook us, flashing and wailing. I watched it, my heart heavy with foreboding. Mel drove one-handed, gave it a silent toast, his glass of port raised.

"They took no notice of us!" Sandy complained.

"It's their loss, dear," from Mel.

We braked suddenly.

"Mel! You've spilled my drink!" Sandy squealed. "Oh, it was *doomed* from the start."

Ahead the road curves to enter Buresford near the church, the black and white cottages in headlights by the river bend. A constable flagged us slowly on. Two police cars flashed impatient lights at rest in Martha Cookson's gateway. An ambulance whirred out of the drive and tore past.

I racked the window down. My hand was shaking.

"Can we go in, Constable?"

"There's been an explosion. I've orders to admit no one."

"Anybody hurt?" The feeling was gone now, only a certainty of tragedy remaining.

"Yes. One member of the family and two anglers." He seemed worried and somewhat lost.

I told Mel to drive through the gateway. The policeman was relieved somebody else had made a decision and waved us in. I honestly don't know what the police are playing at these days, sending bobbies out the way they do. They all seem worried sick and green as grass. No wonder there are criminals about.

We couldn't reach the house because of two motorcycles propped across the drive. It looked like a film set with lights and cables. Three police were talking and scribbling by the ornamental fountain. I made myself observe the lunatic scene yard by yard. A small cluster of people were down by the river. A few others were gathered around the ambulance parked incongruously in the center of the lawn's edge. The ground everywhere was scored by tire marks.

For some seconds the essentials failed to register in my mind. Then I began picking them up more sensibly, one by one. It was as if my mind was checking off items accepted for recognition. The two white-coated figures. A nurse running the few steps into the ambulance for something shiny. Tubes. An inverted bottle of yellow fluid. One doctor with shiny shoes, one doctor in white slipper things. Another constable being told to hold on to the bottle for a moment, please, just like that thank you, and kneeling his creased trousers into the muddy ground, carefully doing as he was asked with sweat trickling from under his helmet.

Smoke pouring up from the river and two fire vehicles blinking redly across the other side of the water. Hoses snaked down and pulsing in time with the throbs from the engine. One fireman in a yellow helmet shouting orders from among the bullrushes. Another ambulance over there, with doors flung wide and two white coats huddled down.

"My *God!*" I heard Sandy say faintly. "Lovejoy . . ."

A policeman was holding me back on the drive. Somehow I was pushing past and saying get out of the bloody way. Then running to the little riverside terrace and the people there.

A long bundle on the ground. Anglers on the opposite bank in twos and threes talking and looking, one with his small son carefully folding a keepnet as black oily smoke rolled among the weeds. Everything was in half shadow, macabre.

Then the longboat. I never realized their hulls were so flat underneath, flat as a pavement. Rust showed and some weeds stuck along the sides. Smoke billowed. I mean that it *billowed* like smoke in famous poems and children's pirate stories, roll after roll from the barge. You only need to see a devastated boat for all the sea sagas ever written to become instantly understandable. Oh, I know a ruined house or a wrecked plane that can never fly again is utterly pathetic. But a crumpled boat is somehow so tragic that even to look is almost unbearable. The crackled windows, the ruptured cabin. The crumpled metal sides, sort of owning up that the gaunt sea creature is actually a thing put together and made of iron plates and logs. The paint already blistering from an unseen fire at one end. Piteous.

It had been creased downward, broken as if smashed from above. Both ends were sticking out of the water, and as I stared a fireman clambered onto the front bit and ran nimbly through the smoke, unwinding some trailing hose along its length. He managed it without falling into the river, jumping over the ruined sunken middle fold and hauling himself up into the smoke. Fishes floated white-bellied in the water.

I crossed to the ambulance, stepping over the steel hawser cut clean through on the grass and pathetically still warped to the angled bow. The weird medical ritual always looks the same, doesn't it? Whether it does any good or not nobody seems to know. I hope somebody is adding it up somewhere.

The long bundle was being stretchered into the slots. A nurse gave me the elbow to reach past. The constable was helped up, still holding the inverted bottle. One white coat was blood-stained to the elbow now, the other still spotless. Car tires spun mud against my legs. A voice spoke from an intercom, horribly distorted. I realized I was coughing because the smoke was blowing back over the lawn now. Whatever the firemen were doing was making the smoke worse.

A police sergeant was ordering the grounds cleared. Somebody else was taking names and addresses. Somebody spoke to me. I said sod off. The man put his hand on my arm and said, "Cool down, friend. I'm Maslow, CID. We have to take a few details, that's all."

Doors slammed and the ambulance rolled away toward the drive. A motorcycle kicked into deep sound. A voice called to clear the gateway.

"He's a family friend," Sandy said. He was ashen. "We're with him."

"The old chap," I managed to get out.

"That was him in the blood wagon," Maslow nodded at the drive.

I turned to see the ambulance leaving the garden. Mel was in difficulties. A constable was making him do a bad-tempered three-point turn. More sulks were on the way.

My mind registered again. The long blood-soaked bundle under the tattered old car blanket was therefore the Reverend Henry Swan. The person of, the expiring person of, or the remains of?

"What are his chances?"

"None, I'm afraid." The CID man was a benign elderly square-shaped man, neat and tidily arranged in a crisp suit. He had a clean handkerchief in his top pocket. I'd thought the nonuniformed branch were all fashionably sloppy and soiled. "You know him, then?"

"A bit." I walked back to the river. The smoke was as bad as ever. They'd got a punt from somewhere and two firemen were

60

poling along the shattered boat. River water was shooting into the fire from three hoses. Why did the engines have to make that piercing whine? Probably something to do with pumping. How pathetic to bring such massive ladders for nothing. Then I apologized mentally when I saw the far tender's ladder was stretched sideways over the river, with a fireman stuck on the end of it spraying his jet into the split barge.

"There was an explosion." Maslow had followed me. Sandy went back to rescue Mel.

I thought a bit. "How can a boat burn when it's made of tin?"

"Steel," Maslow pointed out. "And wood. There's all its fuel."

"It hadn't any."

"Oil generator."

"It had electricity from the house." I nodded to the grass. "There's a conduit cable under there to Mrs. Cookson's."

"Gas, then."

"He'd none."

There was a long pause. We both watched the oily smoke. Oily.

I decided he'd need prompting. "Isn't this where you're supposed to tell me who did it?"

"What's your name?" Maslow asked. He seemed angry.

"Find out," I said. "You're the detective. Where's Mrs. Cookson?"

"The hospital," he answered evenly. "And I would advise you not to adopt that tone with me, sir."

I honestly pity them when they go all official. "And I would advise you to use your frigging cerebral cortex," I heard myself say. "Try."

"Are you impeding a police officer in the performance of his duty?" he intoned.

"Some performance." Sometimes they're just pathetic.

I walked to the drive where Sandy and Mel were arguing. Mel rounded on me spitefully.

"If you think this is a *lift,* Lovejoy," he spat, "you can walk because we're going straight home this instant."

"Shut your face," I said as patiently as I could manage. "Look, lads. I'm going to the local hospital immediately. In this car. And if you've any other ideas, well, let's get the chat over with."

They glanced at each other. I opened the driver's door.

"Into the back, Sandy. I'm driving."

He looked at my face and obeyed while I asked the gate constable the way. I saw Maslow standing on the lawn watching us go. He didn't wave either.

It was the remains of, after all. The Reverend Henry Swan was dead on arrival. A shapely receptionist told us this, sounding really quite pleased everything had gone according to the book.

"D.O.A.," she explained, showing us the admissions list. "Do you wish to see the deceased?"

"No." I halted. "Oh. Can you give a message to Inspector Maslow? He'll be along shortly, when he can be bothered."

"Certainly," she said with pencil poised, sixty-five inches of syrup between two pearl earrings.

"The message is that I want an explanation. And to be sharp about it."

"And whom shall I say . . . ?"

"Tell him Lovejoy." I walked out.

Martha Cookson was being accompanied to the police car. Her back had that brave look. No sign of Dolly. I watched her go. Sandy and Mel climbed silently in.

I can remember Sandy sobbing in the back. Just as well he wasn't driving. I can remember Mel saying with relish that anyway he'd told that awful bitch of a receptionist her nails were a *mess* and her twinset didn't *match*, so there. I had the feeling it was somehow supposed to be a compassionate gesture so I said thank you. I can remember George doing his night round grandly stepping forward and holding up his hand at the chapel, and I can remember driving past without a word.

I got out at my gate.

"I appreciate your help," I told the silent couple. "I'm sorry it was such a shambles. I'll, er, do your scan on the weekend. All right?" Mel drew breath to speak again but finally said nothing.

As Sandy, red-eyed and still catching his breath, turned the car I asked one last favor.

"Should you happen to see George pedaling this way," I said kindly, "persuade him to go home. If he comes knocking I'll break his legs. Night."

I went inside and shut the door.

VII

I thought a lot next day. Now, antiques is a very rough game. Let me explain.

Once upon a fetid hot day in 1880 a daring young captain rode out near Kabul and performed a heroic dashing rescue of three merchants from a fierce and marauding band of brigands. At fearsome risk to life and limb, the gallant Captain F. C. Burton, an appointed Political Resident who had every right to stay nodding safely behind his desk, saved not only these travelers but also certain important bits of their baggage. A brave lad. But the point is that he got nothing out of it, which is especially narking when you realize that inside those bags nestled part of the hitherto fabulous Oxus Treasure, almost priceless. Alas, Captain Burton never got a rupee. There's a lesson hidden in there, fans.

Don't you try telling me that virtue is or has its own reward because it's not and it hasn't. Virtue has a sickening habit of breeding poverty and oppression. Everybody else benefits except the virtuous.

I'm telling you all this because the Oxus Treasure—nowadays

tantalizingly arrayed in the British Museum—is a typical instance of treasure troving. Get the moral? Most treasure's in a minefield of one sort or another. And mines go bang. Old Henry Swan had learned that. And I'm no hero like that brave captain.

It was beginning to look as though the Martha and Henry saga of the Holy Grail was not exactly Lovejoy's scene.

On the other hand, my mind went, you can think of a million examples of people finding treasure and living happily ever after. In dark old England people are at it all the time—ancient flints, Roman coins, hammered Early English silver hoards, priceless early church silver and gold Ancient British torques. Right from our sinister prehistory to the weird present day, mankind's precious works are scattered in the soil, under walls, on beams, in rafters, in chests and sunken galleys, in tombs and tumuli. You can't help thinking.

I got one of those Dutch cigars and sat on the grass to watch the sun reach the tall trees down in the copse. Nurse Patmore pedaled by, wobbling to wave. I waved back, feeling fond of her. Devotion to duty's a wonderful thing, isn't it?

The point is that you have a choice. You can reach for the apple or you can resist the temptation. I felt I'd been warned. All the other antique dealers had been warned off as well. Message over and out. Some things just aren't my business.

"Sleep well, Henry," I said. "Sorry and all that."

I fed the birds some diced bacon rind. I brewed up and got a pastie. There's a low decorative wall where the gravel drive starts. One day I'll finish it, but at the moment it's a convenient place to eat and watch the world turn.

On the *other* hand, I thought as I noshed, did you ever hear of anybody *not* reaching for a luscious dangling apple?

Even God guessed wrong on that.

I had a job to do that evening at the pub. Every year I take on a trainee. Usually they're ghastly. You've just no idea. The trouble is that doting parents can't accept that their offspring have the brains of a wooden rocking horse. Even established antique dealers make the same mistake and send me buffoons who can't tell a Rembrandt from a manhole cover. It's a laugh. They even expect me to turn them into divvies. I take a fee for teaching these psychopaths, which keeps me in calories and helps me to stay, undernourished and shoddy, in antiques. This is important, because antiques are everything. Everything.

By nightfall I reckoned the pub would be jumping and getting ready for Lovejoy. I'd recovered enough to wash and shave and think of facing the ordeal. Tinker Dill sent word there'd be six trainees to choose from. My one good white linen shirt was specially cleaned for the ordeal. I'd ironed it early. The cuffs are fraying, but it's better than these modern fibers which stick to your skin and never leave you alone.

I locked up and started for the pub.

Not every dealer has a trainee. Some don't trust them, and most dealers are so ignorant about antiques that everything they teach is unerring crap. Just remember that. So if ever you're selling Grannie's heirlooms the statistical chances of encountering a dealer capable of distinguishing between a priceless Sung Dynasty imperial jade butterfly and reinforced concrete are so remote as not to worry you in the slightest. Keep telling yourself that however little you know about Chippendale you are at least a head start on zero.

I'm not being flippant. There was the case of the forger who wrote letters in *modern* French, signed them "Plato" and "Mary Magdalen" and sold them as genuine antique letters by those worthies. There was the famous case of Billie and Charlie, who minted "coins" with gibberish inscriptions dated in modern numerals—and did so well they had to start up really serious factory-scale production. As I say, zero.

The saloon bar hushed for a split second as I pushed in. Then the talk quickly babbled up again, people just proving they weren't there to see me picking a pupil out.

Tinker Dill waved an arm. He'd got a drink for me on the bar. It's his day, really. Mostly people ignore him. An event like this is the only chance he has to show off. He'd even taken off one of his mittens to reveal the poshness of the occasion; otherwise he was as grubby as ever. All I hope is that when the archeologists come digging down through the atomic ash for traces of our civilization they don't find Tinker Dill's remains first. Chances are they'll just fill the hole.

"Wotcher, Lovejoy!" He pushed the drink at me. When he offers a drink I always wait for the chance to wipe the rim in secrecy. Luckily, the risk of Tinker buying a round is small so it doesn't happen often.

There was a bigger crowd than usual. Betty Marsham was being determinedly casual in stylish black with pearls and her husband. He looked on about his fifth pint. Liz Sandwell was there bossing her bloke about near the dart board. The size of all these blokes gets me down. Then there was the inevitable good old Alvin Honkworth, Esq., showing his true wit by bellowing out, "Hail! The Conquering Hero Comes!" while sleek Bill Leyde tapped time on his glass. Dolly gauged the performance and my arrival like a referee, measuring distances by eye. The flirtatious Angela was in, giving me the thumbs-up sign of optimism, which I suppose is one way of putting it. Her landowning husband was with her, a thin gray whippet of a man chained to a fine Waltham silver fob timepiece with a modern chain, the nerk. I ask you. Jean Evans was on pink gin, chatting to them both. She was in midsentence but managed a disapproving frown in my direction. Marion and Jed were standing talking to a couple of barkers.

Mel and Sandy were there, whispering cattily about Millie's New One. Millie Kay is antique dress and books. Her husband is a Caithness landowner who shoots birds and brags about it. He set her up in an antique shop down in the Arcade and occasionally appears in leggings and tweeds. He never stays long, which lets Millie off the hook. I suppose it takes all sorts. To while away the midnight hours Millie has intent young gentlemen who arrive in MGs or SS Jags and have long hair and cravats. She goes through them (to coin a phrase) about one a week. Tinker says they then get put out to graze in an old folks' home. We call them all Millie's New One to save us headaches from trying to remember their real names, if any. It would be too much effort otherwise. Tonight Millie's New One was a worried elegant youth of the sort people always call "clean limbed," as if the rest of us never wash. He was gazing about, quite bemused, over his gin.

Brad the flintlock dealer was eyeing up one of the new recruits, a plump young lass dressed plain and elderly with specs and a bun. He has an eye for hidden potential. She sat at an alcove table trying to smile at the other five who'd written in. Funny how some women do their damnedest to look offended before you even start.

"They're all here, Lovejoy," Tinker told me, already partly sloshed. "Three blokes, three birds."

Sundry elbows made way for me at the bar, practically the only time I'm shown consideration.

"Where've they come from, Tinker?" I sipped and turned to see them. They hastily pretended to talk, feeling my gaze.

"The quiet lassie dropped out of teaching college," Tinker began. "Her mum's not keen on the trade." A frosty lady with a new Wedgwood cameo sat vigilantly by the saloon bar fire, knees tight together and clearly slumming in a bad cause. Good legs, legitimate savings and matching tea things. I like older women who're like that. They have a tendency to unused bodily generosity. I gave her a smile. She chilled me by a long straight gaze. I sighed inwardly. Another woman completely lacking in trust. "Those brothers," Tinker growled on, "belong in London, dad on the Belly."

I sussed them in the mirrors. These two lads were cool and flashy, gold sovereigns mounted on tiepins and nineteenth-century Italian intaglios mounted as rings, practically splashed down into scrambled gold by some burke. I hate to see antiques spoiled. You never add value by such fancy work. And as for the intaglios—ingraved pictures carved in semiprecious stones such as quartz, jet or jade—the base would undoubtedly be split from such hamfisted mauling. But having a father who traded on the

68

Belly, London's Portobello road, meant that I could ask practically any fee.

"My fame must be spreading," I told Tinker sardonically. "Tell those two to piss off."

"*Eh?*"

"Get rid."

The saloon quieted while Tinker did his stuff. It got quieter when my shoulder was tapped. I never turn around quickly because it doesn't do.

"Lovejoy?" The elder brother was looking me up and down. "I said," he told me loudly, "are you Lovejoy, the divvie?"

"Yes." We were speaking through the bar mirror.

"Somebody's going to be narked," he said. "Somebody it doesn't do to push around. We're here to get taught, friend. By you." Scientists should harness silence for energy.

"Tell your pappy you're too flashy and too ignorant." I gathered from their sudden gapes they weren't used to being spoken to like that. "I don't accept sham." I gave them a look. They dithered uncertainly. "Look, lads," I said eventually, turning now, "no hard feelings. But if you're going to take a swing get it over with. You can see I'm busy." They gazed about, unsure of the general feeling. They sussed me as a loner but hadn't the nerve.

"You'll be seeing us, Lovejoy," the elder said, licking his lip nastily. They must have been raised on a diet of bad Westerns. "Sykes is the name."

"What else?" I said affably. They went, glancing ominously back.

"In trouble, Lovejoy?" Honkworth yelled, to widespread relieved laughter.

"Go on, Tinker." I could see the remaining four in the mirror. He slurped his pint glass to its echo. I signaled a refill.

"Jesus, Lovejoy," Tinker worried. "Sykes is a bad lad. His lot's a right tribe of tearaways."

I let him panic on for a minute, observing the alcove. The one lad now left was embarrassed and trying to chat to the prim miss, but she'd enough trouble of her own. Her mother, somewhat pale about the gills, had shot across the room and was now whispering feverish instructions into her daughter's ear. She was getting only a determined headshake in return. Quite a little drama. The two other women seemed capable and businesslike (not always a good sign in the antique trade) and were distantly engaged in light chitchat.

"Those two lassies have history degrees," Tinker said. "Both from shops. One's Dredger's niece, the other's from the Smoke."

Dredger's nicknamed for a derelict dredger he sails down—not to say up—the creek on weekends. He's mainly furniture and oil paintings. Nobody's ever seen Dredger smile, but he's a reasonable dealer. I heard this lass had a hunger for porcelain. The London girl was a stranger.

"Mummy's girl's local." Tinker's voice went wary. He cleared his throat carefully. "The teacher sent her."

"Which teacher?"

"The one you're after, with the big knockers."

"Elegantly put, Tinker." Luckily bar hubbub covered his flowery lingo. "Jean Evans?"

"Yes." Tinker nodded and rattled his empty glass on the bar. I paid up. God knows where Tinker pours it. I suppose some capable cells were clanging away metabolizing it all. That obviously explained Jean being here this late. There'd be trouble if I slung her protégé out. "Margaret's sent that chap in."

Hello, I thought, still more trouble.

"Let's get it over with."

Their faces seemed so fresh and alive. The prim lass jumped a little as I slid along the bench. Traditionally spit-and-sawdust, the White Hart had upgraded its saloon to a feeble mock-Tudor plush, but its alcoves stayed wholesome.

"This is Lovejoy," Tinker told them. The bar hushed a moment. I'd glimpsed the CID man as I'd crossed over, his expression one of surprise at all this reverence. How nice to see the CID slumming among us mortals. A few dealers—most of them Marion—crowded closer to hear. I can't help feeling a bit sardonic at times like this. They'll listen all day to me grousing away about the way antiques suffer, but any profit they get as a result of my divvying gets carried straight home. The goon was smoking a pipe, too, just like Sherlock Holmes, eyes everywhere. Some people make you sick.

"Hello."

They said hello back. The prim girl started fumbling for references in her handbag, but I stopped her.

"Tinker Dill's told me who you are," I began. "Let's get this straight. Whoever I take on gets no pay for six months' full-time slog. Okay?"

"In exchange for what?" asked the London lass, cool.

"Learning whether you're any bloody good," I told her.

"How many university degrees have *you* got exactly?" she cracked back, all eyebrows.

I gave her a second for the chuckles to die down. "Bethnal Antiques Exchangery, right?" I leaned across the table, grinning. It's at times like this I'm at my most charming. "Three weeks ago, Clever Clogs, you snapped up a lovely original Wedgwood jasper vase, right?"

"Yes," she said, lighting a cigarette. I stopped to watch.

"Notice the spelling on it?" I said gently, still happy. "Wedgwood never spelled his name like that, with a middle E."

"So?"

"So Smith the forger couldn't spell, love. Always got Wedgwood's name wrong in 1840." She was looking less cool now. I could feel one or two observers nudging each other, grinning. "Maybe spelling didn't matter in your university, love," I commiserated gently, "but it does out here."

The other three were silent.

"Better now?" I asked the truculent lass. She nodded, grinding out her fag. I had to stop to watch that too. "Names, please."

The tough nut was Olive. Her college pal claimed the name Angharad, actually a very distinguished ancient moniker with a lot of mileage left in it. The nervous lad said too quickly that people called him Col. With a name like Lovejoy you learn not to pry, so I just nodded. The prim lass was Lydia. And she looked as if she'd been striving to be a suppressed Lydia all her life.

71

"Mr. Lovejoy," a firm dulcetto cried. "I want to protest at this perfectly preposterous form of interview in a public house—"

I turned. Good old Mummy steaming to protect young Lydia.

"Mummy! For heaven's *sake,*" from Lydia, mortified and scarlet-faced.

"Mummy," I said wearily. "Shut your teeth."

I sometimes think the world consists entirely of twenty-year-olds saying "For heaven's *sake*" to their parents. Mummy stalked back to the fireplace to beam more hatred.

"You get a test tonight," I said. I slid a folded paper between the wet beer mats to each of the four.

"A *test?*" Olive said. She was as scandalized as Lydia's Mum. "You must be joking."

"Just mark a few ticks with your eyebrow pencil."

"Not a chance, Lovejoy." She rose and patted my cheek in farewell. "I didn't struggle through university to get grilled by a rough in a pub."

Some struggle, I thought, eyeing her shape to the saloon door. Three down, two to go. Good.

I said, "All sitting comfortably?"

"Yes, thank you," Lydia said, then reddened. I was almost beginning not to believe in Lydia.

"The test. Then do one other thing. Tomorrow, the Castle Museum. Have a wander. Spot which exhibit on Gallery Six is a cheap—" I hesitated, "—an *expensive* forgery."

"Gallery Six?" Angharad thought, wrinkled. "Furniture."

Lydia and Col drew breath simultaneously but stayed quiet. They too knew their galleries.

"And take your guess to Tinker."

"Where do we find Mr. Dill?"

I smiled kindly at Lydia's innocence. So there was still some of it around.

"Try the George tavern," I told her. "He's thirsty about midday."

Col hid a smile, but Tinker sensed an opportunity.

"A little rum, love, when I can afford it," Tinker whined. "For my bad chest, my dear." He gave her his cadaverous gappy grin. "The war."

This charade was getting out of hand.

"Shut it, Tinker, you stupid burke."

"Mr. *Lovejoy!*" from Lydia, offended. I got up. It had been a long day and Ted was glugging me another drink at the bar. I said good night and left them to it.

A few dealers moved casually to the alcove to see my questions, murmuring among themselves. I wondered how many of them could read. I also wondered who'd got my drink, and found the constabulary at my elbow, which solved that. Sherlock Mark Two, pipe on the go.

"Why are you so broke, Lovejoy?" he asked. "Seeing as you're one of those magic divvies."

"Antiques need money, and I've not got any."

"Are you really that good?" He nodded at the alcove.

"One day I'll find another like me."

He smiled the way bobbies do, meaning watch your step whatever you're up to.

"Not in as much trouble as you, Lovejoy, one hopes."

"I'm not in any."

"Oh, but you are." He nodded at my glass. "Drink up. You're coming down to the station."

"Am I?" These goons really nark me. They'll do anything except use their cerebral cortex.

"Yes. Just a few questions."

"Arrest?"

"Not exactly." A pompous tap of pipe on an ashtray which the universe was clearly expected to admire. "Just helping us with inquiries. I don't want any fuss."

Suddenly it was all too much for me. Maybe it was the fug of the crowded saloon bar after a mad strange day. Maybe it was the indelible memory, suddenly brought back stark and horribly clear, of the pathetic bundle being pushed into the ambulance. Or the image of the anxious faces of Lydia, Col and Angharad hoping to be picked to learn this most fearsome of all trades. Or maybe it was just the sight of Ted taking a glass of rum for somebody down the bar. Old Henry Swan had given me his rum in the hope that I'd stop being so bloody pompous and just bother to divvie some old pewter cup he'd got fond of. I had to fight back an abrupt nausea. I said, "I'm sick of you. Get lost."

"Look here—"

I reached for his drink and spat in it.

"People like you really make me spew." I even dug a finger into his chest. "You're irritated because last night's balls-up won't solve itself. You're like a spoiled brat. Some old geezer got crisped and you haven't a frigging clue what to do."

"Lovejoy. I could arrest you for—"

"Then get on with it, comrade." One day I'll really learn to sneer. At the moment it was a skill I badly lacked. He made no move. Typical. "You think it's time you pushed somebody about and think I'll do," I said. There was an appalled silence all around. "Well you're wrong, mush. I'm narked. So I'll tell you something for free. Suss out the old geezer's finisher fast. Or I'll do your job for you, you pathetic smug bastard."

I told Ted I'd have another in the taproom and pushed through the swinging door. I felt old Bill go. He went quietly, without a single further threat. A bit ominous, that. Still, owing to the hectic nature of our little chat Ted hadn't noticed I'd not paid.

It's an ill wind, my grannie would have said.

I gave the CID five minutes to get clear, then slipped out. The evening had spoiled. Halfway down the lane to our chapel near where my hedge starts a car pulled up, headlights lighting the long trees.

"Get in, Lovejoy." A woman's watch-out-you're-for-it voice.

"Wotcher, Betty." I felt a bit down so I got in and let her drive me to the cottage. She told me her husband had met up with some of his rugby colleagues and chased off on the razz-dazz.

She waited in silence as I got out at my gate. I paused, thinking. She'd probably have to hang around a whole hour before

74

her husband came reeling home after the pubs finally turfed him and his pals onto the High Street. I felt sympathetic. We could probably find something to talk about if she waited in the cottage with me. I cleared my throat.

"Er, want a cup of coffee, love?" I suggested.

She exhaled and gazed my way. "I thought you'd never ask, Lovejoy."

Well, forgiveness is my strong suit.

VIII

I'd better tell you here what the dark secret of Gallery Six is.

When you think of it, it's odd that the great furniture geniuses don't get the praise they deserve. Mayhew and Ince, Lock and a score of others are in the Sheraton-Chippendale class, but outside the antiques trade people are hardly interested. They'd rather take an outside chance on an escritoire being Chippendale than buy a genuine beautiful Mayhew cabinet. It honestly beats me. There's nowt as odd as folk.

Somebody once worked it out that the population in the George III period was about twelve million or so. Assuming there were 140,000 families wealthy enough to furnish their houses by purchasing from the great London makers, why, one might ask, are there so many pieces of this furniture still around in excess of the numbers you'd expect? The answer is, of course, that sinners abound still making "old" furniture. Some are better than others, of course, but all very, very busily plying their sinful trade. We have a saying that the Impressionists painted 1,000 pictures, of which 2,000 are genuine and 3,000 are in America. See what I mean?

Some years ago I was broke. Again. I made a lovely little slide-topped Davenport from new mahogany for a bloke who paid me well, in the days before money got funny. He wanted it aged, please, Lovejoy, to match this valuable antique bureau . . . Stained areas are easy to fake old. To do this I normally use copal varnish and a darking stain, repeatedly wiped gently with glass paper between coats. The unstained areas are more difficult. Take a wet tea towel and stroke the mahogany vigorously till damp. Rush the piece into sunlight. Then take it, after maybe a good half day's exposure, indoors and repeat the wet wiping. Sun. Wet. Sun. Et cetera. If you live where I do and the weather's its usual crummy self, use a sunray lamp. Other forgers use an oven but risk damaging the wood, especially near the dovetail joints. Result? One dark lovely mahogany Davenport. My buyer sold it as an antique. I didn't know whether to be proud or to sulk because he didn't share the profit, but profit only ever belongs to one person in the antiques game.

The reason I'm telling you this is that my Davenport's now in Gallery Six, Antique Furnishings, where I'd sent Col, Angharad and Lydia. They label it as genuine, which embarrasses me, but I don't feel heroic enough to own up. Magistrates tend to get ideas.

I decided to have a quiet morning, richly deserved.

Betty stayed until about one o'clock, when all good people are fast asleep. She'd put her car at the side of the cottage so that our village's prowling spinsters couldn't actually spot it from the lane because the hedge gets in the way. By the time she went home we weren't mad at each other at all, though we had a bit of an argument.

"Aren't you going to get up and see me off?" she whispered, struggling to dress in the darkness.

"No."

"You selfish—"

"I want your warm patch," I explained. You have to be patient with them. "Women always get a warmer part of the bed than me." Mistake, but sleep was on me.

"*What* women, Lovejoy?" No whispering now.

"You. I mean you. Honest."

We compromised. I dashed out once she'd dressed, whisked her into the hall, gave her a quick peck and hurtled back into bed. She whispered I was bloody selfish and I whispered well there's a bloody limit isn't there and that anyway she was all wrapped up and I was starkers. She said typical Lovejoy treatment and slammed out.

I settled into a well-earned doze, thinking that's the odd thing about being holy. It says Love Thy Neighbor. That bit's easy. But sending a neighbor on her way rejoicing's really a very difficult thing to do.

Then the phone rang. At this ridiculous hour.

"Lovejoy?"

"I thought I told you to sod off, Sergeant."

"Inspector," the voice said, but I wasn't having any.

"Do you know what the bloody hour is, Sergeant?"

"That's the point, Lovejoy." We fell silent.

The only event had been Betty, pushing off in a rage. Hey-ho.

"If," he said pleasantly, "you're still refusing to help my inquiries, I shall pay a call on the Marshams and explain—"

"—how you just happened to be outside in the lane and saw Betty drive off?" I filled in uneasily.

"Precisely."

"I might complain to the boss of the local CID," I threatened, scraping the barrel.

"Do," he said, still content. "It's me."

Well, I thought, wise trees bend in a gale.

"How about," he suggested mildly, "I meet you for a quiet cooperative chat? I'll stand you a brown ale."

"Tomorrow dinner time." I gave in. "The George."

"Great," he agreed. "Oh, Lovejoy. Sleep well."

"Sod off," I said, slamming the blower down.

When I climbed in, the warm patch had cooled. There are times you can't rely on anything.

Quiet mornings are marvelous. This particular morning the sun was given to secret gleamings from a half-opaque white sky.

A low mist hung between trees cooling their branches. Hedge-hogs were stooging about the garden doing a final round on lifted pink feet. Some birds bummed about, mostly sorts of pointed sparrows. Till the dew's off the grass I go into my cellar to keep up the good work on antiques. I keep records.

Within an hour I'd found three Swans, curiously all collectors and all about Henry Swan's age. One, a born buccaneer, had written to me offering a miniature of Elizabeth I by the famous Nicholas Hilliard for a lowly price—as it should be, because the original's still in Berkeley Castle. Incidentally, Hilliard loved to paint these rarities (value: about eight times your annual wage, today's minimum) on playing cards, sometimes overstretched with skin of chicks or aborted lambs. So forgeries are pretty easy to spot. The second Swan appeared three years back to win a lovely Georgian pole screen (tip: all things being equal, shield-shaped ones are worth much more than rectangular or circular). The last Swan is well known around here and collects only "frig-gers," small glass objects and figures made by the glass craftsmen from odd bits of glass left once the day's official glassworking had ended. Some are lovely—minute colored glass gloves, dolls, furniture, tiny glass fruit and animals and glass pastry-rollers filled with "lucky salt" blessed to prevent disease or increase fertility. Don't laugh. Some friggers are worth a small fortune. Many were made at the traveling fairs which used to visit our villages—in fact, we have two such glassmakers still at it. But watch out for the cheap Czechoslovakian glass friggers Wool-worth's used to sell before the War—they were threepence then, and I think they should still be threepence now. I keep warning people, but they won't listen.

That accounted for all the Swans in my files. No record of the late Henry Swan. And the only other Cooksons I knew of were two sisters who collect Victorian manuscript diaries.

I tidied away and got some bread for the birds. The garden hadn't changed, but now the morning seemed vaguely sour. The bus was due.

I used the journey to decide what to do.

Sentiment's a queer thing. It gets everywhere, seeps in and out of places you wouldn't normally expect. Last night I belligerently took up the cudgels on poor old Henry's behalf against Maslow. Last night it seemed so righteous to cast myself in the role of noble hero. Now here I was trying mentally to chuck in the sponge. The trouble is you need money to be heroic and as usual I was living hand-to-mouth.

But about this sentiment stuff. Old Henry had used that odd phrase of his twice or three times while we'd got sloshed on his barge. What was it, sanctification by use? An interesting idea, but is it the sort that the Lovejoys of this world go to war about? It bloody well is not.

I can't remember much about our conversation except at one point when he'd said, rheumy old eyes atwinkle, "It's an antique, Lovejoy. Maybe *the* antique," which at the time made me fall about laughing. Some claim. And yet . . .

Maybe old Henry had been telling me that his daft belief about his old pewter cup was exactly the same as mine about all antiques. Thinking, this quiet grayish morning, I thought he seemed close. After all, I reasoned uncomfortably, all antiques only start off a piece of wood, stone, marble or a few pigments mixed with oil and brushed onto rough old canvas, don't they?

What I'm saying isn't an excuse for the terrible things that began to happen. I accept part of the blame, though I didn't start it.

Henry was right in a sense. The love you work into a thing gives it life. On the bus I decided I'd help the CID with reluctance, but getting blown up like Henry was not part of my plan.

I was in the George by opening time.

IX

Margaret Dainty had come from kindness. She is one of the slower age-drifters. She might be twenty-five or fifty, but that plump allure's still there. Hair deceptively casual, always looks a little dressy and overgroomed, but maybe that's because younger women have this crummy modern fashion of looking shop-soiled.

Margaret comes from an old army family, the sort that thinks drinking before dusk's unpatriotic, sinful and stirs up the natives. I don't, so I got some cheap white wine and started on the urgent job of restoring my nerves. We sat overlooking the crowded pavement through the leaded window. Elizabeth the First seated herself precisely in the same spot once upon a time, gazing over the selfsame street. And fifteen centuries before that Claudius the God had ridden past in triumph. I love the human connection —was Bess tired, did she put her feet up? Did Claudius have difficulty keeping his laurel wreath on while his war elephants swayed ahead of his legions?

"Eh?"

81

Margaret was saying something. "You shouldn't have risked trouble last night."

"There was no trouble," I said guardedly. Maybe she'd seen Betty follow me from the White Hart.

"The Sykes boys. And what did the CID want?"

"A football result," I told her, avoiding her eyes.

"Be careful, Lovejoy."

"You know me," I said reassuringly.

We sipped and gazed out. Jimmo walked past carrying a long slender canvas bag and a basket.

"Jimmo's come up in the world." Margaret smiled. "A new two-tone motorcar."

I stared. He'd been broke a couple of days ago.

Margaret smiled happily, always pleased at the success of others. She's unique. "That's his new craze."

"The car?" It had been in a salesman's window yesterday.

"No. Fishing." She was suddenly watching my face. "What is it, Lovejoy? You're all on edge."

Well, you can't help wondering, can you? Fishing equals a river, which equals Stour, which in the dark hours had been disturbed by a savage explosion in which an old dreamer got transmuted. And a couple of drunken bums laughing and getting sloshed in a barge on a quiet river reach tend to converse loudly. An angler who happened to be an eager antique dealer might have heard . . . No. I shook the thought off. We'd known Jimmo for years.

Maybe it was a mistake, but I found myself telling Margaret about old Henry, the explosion, Mel and Sandy giving me a lift and Henry's daft request. So she wouldn't assume I'd gone bananas I didn't admit he thought he'd actually got the Grail. I said nothing about Jimmo. She was commiserating when Tinker showed.

"How do, Lovejoy, Margaret."

"Morning, Tinker. All ready?"

He came belching, still wiping accumulated egg stains from his stubble with a greasy mitten. I waved a pint over. First things first.

"Sure, Lovejoy."

"One thing, Tinker. Just seen Jimmo, off fishing. Where's he go?"

"Oh, Stour, Layer Pits, down the estuary sometimes." He gave me a theatrical nudge, winking. "On the rebound. Broke off with that dollybird called Dolly." He chuckled. "Get it? Dolly, dollybird?" That was news. So Dolly and Jimmo . . .

"A superb play on words, Tinker." I waited gravely for his creaks of laughter to subside. There's nothing you can do about some people. "Sudden wealth, eh?"

"New car," Tinker agreed, gazing soulfully into his empty glass. I got him another to prevent a relapse.

"How come? Jimmo done any buying lately?"

He thought hard—no mean task at this hour—and shook his head. "None I know of."

"He sold a pair of Satsuma decoratives," Margaret put in. "A collector, out Ipswich way. I could be wrong."

"Lovejoy?" Nan the barmaid was pointing. Lydia's interesting silhouette showed against the frosted glass. Sand-etched "frosted" glass pub windows are highly sought after. Those with Victorian or Edwardian patterns mostly finish up installed in nooky orange and gilt parlors as a gimmick to make an impression on visitors. "She won't come in," Nan called.

"Why the hell not?" I growled. Margaret and Nan were smiling. Tinker went out. She came sidling in, frightened to touch the furniture and looking at the floor. She only managed to move her lips soundlessly when Nan called a good morning. With true grit she sat down on a pub chair without giving it a quick polish. Nerves of steel. Her fingernails were clean, just like Margaret's. I closed my hands in case mine weren't.

"What's up, love?" Tinker crashed in cheerfully. "Never been in a pub on your own before?" He cackled a burst of foul-stinking noisy breath, splitting his sides at his light banter.

"No," Lydia whispered. That shut Tinker up. He'd assumed that's where people came from. "Good morning, Mrs. Lovejoy."

"Er, Margaret Dainty, Lydia." I got that in swiftly. These misunderstandings give women ideas they should do without.

"Oh, dear." Lydia half rose in panic, but Margaret calmed her with a friendly word and sent Tinker for some orange juice. He reeled giddily toward the bar, wondering what the world was coming to.

Actually I've been married, if that's the right word. It wasn't bad except that the aggro with Cissie got me down. I'd felt like a half-pint Tom pitted against a relentless armor-plated Jerry. I scrutinized Lydia during the preliminary skirmishing between her and Margaret. They both seemed pleased. Despite Lydia's soft and shy appearance I was on my guard. I reckon women are a very, very tough-minded bunch. Gifted with so much beauty, they nonetheless have a type of low cunning which gives them all the advantages in life. Also, they can be very unreasonable where fair-minded people like me are concerned.

"I *was* married, once," I chipped in, hoping to clarify matters. A mistake.

"Oh, do forgive me." Lydia's eyes filled. "When did it . . . ?"

"No, no." This was all getting too much. Lydia was obviously one of those birds whose conversation gets queerly deformed halfway through. "Divorce. Actually it was my fault . . ."

A woman usually likes this sort of modesty, knowing it can't possibly be true because each thinks all other women are basically undesirables even on a good day. My unblemished humility didn't work this time. Lydia froze.

"Oh!" She switched instantly to outrage, lips thin as a bacon slicer. "I *see.*"

"That reveals my base, carnal nature," I said pleasantly, and saw from her expression that the million warnings she'd had were coming true.

"Miss Evans did furnish me with the advice that . . . *certain* antique dealers were of a *certain* disposition."

I couldn't help staring. She sat there indignantly, full of wholesome fruit, morals and wheat germ. There's a lot of people about who actually talk like this, many more than there used to be. It's probably caught off the telly.

"Good old Jean," I said. "But about antiques, love."

"It's only his way, Lydia," Margaret said.

84

A familiar figure loomed in the doorway and waved. I didn't even gesture toward my wallet. Tinker, on his way back with a fistful of glasses, shied nervously.

"Morning, Tinker," the Old Bill said.

"Why, hello, Mr. Maslow."

Lydia sat watching in horror as Tinker's filthy mittens distributed the glasses around the table. You could see that microbes were suddenly on her mind.

"Maslow, Lovejoy," Tinker whispered. "A right bast—er, a real grouser." Street traders' slang for a bobby of serious and unpleasant disposition. My own feeling is that there's too much law knocking around these days. It's invented by secluded crowds of schizophrenics who play at making rules for some imaginary world in the sky. The pity is that we've no way of pointing the law in the right direction.

Maslow stood at the bar chatting to Nan, his back toward us. On the Continent he'd have been stymied, but you never get an English pub without six thousand mirrors on every wall. He could see in everybody's earhole.

I nodded for Lydia to start up. She drew breath.

"There's something wrong in Gallery Six. A Davenport in the central display."

"But that Davenport's beautiful . . ." Margaret halted abruptly when I gave her the bent eye.

"It's . . . it's an excellent piece of work," Lydia said. "Lovely. The texture's almost right and the colors exquisite." Her eyes were glowing now behind her bottle lenses. "Somebody has created it with such . . . well, feeling. But it is modern, not antique."

"Sure?" I said.

"Yes." She examined her hands and said nothing.

"What tipped you off?" You have to be ruthless at this stage.

"I . . . I just don't know," she admitted. "The poor thing. So beautiful, yet basically a . . . well, just a trick, isn't it?"

I gazed at her in silence for a moment. Tinker gave me her answer paper, a lined sheet torn from a spring notebook. Eight out of twelve right. Only an average knowledge, but knowledge is only a small percentage of knowing after all.

"Have a look at this." I gave her a dazzling little 1598 leather-bound copy of John Wylie's madrigals. Margaret had lent it. Lydia flipped it carefully, guessing it was special from my handling, but clearly bemused.

"An old book." Quite lost. "Is it genuine?"

"Yes. Rare. Superb. Brilliant."

"Oh. I'm afraid I know so little—"

"He was inspired by an illicit love affair. Lady Mary of Saint Osyth. They were always at it." Lydia hastily dropped the book, reddening. "You win," I said. "Look, love. If you come to learn from me you work like a dog as and when I say. I'll take you on for three months, then I might give you the push. No wages. A share in a nonexistent profit. No expenses. No grumbling. And no comeback if I sling you out before time because I suddenly take umbrage." She listened, still as a squirrel. "Everything else comes second to antiques. And one last point. I don't like criticism." I waited. "Well?"

She nodded breathlessly. "Am I . . . taken on?"

"Yes."

"Col will be so disappointed," she said sorrowfully, her eyes filling with tears. "He was so thrilled, brimming with expectation." Oh-ho, I thought. No tears for Angharad, only for Col.

"Tinker. Find Col and Angharad and tell them sorry." Tinker nodded and started draining his pint glass. "Margaret, would you explain basic survival? I want a word with Maslow."

Lydia rose, figure meticulously tidy and handbag on guard. "Thank you, Lovejoy," she said politely. "As your apprentice I shall endeavor to fulfil whatever promise you see in me, and perform—"

I got up and kissed her cheek and Margaret's.

"Welcome, love. Meet me on the gallery in thirty minutes."

"Lovejoy!" she was starting up indignantly, but Margaret hastily whisked her out as Maslow came over.

"Wherever I go you're grilling young ladies in some tavern," he quipped.

"A merry jest, Maslow."

"Still in that public-spirited mood of cooperation, I see, Lovejoy," he said. He did the fire spectacle to pollute the pub's fresh atmosphere, twinkling merrily, silly fool. He knew he was nettling me. "Betty any good?"

I ignored that. We sat facing across the narrow table like gamblers. Nan was round in the other bar. It was too early for the regulars. Just me and this nerk.

I asked, "Well? Who killed the old geezer on the boat?"

"Which is where we left off," he prompted. "What makes you think he was killed deliberately?"

"No fuel. No gas. No explosives." These pedantic civil servants really get me. "Does that add up to kerboom at the police college?"

"Boats have stoves, and petrol, oil. Old boozers drop matches."

"Immovable boats don't."

He shook his head and wagged his finger. It took all my self-control not to break it off. "Engine-driven boats are always movable, Lovejoy," he explained as if to an imbecile. "A flick of the wrist to cast off. The North Sea," he said, ramming it home, "isn't all that far downstream."

The bleeder actually sneered as he poked my collarbone with his pipestem. These pompous warts really chill me. I took his pipe away and dropped it into his beer with a succulent fizz. Second pint of his I'd ruined.

"Concentrate. The estuary," I corrected, "might as well be on Saturn. The barge had no engine." Like I say, sometimes it feels like we're ruled by Neanderthals. I saw I'd have to explain. "Engine number PDK oblique YOZ oblique 43315M oblique 229 was removed for scrap years ago. Longhelp Mason's, bargeyarders of Belchingham, Lancs. They're on the telephone and everything, very willing ordinary people keen to help with the most simple routine inquiries. I phoned them. And one other thing, Sanders-of-the-Trail." I managed to stand up. I knew I was brewing the wrong exit line, but I was trembling with fury.

"Look here, Lovejoy—"

He tried to stand, but I slammed him down. "If your shambolic gaggle of bumblers isn't going to bother, then I am."

"Are you sure about—?"

"When you've done some thinking, Maslow," I said, "call on me. Until then, leave us common folk to get on with dishing out the justice."

"Just you dare, Lovejoy."

I was halfway to the door but found I'd swung round. "Oh, I dare all right, Maslow," I said. "I dare." I even felt pale. I went meekly out, not a little embarrassed at the contumely. Notice that expression I just used, "not a little embarrassed at the contumely"? That's what listening to people like Lydia does for you. For some reason I was mad at her as well as Maslow.

It was high time I put my mind to trying to remember what old Henry and I had talked about when we were drinking ourselves paralytic. I always knew it would be left to me. No wonder I'd been so on edge.

"Excuse me." A traffic warden barred my way in the alleyway. "Is that your car? It's illegally parked—"

I kneed him and propped him gasping against the tavern wall. "Piss off," I said. I nodded a breezy good day to two old biddies gaping at the scene and stepped off feeling better already, though I knew I'd worry all day in case he was a friend of Brenda's.

Having alienated practically everybody I could think of—as usual not my fault—I drifted into our town library to suss out books on the Grail.

Lydia was waiting patiently on Gallery Six. I'd never seen so many people in the museum. The galleries were crammed, at least a score of people and children to each.

"Can't you see?" she said, pointing excitedly. "How . . . *guilty* the poor thing looks?"

"You're right," I calmed her.

For the next hour I took her around the galleries, becoming more resigned every second. Lydia had the knack beating fervently inside her, but it was a furniture knack. I showed her the ancient Galileo pendulum hanging from the museum's glass ceiling to head height. It is really only a massive lead weight on a wire flex. Set swinging it shows the rotation of the earth. Naturally our museum authorities forbid this because children are always playing "chicken" at it. Lydia thought it stupid and ugly.

"How do they *clean* it?" she demanded. She also gazed blankly at a blindingly beautiful Thomas Tompion clock worth a fortune. She was merely puzzled by a rare collection of cased smoking pipes for a Georgian lady—ivory and gold decorations, silver-and-pearl-embellished tobacco pouch, of the kind occasionally put on sale as snuffboxes—their greater size gives them away. She was bored stiff by a precious excavated set of Roman surgical instruments owned by the doctor of the famed—and doomed—Ninth Legion. She gazed, fingers tapping signals of boredom on her handbag, at a display I'd helped to arrange in the English Civil War section.

"See," I enthused. "English doglocks are so very rare."

"Mmmm."

"Those two little heaps of powder I put there to show the ingredients of gunpowder," I explained enthusiastically. "I left out the charcoal because it might get wafted about onto those uniforms."

"Mmmm."

A little kid pulled at my trouser leg and held up a bar of chocolate. I bent down and took a mouthful. It trotted off, pleased.

"The curator made me take out the flints because he said —"

"*Lovejoy!*" Lydia said, incensed, pointing after the infant.

"—it disturbed their line, made them look too much like weapons—"

"You ate that baby's chocolate!"

"—which is what they *are*. Eh?" I homed in on her outrage. "I know. It insisted."

"You . . . you insufferable, greedy . . ." she stormed.

"Here endeth the first lesson," I said wearily. "See you." And left.

I can't understand what women are on about half the time.

There are garden seats placed on an especially windy corner of the market square. I flicked through Ashe's book on the Grail for half an hour and finished up no wiser. Maybe I needed the close assistance of a desirable Ph.D. in ancient history.

I strolled off, deciding to chat up Lisa. But no silly obvious questions about the Grail, because a lot of other antique dealers see Lisa very, very often.

X

But how does an entire civilization lose the Grail, for heaven's sake?

The whereabouts of all antiques isn't necessarily known, even if they are very, very important antiques indeed. In fact whole palaces full of them have even gone missing, like Nonsuch Palace, lost by the notorious Barbara Villiers, otherwise Lady Castlemaine of glamorous renown. This famous beauty, cold and grasping down to her very bones, was a profligate gambler. She had acquired the lovely Nonsuch Palace by means best not gone into, and immediately considered the alternatives: to sell for hard cash, or to hang on to, this exquisite wonder of the Royal Tudors, crammed as it was with the breathtaking craftsmanship of the glittering age of Henry the Eighth and Queen Bess. If it was money or beauty for Barbara, there was no contest. Money changed hands, and even the stones were savagely plundered. Finally the palace was gone, vanished. I can't really be glad that Barbara got in trouble when, as an interesting widow of sixty-three, she was tricked into a bigamous marriage with Beau Fielding, a handsome layabout of the time. She's one of the historical beauties I sob least tears about. Mind you, she must have been a cracker.

Well, if you can lose a palace you can lose a pewter cup, can't you?

I tried to calm down and forget my worries, wandering about the Arcade and chatting till Lisa finished serving. I saw Jason, a retired army man turned honest, and made him blush by telling him that the "Linen-and-Calfskin Guinea-Pouch" he was advertising was an early contraceptive.

"They waterproofed them with linseed oil," I told him affably. "Sometimes even tar."

"Is it *really?*" he said, awed, gaping at it.

"Making them impervious was the difficulty." There were other more natural ways, if you follow. I gave Jason a few details. Bill Shakespeare's Dark Lady Emelia Bassano avoided, er, the issue (so to speak) by diverse other skillful practices, about which I'd better not digress. But it's interesting that antique contraceptives, flea boxes and the like have to be called something else in order to sell them nowadays—we label them "sovereign-purses" or "snuffboxes," or some such, often unknowingly. Odd how our hang-ups still haunt us.

You have to laugh at some stuff, though. Every day you find a piece which sets you falling about. Today's gem was a plate of Spode type, priced high by Lennie. He hasn't a clue, but hope beats eternal in the human breast. He called me over. His mother-in-law, Jessica, was with him and glamorous as ever. She has him in thrall, owing to the fact that he's penniless and she's aggressively rich. Lennie is said to be utterly obedient to her every whim. Jessica has somehow managed the older woman's perfect triumph—a kind of marriage by proxy, with every known practical, material and bodily gain. Ah, well, young love. I've never even seen her daughter, Lennie's wife. I sometimes wonder if Lennie ever has either. Jessica rides him pretty close.

"Lennie's found a superb piece, Lovejoy!" she breathed proudly. "Spode. Believe it or not, 1732!"

She moved ahead of me into the shop wearing a ton of gold bangles. I'd never inhaled so much perfume at one go.

"Hiyer, Lovejoy." Lennie looked bushed. It happened more and more frequently since Jessica had taken him in hand.

And Jessica was right, in that the blue-printed earthenware Spode plate was marked A.D. 1732, which was a considerable achievement since Josiah Spode wasn't born till 1733. I explained this slight technical flaw. Jessica saw Lennie's face fall and pulled me quickly to one side as Lennie blundered eagerly toward two customers.

"Look, Lovejoy," Jessica said softly. I reeled from the scent but listened gamely on. "I know Lennie's not too lucky at antiques." She squeezed my hand gently. "But couldn't you just see your way to . . . well, *suggesting* Lennie's successful for once? Made a really marvelous find?"

"If I could, I'd have done him that kindness years ago."

"I quite understand." We were suddenly eyeball to eyeball. It's a very disturbing sensation because Jessica's shapely and somewhat overpowering. She stroked my arm to a clang of assorted bracelets. Modern, I observed, disappointed. "Come in one day, say tomorrow. Use a lot of money to buy one of Lennie's pieces. Anything."

"I've no money."

"But," she explained, looking carefully like they do, "I have."

"Look, Jessica, love . . ."

"You need clothes, Lovejoy," she breathed softly. "And other things. A woman always knows when a man's so clever he can't . . . find for himself. And you need more than just money, sweetie."

"Er, look, Jessica." My words stuck.

"Think it over, Lovejoy."

I escaped thankfully, saying I might.

For an hour I went round the town, looked in at the viewing day in our local auction. Some good stuff, some utter dross. Lennie would be down later, quite unable to recognize the Gillow bureau, though it stood there among piteous rubbish shrieking its class and scintillating quality. Still, he had several compensations I lacked, Jessica, for instance. Liz Sandwell was casually inspecting the porcelain.

"Spending your ill-gotten profit, Liz?" I joked, meaning the Irish glass.

"Precious little profit from you, Lovejoy."

"Jimmo been in?"

"No." She hesitated. "Lovejoy—those vases."

Genuine large Second Satsumas, big with ostentatious white slip. I've already told you how little I think of them. They were nothing special, though honest Japanese nineteenth-century. Holland's full of them.

"Ordinary Satsumas," I told her. "Interested? When in doubt, Liz, buy." Smiling I quoted the antique dealers' old maxim. It's good advice, but only sometimes.

"I could have sworn they're the ones I sold Jimmo a fortnight ago. I heard he'd sold them on the coast for a whacking profit."

"Well, good for Jimmo. He's learning."

"So why are they back?"

I shrugged. Double deals are common. You often handle things twice.

She was still doubtful, though. We chatted on about some French marionettes that were rumored about town and then parted, both of us spicing the chat with cheerful falsehoods after the manner of our kind. I promised to see Liz for a drink on Saturday when I knew her bloke was splashing around a rugby field in Essex.

I tore myself away when I was sure Harry the attendant had popped out. Sure enough he was next door, where thoughtful brewers had guessed right six centuries back and built the Rose and Crown.

"How lucky to find you here, Harry," I said, and persuaded him to a pint of beer. It took little time and less skill. He was busy at his newspaper with a pencil stub. "The Satsumas," I said. "Left side of the Victorian bookcase."

"Yeah?"

"Who sent them in?"

"Gawd knows." He dragged his eyes from the list of runners. "Want me to find out? I heard tell it was Caskie."

I made a great show of thinking, finally shaking my head. "No thanks, Harry. Just thought I'd seen them before."

"Cheers, Lovejoy."

I walked back up East Hill and sat in Saint Peter's churchyard to watch the motorcars go by on the distant London road. Some children were playing in the Castle Gardens across the way. Shoppers were streaking into town and trundling out again laden with bags. A really normal average scene, the sort I usually like to sit and enjoy for a minute or two. Happy and at ease.

But, folks. Old Henry dead and Jimmo suddenly well off.

Suddenly Jimmo has plenty of time to neglect his mediocre antiques business and go fishing in a new two-tone motorcar. Second Satsumas are not worth much, and that seemed to be the only business Jimmo'd done. But again, so what? So Jimmo's made a few quid. That's the game, isn't it?

I rose and walked back through the alley toward the Arcade. Lisa saw me from the window of Woody's. I waved, signaling. I drew a deep breath so I'd have enough oxygen and opened the glass door of Woody's. She slipped out.

"Hello, Lovejoy."

"Lisa. Do something for me?"

"Yes. Do hurry. Woody'll go spare. What is it?"

"Find time to go to Lennie's. Know where?"

"Yes. Him and Jessica." She obviously disapproved.

"That's the one, love. Get Jessica alone, so Lennie doesn't hear you." I was glancing about like a bad spy, in case some other dealer overheard my skullduggery. "Tell her from me the deal's on."

"With her, or with Lennie?" I saw that antiwoman frown developing on Lisa's brow.

"It's to do with antiques. Honestly."

"It had better be. She's a right vampire."

"Shut up and listen. Tell her to buy the Satsumas at Gimbert's auction tomorrow, and that if she does I'll go through with it. Okay?"

"The Satsumas at Gimbert's, and you'll go through with it," she repeated. "You still all right for the fireworks?" She saw my blank expression. "Our date. Castle Park."

"Eh? Oh yes. I've not forgotten," I said, having clean forgotten. Woody appeared at the window in a rage. "Er, well, I'm a bit busy—" I began but she had plunged back into the blue fumes. I should have scuppered that because the fewer complications the better. And young Lydia should be turning up for work. I'd glanced in at Margaret's as I passed. Lydia and Margaret were going through some Victorian tapestries, one of today's seriously underpriced antique items.

Getting Lisa to fix the arrangement with Jessica gave me half an hour to telephone Martha. It took a lot of nerve, but it had to be done. Mercifully she was glad to hear me and said could I come over please as soon as possible and had I heard the terrible news. We arranged to meet at a café on the Buresford road in thirty minutes. She said get a taxi and she would pay.

There'd been one whole day between my two visits at Martha's house. It was high time I found out what Henry had been up to in that time. Whatever it was, it had got him crisped. And one other realization came to me as the old taxi trundled down the northside hill out of town past the railway. If Henry had an old pewter cup which he thought very special, well it couldn't have vanished entirely, could it? Henry might have gone, but his pewter cup was still around somewhere.

XI

Gun Hill's summit now has a little walled garden, café, roses and fountain with trellis to trip the unwary at every step. It's a quiet place overlooking a valley and woods with sheep and barley fields adding local color. Really average. Martha was waiting.

"Henry and I used to come here."

"I'm so sorry, Martha." You never know what to say at these times.

"You've just no idea, no idea." She blotted her face a minute while I gazed at the revolting rural scene below. "We were so happy."

"Martha," I said carefully. "I'm not after his pewter thing—"

"Grail."

"Grail, then." Let her have her way. "Honestly I'm not. But one thing keeps nagging in my mind." I weighed Martha up. Maybe it wasn't the right moment to talk about killing. "Is it possible that . . . well, that Henry had something really valuable? I mean, did you ever see his, er, Grail?"

"No." She shook her head.

"Didn't he show you a picture, draw it for you, anything?"

"No." She was looking at me, though I tried to stare casually into the middle distance. "Lovejoy, what is it?"

I shrugged, wondering how best to go on. For all I knew Martha herself might have . . . no. Impossible. Look at the woman, for heaven's sake, the state she was in. I decided to plunge.

"The boat. It was just a hull."

"So?"

"So tin boats only explode when there's something to explode."

I'll say this for Martha Cookson. She's pretty cool. She sat there a full five minutes, occasionally lifting her head as if to speak but saying nothing and letting her eyes wander about the garden. She was very pale.

"You believe . . . ?" she tried finally.

"Yes, love."

"Have you told the inspector?"

"I've tried to, the pompous sod. He takes no notice. I've had a go at him. Look." I leaned across our table earnestly. "Henry said he'd fetch something back, right? A day passes. Then a . . . er, a tragedy. See what I mean, Martha? Henry said he was going to fetch something precious back. Well," I ended lamely, "maybe he did, see?"

"You mean—?" Martha faced up bravely.

"You know what I mean, Martha. No need to say it." We obviously had to go in stages or she'd be shattered. "Where did Henry go that day?"

"I don't know. He took some money." She wept a steady minute or so, remembering. "Henry isn't—wasn't—a very worldly man. I always had a tobacco jar in the living room with money in it, so he could take whatever he needed. It's empty. He was pleased that day, very quiet. Kept to himself." Again the slight defiance. "He prayed a lot. And before midday he went to church. They don't burn candles or anything hereabouts, so he does it in the stables."

"He *what?*"

Martha fidgeted, obviously wondering if she was being disloyal to reveal Henry's foibles. She decided I could take it.

"I was always having to buy candles. He had rather a thing about sanctification, you see. I can't say I quite understood entirely." She sniffed again while I pondered the rum image of an elderly reject lighting candles in a stable. Some symbolism there, I supposed, if you bothered to look.

"Always in the stables?" I asked shrewdly.

"Not necessarily. The boat, the stable, the garden shed sometimes. On the little wharf, the riverbank beneath the big willow trees there, if there were no anglers out."

"Where would Henry actually *keep* it though?"

"He only ever brought it once before, that he ever admitted." She smiled, full of tears. "About six years ago. Twenty pounds of candles, all in one week. You see, the church . . ."

I nodded. East Anglia's so Low Church you've got to be careful blowing your nose in evensong—the merest flash of a white linen hankie's enough to set people worrying that papists are smuggling altar cloths in.

"Those two friends of his," I asked. "The ones I met at your house after lunch?"

"Sarah and Thomas?"

"How often did he see them?"

"Very rarely. They never stay, only maybe an hour or so. You know how old college relationships decay."

"Show me?" I asked. She thought a bit, nodded and discreetly paid the bill.

She let me poke about on my own outside.

The stables were a short row of three, but now they were connected. Henry or somebody had removed the intersecting walls. It was quite a large roomy building, single windows to each third and those daft half-doors horses like to gaze over, only there were no horses. Sure enough you could see black smudges and opaque white droplets where his untidy candles had burned on the sill. He had erected a trestle table for a crude workbench at the far end. I couldn't resist going across, though it seemed an intrusion.

A spindle, hand drill and a few small saws. A power drill. A

99

good piece of thickish mahogany. A lathe. Underneath a table was a chair, in pieces. I picked up a loose leg, lovely African mahogany. Though you can't really tell without seeing it entire, it had the feel of a mid-1880 English withdrawing-room chair by a good maker. Its weight puzzled me until I found the plug. "Whoops. Sorry, Henry."

I'd intruded further than I wanted to. You fake old furniture by increasing its weight, making vigilant would-be purchasers think they are buying heavy and dense (and very rare) hardwoods. A really skilled faker will drill *down* the interior of a chair leg and insert a beaten lead cylinder, carefully plugging the hole up with filings glued in place by an epoxy resin, or plastic wood stained under a coat of hard polyurethane varnish. It isn't too easy to spot by naked eye alone if it's done really well, but I've never seen a "reamer," as it's known in the antiques game, you can't detect with a reasonable hand lens.

"You sly old dog, Henry," I said. He wouldn't want the evidence found after his promise to Martha to go straight. I mentally asked Henry's permission to come up one day when Martha was out. I'd finish it for him. "No good leaving a job half done, is it?" I asked the bare ceiling innocently.

There was also a drawing. An emigrant miner's brooch. It looked as though Henry was a regular contributor to the world of so-called antiques. These brooches are lovely small solid gold works of art. Cornish miners off to South Africa's gold fields in late Victorian days made these precious brooches and pendants, often including a South African gold coin of the year in the design. Mostly though it is crossed shovels, picks, lamps, flags and suchlike. Naughty old Henry was obviously intending to make one. I scanned around, but no gold.

The stable floor was beaten earth. Bare beams in clear view. No signs that one part of the whitewashed wall had been repainted lately. I went out onto the cobbled courtyard to see the two loyal yokels duck back behind their kitchen curtains.

The shed was a blank. Hardly anything but garden tools. I meandered about to get the feel of the place. From the workshop bench in the stables you could see the shattered longboat and its huge tethering willow tree. I lit the stump of a candle and put it in a broken plant pot for safety before heading back in. Martha would be wondering what I was up to. I was careful to walk all around the house first.

"Did you see everything?" She'd made hot crumpets, for heaven's sake. I like them but get covered in butter. Everybody else never does.

"Almost."

"I suppose you have questions to ask, Lovejoy."

I drew breath. "Outside the house there are two sets of stapled wires leading up to one of the windows."

"That was Henry's idea."

"An extra phone, aerials?"

"No." She smiled, embarrassed again, but defiant. "Henry's hobby was badgers, owls, wildlife. He had night cameras and bleeps. They used to wake . . . us up."

"And . . . ?"

"He'd sometimes photograph them."

"At night? In the dark?"

"Oh, yes. From our bedroom window. And night glasses by the bedside."

She showed me Henry's elementary electronics center upstairs. One was a commercial warning device, an interrupted ray system. Anyone walking between an issue and receptor activated an alarm by their bed. The other was a battery-operated bell for the outside trip wire, crude but good. Benign old Henry was pretty vigilant.

"Did Henry set them every night?"

"Without fail."

I asked to see his books. They were theological, travel, literary and biography. But who ever heard of a wildlife enthusiast with no books about wildlife? Outside I walked to and fro across the garden. The electronic cells were set in the mortar of the balustrade. You couldn't reach the boat's mooring without activating the alarm. The trip wires ran from the river to the house. However you reached the boat you'd create *some* sort of a racket. I had one crumpet for the road, and said my thanks.

"Are you any nearer, Lovejoy?"

"Give me time, Martha, and I'll say yes."

Martha gave me a lift back to the village. I waved at the lovable Constable Jilks to brighten his day and got Martha to drop me at the chapel to show the constabulary what posh friends I'd got.

Lydia was walking around the cottage. She jumped a mile when I bowled up.

"Admiring the view?" I joked. I momentarily wished I was in a Lagonda in which I could screech to a stop like Honkworth does in his massive roadster, but caught myself in time. Man's desire to impress a bird has a very bad record.

"Yes," Lydia said, all misty, gazing at the obnoxious view. "Isn't it just beautiful?"

"Eh?" I peered, but she meant it. I cast a glance at the river below, the valley's green shoulder, the woods and fields and a few cows noshing grass. "Do you mean the viaduct?"

A lovely railway still runs over the river a mile off, but trees obscure full sight of it. There are seven graceful brick arches soaring from the fields so the railway can straddle the obnoxious countryside and passengers need not notice it if they don't want.

"Of course not." She smiled at me. "The fields. The farms. How lucky you are."

"Come inside," I said, thinking I've got another nutter here. I always seem to draw the short straw. "None of that's man-made."

"But it's still beautiful."

"How can it be?" I decided to brew up for her. She was the sort who'd admire my domestic skills.

"Because it's alive, and pretty." She shelled off her coat and was stuck for a place to hang it. I pretended not to notice because I've only one peg and that's snowed under. People should learn not to depend on me so much. "You can't call a viaduct pretty, can you?"

"Yes." I got the kettle on. She came into the main room

carrying her coat on her arm. She'd brought a bag full of note-books and learned tomes.

"That's absurd."

I took her gently by the shoulders and sat her on the divan, to her alarm. I saw Jean's dire warnings streak into her eyes.

"Listen," I began savagely, more than a little narked at such ignorance. "Once upon a time this valley was just as you see it, but without the wires, the bridges, the viaduct, the roads. Then a gang of hard tough men came hauling stones. They scrabbled in the fields and splashed in the water, flinging up a beautiful arching roadway from hill to hill. The cholera came and they died in their ramshackle tents by the score. They drowned in the floods and some are still crushed under the landslides of that terrible winter. They froze in the snow and shattered their limbs under massive stones. Their women worked with them, carrying hods of bricks and iron rails. Their children were dosed with nepenthe so they slept in peace and didn't cry from their hunger gripes. They slogged twenty hours a day, love, and mostly died drunk and penniless." I could see the fear of rape had dwindled. "Now, love, don't you try telling me that a bit of dirt and a blade of grass is beautiful when there's an old viaduct to look at. If mankind made it by his own gnarled hands, it has love in every crack. And love's all there is. Love's not a casual glimpse of a posh field or a bored cow."

She said nothing. I let her go and rummaged about for books and catalogues to give her. She went all quiet making the tea. I gave her a summary of reading, starting with Savage on antique forgeries, Crawley on furniture, Bainbridge on antique glass, J. N. George on short and long handguns, and a collection of catalogues of some famous antique auctions of the past decade.

"Read that lot fast. I want to teach you to buy later on this week." I rather hurried her after that because I wanted to find out who was at Cambridge with old Henry. She said a friend was calling for her at the chapel crossroads and she'd get home all right. He was sure to be a fine clean-living lad. I watched her down the drive. She gave a half glance toward the viaduct span-ning the river valley.

"So long," I called after her. She hesitated at the lane as if to wave, but her hand never quite made it. Ah, well.

There was nothing for it. A couple of minutes to lock up and I cranked up the Ruby. It notched a pacy fifteen up the lane. Your friend and mine stepped forward, hand raised, once more to enforce personal prejudice. I pulled in obligingly, smiling.

"Got you, Lovejoy!" George squawked delightedly, hauling out a notebook. Being already chained ostentatiously to a pencil he was all prepared. I watched the little ceremony with interest. They're teaching absolutely everybody the alphabet these days.

"Doing what, Constable?" I asked innocently.

"Driving your car while—" He paused.

I said, all patience, "I know you've reported me for drunken driving, George, but my case isn't heard till next week."

"Get out," he growled, jerking his thumb to show he meant it.

"If I do, George," I said gently, "I'll kick you silly." We waited. "Well, George, what's it to be? Me resisting wrongful arrest and you with your leg in traction, or a general return to sweetness and light? Maslow will be very vexed."

"Maslow?" They go all shifty when you've got them. He'd heard of Maslow, obviously a right bastard to everyone, police and all. It wasn't just me.

"You know him, surely?" I chatted. "Burly bloke, about middle age, smokes—"

"One day," our law-abiding constabulary threatened, uttering foul obscenities. "One day, Lovejoy."

"Any day you like, George," I offered back, "but remember that I'll leave you seriously in need of an orthopedic surgeon. Agreed? Mind your piggies." I'd unlocked the hand brake while passing the time of day and zoomed off with a surge—well, a flick —of power toward the Cambridge road.

War, folks.

XII

East Anglian roads are a rum mixture of corkscrews and rulers. You're bumbling along a stretch running straight as a die over the low hundreds, whistling and thinking how good it will be to reach the next antique shop, when suddenly you're fighting to stay on the most macabre switchback roads on earth. They twist and turn, lunge and soar, narrow to incredible thinness, then spread oafishly in demented straggly tree arches. Just as you're at screaming pitch the madness ends and you're clattering serenely level again. The straight stretches we owe to the good old Romans. The crazy bits are legacies from the Ancient Britons or rearrangements carried out by the Early English, undoubtedly history's most forgetful organizers. They had an unenviable habit of losing parts of the Roman roads, or just simply deciding that too much straightness was a drag and that there were prettier views elsewhere. An artistic attitude, but death to sane travel.

My Ruby spluttered thankfully to a stop in Cambridge. We were knackered as each other by the journey. I streaked into the town library for an hour, then strolled to Selward College.

A hoary old philosopher led me through beautiful ancient

doorways and across quadrangles to an office containing a choice
of a luscious bird undulating at one desk and a decrepit ancient
crone withering away at another. He deposited me with unerring
foresight at the crone. I explained the problem, my poor Uncle
Henry dying. I wanted to get his obituary details right.

"Good heavens!" she squeaked. "We were notified only yesterday! He was one of ours! How very sad! You must be so
upset. May we express our sincerest condolences?"

"Er, thank you."

"Same here," said the luscious bird from the other desk. She
didn't look sincerely condoling at all. She was doing things with
a lipstick. I forgot to be downhearted.

"I'll get the records for you." The crone wheezed off into the
middle distance. I sat on the luscious bird's desk.

"Look, comrade," I began. "Old H.S. was no more my uncle
than you."

"So?" She pretended to be busy typing, but I put a stop to all
that by taking the paper out.

"So you have a golden opportunity to help me."

"Cheek." She wound some new paper into the machine, but
I could tell she didn't much care what went on it.

"Your reward will be a slender chance of making me, on some
future nocturnal occasion," I said, "and the benefit of knowing
that you've soared in my estimation of you—already very high."

"Stop looking like that."

She made a great show of buttoning her twinset.

"Send me a list of old Henry's class."

"*She's* doing it for you," she said, jerking her head. Women
don't like each other. I've often noticed that.

"Ah," I added. "I want their full addresses and other personal
details, you see."

"That's not allowed."

"That's why I came to you, Joyce, love."

She gave me a quizzical glance and typed a line in low spirits.
"What do you want it for?"

I could hardly tell her I was going to report one of the people
on her list for complicity in murder.

"It's to do with a will," I admitted reluctantly. "The old man was a millionaire. He has all these houses and big estates and that. His daughter's being done out of her inheritance by this old woman." I thought of calling the old woman Mrs. Blenkinsop, as that was the name on the crone's desk, but decided it was stretching the story too far. I shrugged, half disclaiming. "It's really none of my business, I suppose. But I was . . . well, friendly once with the old man's daughter, though we broke up, and . . . er, and . . ."

"And you still want to help her, don't you?" the little helpful darlin' finished for me, all misty. "Despite having parted," she prattled on, "you can't let that grasping old bag do her down, and you've come here trying to protect her, though deep down—"

She rambled away adoringly while I looked cut to the quick but noble with it.

"I'll be outside the main gate, if you can do anything, love."

I had a hard time tearing my eyes from her as the crone creaked back carrying a blue volume. We disengaged hands just in time.

Mrs. Blenkinsop confirmed old Henry's dates. I quickly scanned the class photograph and the list of names, all casual. I thanked her, bowed gently toward Joyce's desirable shape and strode nobly from the room. It can be quite pleasant inventing the odd falsehood. The trouble is I start believing the bloody stuff. I was out into the college grounds before I could stop seeing myself as a heartbroken lover and made my way to a pie shop opposite Selward's main gate.

She was almost an hour and arrived breathlessly, carrying a thick brown envelope. It took another hour prizing it off her. Still, it was effort expended in a good cause.

There were maybe sixty names. Haverro was there, and Devonish, but no other I recognized. So Thomas Haverro and Sarah Devonish's late husband had been at Selward College as undergraduates when old Henry studied there. I drove south, angry at myself. I'm always like this when I'm worried sick about something, collecting facts that seem important but usually turn out no use at all. Thomas, Devonish and Henry Swan were old chums, but again so what? I tried to concentrate on the Satsuma-Jimmo problem, but that only got me madder.

Some sleuth.

XIII

I rattled home, resisting the temptation to call in at Liz Sand-well's place at Dragonsdale. Every light her shop possessed was on. Gimlet-eyed and stoical, I drove noisily past. Sooner or later I'd have to see Liz made an honest man of me, as long as Marga-ret didn't find out. And Betty. And Lisa. And Jean. And their tough male hangers-on. Thinking what a rotten unfair old world it was I eventually chugged into my garden, all prepared for hot pasties a foot thick knee-deep in sauce.

Once you try to put a thing out of your head it only returns with renewed vigor. Ever noticed that? As I hotted my frozen grub and washed up enough crockery to make noshing a respect-able enterprise, people's faces kept haunting me.

Sarah Devonish is the sort of woman a man can't help going for. And J. H. C. Devonish was one of the names under the photograph of Henry's class, though I hadn't been able to locate which young smile had been his. Sarah must have been a lot younger than good old J. H. C. Yet for a forlorn widow she seemed particularly belligerent and nastily knowledgeable, which makes a bloke wonder why she'd been the main mouthpiece that day, telling old Henry to shut up and all.

I cleared a couple of square inches of table free of debris so I could eat. Hardly worth laying the table just for me. The kettle boiled. I made some evil coffee and sat waiting for the oven to signal that my taste buds were again about to be tantalized. Thomas seemed utterly benign and apologetic for all that he was a medical scientist. Well, even that's still legal. The oven clicked, but I telephoned Martha to ask about Dolly.

I cut through the chitchat. "That day Henry and I were, er, sloshed, Martha. You said something about Dolly's friends calling for her."

"Well, yes." Her voice leveled from the tremulous. "It *was* rather shameful, Lovejoy—"

"Yeah, yeah. *Which* friends, Martha?"

"The one with the big car. I find them somewhat . . . well, showy isn't too strong a word, is it?" She thought a second. "He has a funny name."

Big car, showy, funny name. "Honkworth?"

"That's the one. Though he was so kind helping Henry that one often wonders if indeed one is somewhat prejudiced . . ."

"One does," I agreed. "Hang on." I went and put the oven back on to give myself time to think. The Dolly-Henry chain had suddenly lengthened by a few links it shouldn't have had. "Er, helped? How?"

"Giving him a lift back from the station," Martha explained. "Didn't I tell you? He was so terribly late, and getting a taxi to meet the last train's absolute hell."

"But you have a car, Martha." I had a funny feeling even before she said it that I'd missed something terribly obvious.

"Oh, yes. But Henry never learned to drive, you see." Served me right for not checking.

We went round and round this same conversation a couple of times before ringing off because I wanted to drive the main facts into my thick skull. My pasties were practically radioactive from the heat by the time I settled down. Honkworth had not only seen Sarah, Thomas and me at Martha's house, but knew enough to be waiting in his flashy crate when Henry was stuck at the station. And give the old bloke a lift home, the crawler. Now supposing Henry had been carrying something precious, what then? A worm like the revolting Honkworth might be tempted . . .

It was midnight before I locked up and pulled the divan out for a bed. Some problems are better slept on, I told myself piously, wishing Margaret would happen by.

The police disagreed. Maslow rang at four in the morning and told me to get down to the Arcade fast. I never refuse an invitation, so I went.

You can smell malice. The stench of spite pervades the very air you breathe and stings your eyes. It's as horrible as that, something foul and stinking, exactly like the ancient medievalists sensed the corruption of evil. I nudged Tinker Dill awake at the High Street. He was already mad because I'd roused him from his drunken stupor and made him come with me.

"Nip down to the post office," I told him. "Keep an eye on me, for Christ's sake. If the Old Bill hauls me off you know what to do."

"Bloody four in the bloody morning," he muttered. One thing, incredible to relate, he looks better in daylight. He shuffled off into the darkness, merging with the gloom across the way. I parked the Ruby with flamboyant defiance on the main street. Just let Brenda or Jilks give me a ticket, I thought piously. Two police cars were parked by the Arcade, disturbing the peace with radios and blue lights irritating. Half a dozen bobbies stooged about wishing there were cameras on the go.

"Can't you manage without us civilians, Maslow?" Always start as you mean to go on, I thought, watching him pause at hearing my well-loved voice. I got a jolt by noticing that the activity seemed centered on Margaret's place. Lights blazed. They'd rigged up two spotlights to shine through Margaret's window on the antiques, what was left of them. A tired man photographed inside the shop, over and over. Lisa and Woody were there talking to Jimmo and Marion. The bobbies had called out everybody they could think of.

"Not really, Lovejoy." Maslow gave me a bleak smile. "We need you."

"What did you let them do *this* time?" I asked, telling myself not to get talked under.

"You have a chance to shine, Lovejoy."

"At . . . ?"

"Why at what you're so good at." He pretended surprise. "Knowing exactly what went on." His smile became more aggressive. "When the rest of us don't know anything of the kind." He tapped me with his pipe. One day I'll lose my wool and he'll go about left-handed. I can see it coming. "Take a gander inside, friend."

Margaret was speaking in a flat undertone to a scribbling constable. A policewoman was having difficulty with a portable tape recorder whose microphone wouldn't fit. Typical. The place was wrecked.

Porcelain pieces crunched underfoot. Chairs and cabinets had been hacked into splinters. Margaret's collection of dolls were smashed and torn. I choked on fumes I couldn't identify.

"Acid, Lovejoy." Maslow actually sounded pleased. "On the antique medallions. Ruined."

The main window was broken, probably done last in case of the noise. A lovely Mayhew and Ince Pembroke table was fragmented. I found myself on my knees trying to fit pieces together.

"No use, Lovejoy. No use at all." Maslow motioned me outside into the covered way. I gave Margaret a hopeless wave to show I'd stay around and followed.

"Which of these nerks," I asked, "was on the beat when it happened, Maslow?" I pointed to the lounging constabulary.

"None. We've withdrawn the beat constable." He liked the question as much as I liked him. "He can cover the ground in a car much quicker."

"And in twice as much ignorance."

"Look, Lovejoy. Until now you and I haven't seen eye to eye."

"Oh, but we have. You try to push me about. And I tell you to piss off because you're useless." I could see him struggle for control. A constable within earshot started getting out of his mobile rest room, but Maslow gestured angrily and he retired into the car all hurt at not being allowed to play. "Maslow," I said. "If I emerge with a few broken bones, a certain friendly barker watching eagle-eyed in the shadows will give my Member of Parliament a rude awakening."

"I'm . . . I'm prepared to admit," he tried to say evenly, "we've made very little progress."

"You checked the boat yard," I said encouragingly. "Quite bright."

"How did you know?"

"I used the clever electric talking machine and asked the foreman."

"Okay, Lovejoy. A truce." We thought about it for a while. "Whatever's going on seems to do with antiques. And you."

"Not me, mate."

"Oh, yes," he nodded. "And you, mate. *Your* friend here gets her place done over. *Your* old pal Reverend Swan gets his boat blown up and goes early to heaven. And busy little Lovejoy's been sniffing around old colleges, hasn't he?" Oh-ho, I thought. Cambridge.

"A casual call," I said airily. "My old alma mater."

"Tomorrow—by which I mean early dawn, lad—you'll call casually on me."

"Will I?"

"And enter into a partnership with us," he went on, tough now. The uniformed man was out of the car and stayed out this time. "You'll disclose all you know or suspect. If not I'll arrest you by six this evening. Understood?"

"Marvelous man, your inspector," I said to the constable. "Useless as the rest of you, but goes after the innocent like a tiger." I put my head around Margaret's shattered door. "Coming, love?"

"She's needed here," Maslow said curtly.

"I'd better stay, Lovejoy," Margaret called, looking up from a list. Maybe something to do with insurance.

"Okay." I meandered across to chat with the others. It took

about ten minutes of muttered asides to vanish into the darkness with Lisa. The Ruby's oil lamps were still flickering when we reached it. Tinker emerged from the darkness abusing everything.

"What the bleeding hell's going on, Lovejoy? Wotcher, Lisa."

"They've done Margaret's over."

"Christ." His groan was as much criticism of my extra passenger as sorrow at a dealer's plight. "Did they break them two matching devs?" He meant the small devotional soft porcelain fonts, Continental, eighteenth-century and valuable.

"Yes." They were the first things I'd noticed.

Lisa was furious.

"Charming," she snapped. "Is that all you two can think of, antiques? Neither of you so much as asked about Margaret."

Tinker rolled his eyes heavenward.

"Er, how's Margaret, Lisa?" he tried courageously, but Lisa was mad and wouldn't reply. "What about that little Ukrainian ikon?" he asked me in a hoarse undertone.

"Ruined. Some sort of acid. On her medallions, furniture, on the bloody walls."

"Christ."

We were finally crammed in somehow and zoomed off down the hill. The pong from Tinker's horrible gear was indescribable. I remembered to stop off and let him out on North Hill.

Which left Lisa and Lovejoy. Well, it's an ill wind and all that.

Lisa is trouble. That doesn't mean I don't like her. You can classify women only two ways: trouble and very much trouble. The first kind's Lisa and Margaret. They're moderate trouble no matter what. Wherever you are they're in the background being vaguely irritatingly troublesome, like a gentle rain that trickles down your unsuspecting neck. The VMT model's the Betty, Jean Evans and Lydia kind. As soon as you clap eyes on them it's a shouting match and pistols at dawn. The first sort you never get free of and sets up immediately as a sort of chronic niggling part-time pest. The VMT is nonstop Typhoon Emma. Meet one at a vicarage tea party and you finish up pinned in a corner like the baddie in *Zorro*. It can be very tiresome because you're knackered every single minute of every single day while one's about. I have difficulties with both kinds, which is a drag because I live like Hereward the Wake as it is, always one terrified eye open. My difficulty is I have this undesirable knack of looking guilty even if I've done nothing. I reckon it attracts them.

Next morning Lisa made the bed and swept up. She fried things and flung the doors and windows wide, then had us both breathing in time to a broadcast tune some maniac was tinkling on the piano before the eight o'clock news. I felt a fool, but she said it was good for my lungs. She complained the vacuum cleaner was on the blink and the sweeper needed oiling. I hadn't any. "Nil out of ten, Lovejoy," she admonished sternly, washing the dishes in a noisy clatter. She thought the little alcove, which is my entire kitchen, a health hazard and told me off because I'd no washing-up stuff. She insisted on stripping the bed and hanging the sheets on the line, though somebody only has to put them back on again. I tried telling her it was counterproductive, but she wouldn't listen. By the time she'd taken the curtains down to soak I was in the garden, thinking. Lisa came out to bang a rug on my unfinished wall and pollute the lovely smog with dust. For a second I became quite interested.

"I didn't know I had that rug, Lisa."

"I'm not surprised," she said curtly, slamming back in. So much for the friendly approach.

The robin came on my arm for its cheese. It listens while I think aloud but has unnecessarily cynical views judging by the glances I get. I ran quickly over recent events, starting with my Cambridge run and the vandals doing Margaret's place over.

"But suppose," I said softly, "it wasn't a casual mob, eh? Suppose it was some lads sent by a big bad London dealer who wanted his two Neanderthal brats educated." It gave me the bent eye, mistrustful little sod. But I obviously had to visit Sykes and have a brief word. I'd start politely with a gentle request and go on from there. Sykes and his merry men were a hard lot. I knew that. On the other hand, I can be very, very treacherous indeed.

One thing was worrying me. I'd have to call on Margaret. I

needed an estimate of the damage the Sykes lads caused, otherwise I'd have no way of balancing up. It's called retribution.

Lisa called, "Lovejoy, I need some help with this divan."

"Coming, love," I said, putting the robin down. I tiptoed away, quickly cranked my minuscule zoomster and rattled out into the lane toward town.

Lydia was already clearing up in the Arcade. She told me Margaret was asleep at home, having had a tiring night. There were barbs in them there undertones. A score of dealers and barkers were assembled to ogle Margaret's misery. They were concealing their heartfelt sorrow so effectively you couldn't tell they weren't actually delighted.

"I go to the Smoke early tomorrow," I informed Lydia. The mess was enough to make you weep. "You've a job to do for me, love."

"Very well." That flinty voice again. She'd fetched a pinafore, dusters and polish, dustpan and a set of brushes.

"Er, sorry." I'd been staring. She really was a lovely shape. God knows why it seemed to dismay her so much, but she did her utmost to hide it.

"I think you ought to know, Lovejoy," she said, facing me bravely, "that I called at your cottage earlier."

"Er, great." A significant pause. "Why didn't you, er, knock and stay for coffee?"

"I could hear . . . two voices." Lydia's face was scarlet.

"Er, *two* voices? The radio, probably."

"Not the radio, Lovejoy. Lisa's."

"Now I remember," I said, smiling easily. I laughed a light airy laugh. "She'd called with a message from Tinker."

"I told a *lie* for you, Lovejoy." She was saving porcelain pieces in a cardboard box.

"Er, well, thanks, love."

"Don't thank me! I should have done no such thing."

"Course not, love. Er, what was it incidentally?" I had to ask. Truth can always wait a little, but lies can be very important. She avoided looking at me, busy.

"I advised Woody that Lisa was unable to come to work."

"Bless you, Lydia." Good old Lydia. Trust a woman to be devious and full of clever little falsehoods. I tried to show how pleased I was, but she was all prim and disapproving and stepped back.

"I realize your . . . disposition to carnality is not altogether your fault, Lovejoy," she went on, getting more steam up, "but you really must acknowledge—"

The rest is lunacy of the sort only Lydia's ilk can invent, about being less reprehensible and suchlike jazz. I listened as long as I could stay meek and mild, then interrupted when I'd had enough.

"Love, go to Lennie's. A pair of Satsuma vases. He'll have bought them at yesterday's auction. Say we're interested, but tell him the price is too much—"

"How do you know without having seen—?"

"It's *always* too much, love. Put a few quid deposit."

"Why?" She was looking at me with that look.

"Well . . ." I hesitated, exasperated. She was so charming. "Why not?"

"Because they're cheap and nasty, Lovejoy," she said with asperity. "Those . . . the strange gentlemen said so." She must mean Mel and Sandy, judging from her sudden bright pink face. She pointed to a volume resting on her handbag. "And that."

"You've been reading what I wrote!" I said indignantly. She'd got hold of my bloody book, the one I'd written on faults in antique collecting.

"If I'm your pupil—" she began severely.

I slammed out in a temper. Lydia has the makings, I decided angrily, of a very treacherous woman.

I wanted to find Honkworth. Maybe if I rang Martha and asked where Dolly would be I'd scoop the pool and get Honkie and that creep Leyde too, but I'd bothered Martha enough.

"How do, Lovejoy," Woody yelled through the smoke. I settled at a table, peering about for Tinker Dill. The place isn't big enough to swing a cat, but I've never yet managed to see all the way across to the opposite wall.

"Tea, Woody," I shouted through the hubbub. "And a fresh

table napkin. This one doesn't match your Nantwich lace cloth."

Jason and Marion laughed. Hello, hello, I thought, where's Jed this sunny dawn?

"Morning, Lovejoy," Marion said. "Watch it. Woody's in one hell of a temper. Lisa's off."

"Tut-tut," I remarked. "Nothing too serious, I trust?"

"You seen Lisa, Lovejoy?" Woody belligerently splashed a chipped cup of oily liquid down before me.

"Me? Not since this morning," as true as I could get. He glowered suspiciously.

"That bird of yours came full of excuses, and me with my hands full."

"A thoughtful lassie, Lydia," I said proudly, paying him.

No sign of Tinker or Honkworth, but in the next few minutes Liz showed up for a quick coffee and Jenny Bateman arrived excited at having found a Wheatstone Viewer. Sir Charles Wheatstone invented a stereoscopic gadget in 1832. You still see cheap modern cardboard ones, but the originals were lovely brass and walnut things like a splendidly tailored gunsight. You see them in toy museums like Pollock's.

"Very nice, Jenny," I praised. They're not worth a lot, but you can't help lusting.

It made us all think, because the previous week a zoetrope had been sold at Gimbert's auction, as if a serious collector of "visuals," which the trade calls these things, was starting to unload part of his stuff. A zoetrope's a sort of very early picture show. We'd fallen silent. Nothing pains an antique dealer like luscious bargains falling into the hands of the undeserving. From there talk began again, of chances passed up because fickle fate's never to be trusted.

Finally, just as I was losing hope, the door creaked open and Tinker tottered in. Remember I said a bit ago that he looked better in daylight? I take it back. He looks horrible in daylight.

He shuffled across and practically fell into a chair. The smog instantly reeked of the habitual drinker's bitter breath.

"Chips, peas, sausages," the apparition growled. "And fried bread. Bacon. Fried egg. Tea."

"Coming," from Woody, blundering about in the smoke like a fiend from a Teutonic opera.

"You forgot the custard," I joked. Tinker's bloodshot eyes wobbled.

"Hello, Lovejoy. You got me up at four o'bleeding clock," he accused.

"I've not forgotten. I owe you. Look, Tinker." I had to get out before the ghastly plateful arrived. "Where will I find Honkie?"

"At that old pub, the Bellman, on the canal. His barkers meet him there, and his popsie, the one with the big—"

"Yeah, yeah." I told him as a parting shot I was going up to the Smoke street markets in the morning to have a harsh word with Sykes for letting his lads do Margaret's place over.

"You're a goner, Lovejoy." He shook his head when I grinned. "You never bleeding well listen."

I was crossing to the Ruby when Mel and Sandy's multicolored motorcar streaked past, slowing a fraction for Mel to stick his head out of the window.

"Lovejoy, baby!"

I tried to dodge back among the crowd, but Sandy braked to a halt. Other cars screeched and swerved, a right hullabaloo.

"Did you see we've done the wings mauve and orange?" Mel cried, waving and pointing. "Don't you just *adore* it?"

"Er, great." I began to retreat into the Arcade. There's another way out across the pub yard at the back. It leads into the old marketplace, where no dazzling motors may follow.

"About those poxy Satsuma vases," Mel shrieked. "Lovejoy! Come back!"

I hadn't time to listen to their fantasies. Lydia had already told me they'd given her the benefit of advice.

I escaped thankfully past Margaret's wrecked shop. Lydia looked up as I passed. I blew her a demonstrative kiss. She stared at the floor, but I definitely saw her hand flick upward in the slightest shyest wave on record. Well, progress. Almost negligible, but very definitely progress.

Honkworth, Esq., was holding forth in the saloon bar. Note that phrase, please, holding forth. Only people as grotesque as Honkworth can hold forth. Other people have to simply manage with speaking. Bill Leyde's glittering waistcoat had clearly been woven by transalpine virgins among vine groves. The blond popsie and Dolly were tittering at Honkworth's jollity. A few canal men were knocking pints back and smiling with quiet amusement.

"If it isn't my old pal Lovejoy!" Honkworth boomed. Leyde's piggy eyes took me in while the two birds fell silent in pleased anticipation. Under the glare of all this attention I made the best entrance I could manage.

"Can I have a word, Honkie?"

"For you, Lovejoy—anything! Well," he twinkled caution at the assembled multitude, *"almost* anything!" Roars of merry laughter followed.

"Come over here then." I got a noggin from an intrigued barwoman. "Sorry about Henry, Dolly."

"I believe you've been filling Aunt Martha's head with silly ideas," she said, frozen-faced.

"Your beliefs are beginning to get me down," I said. She took a swipe at me as I turned. It caught me off balance and I went flying, the glass shattering on the wall near a sea engraving by Woollett, the sort English pubs so riskily have littering their dusty walls. Luckily the glass was modern pressed rubbish and the print got none of the impact. My head was ringing when I rose. The rest were still. I recovered and headed for the fireplace where Honkworth was waiting, hands on hips, belligerently. "About the Reverend Henry Swan, lately deceased, of this parish, Honkie."

"Who?" He was glancing from me to Dolly.

"You gave him a lift from the station. The last London train." His frown cleared. "What about it? What's up?"

I was suddenly fed up with all the fencing.

"What did you talk about?" I asked. He stepped back, watching me carefully. "Tell me now, Honkie, or I'll be cross."

"He'd been to London."

"Anywhere else?"

"Cambridge, I think he said." He was still wary, though now Leyde was at my elbow.

"Did he say why?"

"No." He thought further, shook his head. "No."

"Who'd he seen?"

"Why the hell should he tell me?" he demanded, working up to indignation.

"Was he carrying anything, Honkie?"

"What *is* this, Lovejoy? Get lost." He tried to push past but accidentally stumbled somehow and got my knee in his groin. It really was an accident. Honest, hand on my heart. He folded like they do and clutched at a bar table, gasping and whey-faced. It's very painful. Leyde moved in, but he accidentally stumbled as well and got my elbow on the bridge of his nose. He fell back with his eyes streaming. Furniture clattered. I dropped a small table on him to keep him occupied.

"Any more for any more?" I asked gently, my back to the fireplace. People said nothing. The canal men weren't looking my way with anything like anger so I hauled Honkie up by his posh cravat. "I asked you was he carrying anything."

"A newspaper," he gasped. I pulled his face close to peer into his eyes. "Honest to God, Lovejoy. Not a bloody thing." He seemed truthful and I believed him, the lucky lad.

I let him go. He fell against a stool with a crash.

"Of all the—" Sudden indignity brought Dolly forward at a run, thinking perhaps to repeat her lone success of a moment ago. I gave her a clout to shut her up, spun her around and tore from the top back of her dress down toward the hem. It split neatly along the zip stitches from her neck to the waist, which only goes to show the sort of rubbish people buy nowadays. You could never do that to a hand-stitched Victorian garment. The ice bucket was only half empty, but I upended it inside her petticoat just the same. I handed the bucket back to the barmaid.

"Keep it filled in future," I told her amid the shrieks and groans.

I decided to go back to Lisa at the cottage. I'd need to be off about midnight to catch the London street markets. Only mugs or the genuinely innocent arrive late because by dawn most of the good antiques have vanished like the snow off a duck. I'd need a well-earned rest. Lisa would see that I got it, perhaps.

Ice buckets that are only half full really get me. There's no proper service these days, not like there used to be.

My spirits were dampened by Maslow, who rang joyfully the minute I got back to the cottage.

"Who's been assaulting whom, Lovejoy? Maslow here."

"Go on," I said. "Whom?"

"You, lad. I've a summons against you for common assault."

"I'm delighted you're happy, Maslow." Good old Honkworth had evidently done his duty. "Giving pleasure to people's one of the joys of life, isn't it?"

"I gather he was today's suspect, Lovejoy. Well, cross him off."

"Why?"

"He got a ticket for speeding that time he gave the Reverend Swan a lift."

"So?" I said, sick to my soul.

"So he's on police record as the last person having been seen with the deceased alone. No murderer's that dumb, to murder when he's the prime suspect." He chuckled into my silence. "If you'd asked, he'd have told you all that. And Reverend Swan spent all that day in the Guildhall Library, quite innocently. See you in the dock, Lovejoy, you stupid sod."

He banged his end down before I could think of a witty ending.

XIV

The inquest was held in Buresford village hall. Our coroner's a portly little man with fussy mannerisms. Glass partitions rolled back gave the hall a ludicrous gymnasiumlike appearance. His secretary kept smiling meaningfully at the doctor giving evidence, but he wasn't having any and did his stuff without a falter. We had the indefatigable Maslow and a few uniformed bobbies, sundry fire officers and a secretary from the local angling club. And Martha and Dolly. And Sarah and Thomas, the latter falling over people's feet and apologizing.

We were called to order as if we threatened anarchy.

"What's that man doing, Officer?" the coroner demanded.

I became conscious of an atrocious yet familiar pong. A filthy mittened hand clutched my shoulder.

"Lovejoy," Tinker's voice growled in my ear. A report of antique bargains he'd sussed out. "Three Shunga prints by Utamaro, all showing people shagging like monkeys. Brad has them, for a swap. He'll accept porcelain or flintlocks, cashjacked. Big Frank's got option on an eighteenth-century marquetry longcase—"

A belligerent bobby started tiptoeing through the throng.

"—clock by Scholtz of Amsterdam, nearly mint. He's asking the frigging earth for it and the whisper is Jenny and Harry Bateman picked up—"

"Not a witness, sir," the constable intoned. He had hold of Tinker now, but there's no stopping a barker reporting in.

"—a host box, Irish silver, but I can never tell what the bleeding marks mean—"

"Evict that man, Constable."

"—and an old lead cistern with a coat of arms is in Gimbert's auction for next week and a Pugin satinwood parcel-gilt table by Grace and that's about it—"

His voice receded and a door slammed. Sometimes I'm really proud of my friends. Devotion to duty is what makes a genius of Tinker. Whether he stinks to high heaven or gets evicted from every joint on earth makes no difference. Sometimes our shoddy human race warms your heart. I noticed Sarah Devonish smiling and trying to conceal her amusement with an elegantly gloved hand. Well, well, I thought, human after all.

"I will remind those in attendance," the coroner said, "that this is a court established under the Monarch's direct authority. Anyone creating interruptions will suffer immediate penalties." You could tell he was peeved, but to me Tinker is an example to us all.

As Maslow chirped a load of rubbish for the coroner's records I ran with wistful love over the list Tinker had faithfully reported in. The Japanese Utamaro prints are never that few—a full set would be about a dozen. But they're sought after avidly by collectors of erotica as well as artists. The Scholtz clock was beyond my reach.

The designer Pugin's furniture were made by Grace about 1850. You can see the same sort of scaly decoration (which I hate) in the House of Lords, if you're ever along that way. A host box is for hosts, as in the orthodox Mass, mostly Irish, of about 1730 to 1775 or even later. I'd heard that one by Fallon of Galway was somewhere in the offing.

In the end I wasn't called as a witness. Maslow could feel my hate-filled gaze on his fat neck throughout the entire proceedings. I was gratified to see his ears redden. Everybody gave evidence about how good, kind and careless old Henry Swan had been.

The coroner had no alternative. The Reverend Henry Swan went down for all time as a slipshod drunken old bum. The coroner commiserated with the next of kin. The fire services and police were praised.

It was at this point that I found myself pulled at. Some force had me on my feet and people nearby were plucking at my jacket and whispering sit down.

"Is that gentleman unwell?" the coroner called.

"No thank you," I heard my voice say. "Is that the verdict then?"

"The court is closed," he said, puzzled. "Did you have anything to contribute?"

I stared at Maslow for a long time.

"Not now, sir," I said. "Not anymore."

"I quite understand," the coroner said sympathetically. "All who knew the deceased are deserving of our condolences at this time."

Outside cars were starting and people chatted in groups. Sarah was waiting. Thomas Haverro was having a word with Martha over in the school's playground. The scene had every appearance of Thomas clumsily saying the wrong thing and Martha weeping at the good will everywhere. I suppose as a doctor he has a collection of useful phrases for occasions like this.

"Good day, Lovejoy," Sarah said. Well, at least it was better than her usual elbow. "I gather from your display at the end you're unhappy with the verdict?"

Honkworth's motor breezed in just then. Martha was being given a lift. Dolly took her aunt in hand and was obviously urging Thomas to come along. He gestured at a car, probably his. Bill Leyde the geltie was with Honkworth, but the blousy woman had been left out of today's jaunt, poor thing. Maybe she'd have lowered the tone. The big car thundered off.

"There's something wrong, Sarah." I searched for the easy

words, but they didn't improve with waiting.

"What else could it have been but accidental?"

"You tell me."

Dr. Haverro pulled alongside. "Coming, Sarah?"

"This minute, Thomas?"

"I've to follow Martha back to her place." He gave an embarrassed laugh. "Somehow I always get myself into a quandary."

"I'll give you a lift, Sarah," I offered suddenly.

"Better come, Sarah," Thomas said quickly. He opened the passenger door. I felt Maslow's deliberate advance from the right. The coroner's black limousine hissed placidly from the playground and onto the road. A constable saluted the Royal coat of arms and relaxed as the car dwindled toward the motorway.

Sarah suddenly surprised me. "No thanks, Thomas. Maybe I'll come on later."

"Are you sure?" He too could be determined.

"Yes. Give Martha my love."

Thomas darted a smile at her, but the flash deep in his expression was without humor or even hesitation. It got to me for a split second. I put it down to being on edge. Surely it couldn't have been a look of warning. How could benign old Thomas be warning anyone as self-sufficient as Sarah against innocent old Lovejoy? It didn't make sense. He smiled, full of understanding, and was out of the way by the time Maslow hove up. Maybe I'd imagined that gleam.

"Lovejoy."

"What is it now, Maslow?"

He was very angry. I was glad about that, because I don't like being angry on my own.

"What the hell did you mean by creating a disturbance—?"

"We've an appointment to keep, Inspector." Sarah linked my arm. "Would you excuse us, please?"

She whisked me toward my crate, leaving Maslow sizzling. We hurried off, though the engine took six goes and a push from two passing farm lads who were on their way to a football match. They thought the car hilarious and made jokes.

126

"Thanks," I told Sarah. Then, on the principle that it's safest to own up to what women are going to suss out anyway, I added, "I had this odd idea that we weren't friends."

"And you are correct, Lovejoy, so far." She was smiling, though. "Hadn't you better explain?"

So I did, practically everything that had happened. Some parts she guessed even as I spoke. Other bits she couldn't see until I'd explained them over and over.

"Why are *you* so obsessed, Lovejoy? The antique cup?"

I found myself stumbling for words. "It's Henry. Whatever it was he had, a ten-year-old kid could have nicked. Henry couldn't have stopped a bus. Yet they killed him."

"I see."

"No you don't, Sarah." I pulled the crate to a tipsy stop in a layby. "He had these daft ideas about . . . about mankind being able to sanctify things. Any bloody thing at all, just by using it right." I saw her expression clear with sudden understanding.

"Like antiques, Lovejoy?" she smiled.

"Well, yes." Why do I always go on the defensive? I make me mad sometimes. "What about it?"

"I see." She was staring at me full face. "I do see, Lovejoy. How beautiful. How very beautiful."

"Eh?" Women make me suspicious when they switch moods like this. I took my hand back from where she'd reached for it. There's no halfway house.

"I mean, so we're fighting for sanctified love?" I didn't like that plural. "How can I help?"

I thought a minute or two, then decided to trust her. "Tell me all you know about old Henry and this cup thing."

"Have you somewhere we can go?"

"Martha's?" I suggested lamely.

"Possibly not," she said, frowning. "There are too many people there. Your cottage."

"Are you sure?"

She fell about laughing. "Yes, I'm sure, Lovejoy. Even without a chaperone."

When I have somebody like Sarah home I'm always embarrassed. Not that I'm uneasy fetching a woman in. In fact, trying to achieve this occupies a large part of my waking hours. Women of Sarah's class will never complain about the state you've got yourself into, the way somebody like Lisa does, for example. But that only makes the general grubbiness seem worse. And the more you try to cover up the worse things get. I said to look about if she wanted and started to brew up. She went out into the garden.

"I don't like to do much to it," I explained to forestall her when I knocked on the window to call her in.

"So I see." She was smiling again. "No gardener."

"Well, it's done nothing to me." I carried a cup for her. She sank gracefully on the divan without giving it a glance.

"How wise you are, Lovejoy." She didn't appear sardonic to my brief look. As I went into the alcove for mine I realized she'd caught my eye. "It's time to make amends."

"Eh?"

"Come and sit down." She folded her legs under her. You can't help admiring the way their legs finish up in curves and sleek lines. I did as she said and stared gravely somewhere else. "I must apologize. When we first met I supposed you were a . . . a chiseler." She brought it out with a gratified smile.

"No need to apologize."

"Yes there is." She pulled a face after a sip and moaned. "How absolutely *terrible.*"

"It's the water," I said defensively. "They put chemicals in for our bones."

"I was insufferable."

"Forget it."

"I think Thomas would have been kinder to you—if I'd not been so suspicious the day we all met." She took off her hat and dropped it carelessly aside. I like how they loosen their hair. "As I see it, Lovejoy, Henry's hitherto useless friends—Thomas, myself, Martha and her unsettled niece, Dolly—ought to do what we can to help."

"How?"

"Let's be practical." She rose and wandered about the room. "Your garden's unkempt, and your cottage. But that might be explained by your . . ." she paused, then added, "your, shall we say, solitary mode of life." I knew she'd spotted some of Lisa's things. I thought I'd hidden most of them. "You can afford a car, of sorts. You are therefore not destitute. On the other hand you are obviously less than affluent, despite your intuitive gift where antiques are concerned."

"Maslow asked why I don't make a fortune."

"That's because the man's an imbecile," Sarah said. She sat down, doing the leg twist thing again, almost as if she hadn't noticed my difficulties when she attracted my attention this way. "I'll pay you."

I paused at that. She was smiling.

"An allowance. Nothing sinister."

"Antiques?" My mind began to race happily ahead into those meadows of buying and selling where antiques blossom like flowers in springtime, but she was shaking her head.

"While you find what actually happened to Henry."

"And his Grail?"

"That too. But it comes second, a long way second. Agreed?"

I told her I agreed, though I had no right. Antiques naturally come first every time.

"I'll have my agent send you a weekly sum, payable from now."

"Er, can I have some on account?" I asked, trying to be off-hand. "I'm a bit strapped at the minute."

She laughed and clapped her hands delightedly. This is an unusual response, but women are odd.

"And tell me about this thing Henry lit candles for."

She did, only getting into her stride after she'd rolled in the aisles some more while giving me a week's advance.

Henry Swan, Thomas Haverro and James H. C. Devonish had been undergraduates together at Selward College, Cambridge. Mainly for religious studies of the Established Church, it had tolerated Thomas when he had bumbled his way into the medical

129

faculty across the way. In contrast, James and Henry went straight, but only Henry served the Church. Devonish went on to become an adviser in the prison services and worked gallantly for malcontents till he died in a road accident. Sarah was the result of a chance meeting with an old friend. Though much younger than Devonish, she'd married him and they'd had a few years of happiness together before the accident.

"James told me about the Grail," she told me reflectively. "I remember it quite clearly, the odd story, even the words he used. An open, lovely man. But it was only in our last year he explained."

As undergraduates the trio went on holiday to Berwick. A crumbling old church by the lovely Northumbrian shore captured their romantic imagination and they made quite a thing about trying to have the authorities restore it. Naturally, as with all such brave attempts, they failed. But it was there that they came across the Grail. With romance burning in their youthful souls they decided to adopt it there and then.

The church was obviously derelict. That particular bit of coastline is favored by curious spells of beautiful pacific weather, dull gold sunshine and skies clear to the planets and back. The seas were clean and dark, the sea stones tumbled sharp in heaps on miles of crisp sands where birds fly flock after flock and distances from each inlet to the horizon seem infinite. I know the whereabouts of the ruined church but couldn't recall having seen it.

"South of Berwick?"

"James described it as a few miles from the Tweed estuary. He said you could see the sandbanks clearly from the churchyard. They used to cycle out and have picnics on the shore."

An elderly man met up with them one day, the second holiday they took in those parts. He had heard of their attempts to rescue the old church and sought the trio out. He told the youngsters he had the Grail, passed down according to tradition from hand to hand. Listening to Sarah's secondhand account, I had more sense than to ask how it had got from ancient Jerusalem to modern Berwick.

"That's near Holy Island," I remembered suddenly. "Lindisfarne."

This long promontory runs into the ocean from the coast, roughly southeast. At the end is a cluster of houses, a post office and an old monastery. It's where the magic and mysterious Lindisfarne Gospels hail from, those dazzling intricate pages made and embellished by the devout hands of saints themselves. I shifted uncomfortably. All of a sudden silly old drunken Henry seemed less daft.

"This old chap—?"

"Was the last priest of that particular church."

"Shouldn't he have given it in? Surrendered it to the local archbishop, something like that?"

"He distrusted the Church. In its immensity he feared the Grail would be lost, derided—" She shrugged. "Henry felt the same. That's the reason James never took a parish."

In a way I could sympathize with a tired overstretched bishop, facing his millionth report of the Grail's finding yet again, knowing as he wrote the report it was only the start of another epidemic of identical reports.

"And did this bloke just haul it out of his pocket and hand it over?"

"No. It took a year," Sarah explained. "He insisted on having them stay in his house and talk, explain their motives, beliefs. James used to joke about it, said it was worse than his Cambridge finals."

The elderly priest showed it to them. From Sarah's description they were all chastened, Henry most of all. I suppose, reading between the lines, three young students can't really be blamed for a certain amount of cynicism. Maybe they'd even secretly joked about the mad old parson among themselves, in the same way as I'd thought how cracked Henry was.

"James was partly convinced," Sarah said. "Henry was utterly sold. I can imagine it. The very beauty of the idea *is* transfixing, after all."

"And Thomas?"

"Well, scientist," Sarah said defensively. It made me look at

131

her. She laughed, embarrassed, for once caught out of her stride. "He was bound to disbelieve, wasn't he? He went along with the other two, though. Paid his share." I couldn't help thinking. Sarah and Thomas Haverro . . .?

"Paid?" My voice must have sounded ugly because she cooled me with a brief chilling stare.

"Nothing like that, Lovejoy. It was a gift. In trust."

She began to explain.

The cup was merely battered old pewter, "shallow as an egg-cup," James Devonish had described to Sarah. It had come to light somewhere in the Great Civil War, about 1643. Unaccountably the legend stuck like glue to the little vessel. It apparently seized the religious admiration of the time throughout the district. It became a small focus of local miracles, was even worshiped. Pilgrimages were made. In the Restoration a Mercian prelate threw his conviction behind it and had a tiny silver casket constructed to contain it. The casket was tree-shaped, probably intended as religious symbolism.

"It was sealed in," Sarah said. "You could only see through the crystal trunk. The cup was fixed."

"Crystal windows, like an old lantern has?"

"Yes. That was how James explained it." I switched the fire on to give us something to stare at. I was scared of interrupting Sarah's flow of reminiscence. Her face looked quite beautiful, lit by the red glow and smiling wistfully. "Before then," she went on, "it had just been on a tiny gold plinth."

"And after?"

"Oh, as it was handed on each generation seemed to have added to it." I said I didn't follow. "Well, made it more precious," she said. "Remember, I never saw it. But the old vicar had a list of the main things that had been done."

"Are we still talking about a small pewter cup?"

"Why yes, of course, but I suppose the value of the casket was extremely high." I cleared my throat and blinked a few times. The fire was drying my eyes. "Because of the additions, you see."

I saw all right.

"Who?"

"I can't remember all the names James told me. Different jewelers and suchlike." She smiled reflectively. "Thomas Tucker was one. Another was called Sweet. They made me laugh."

"And *they* did some work on the Grail?" My throat felt raw.

"Yes. It must have been beautiful."

"Do you remember any other names?" Tom Tucker's about 1692. Sweet was one of many West Country silversmiths of that name spanning the period.

"Hester somebody."

"Bateman?"

"That's it. And Fabergé, of course, in later years."

I went giddy. She couldn't remember any more, but I'd been told enough.

The idea was good. Where a worthless object needed to be preserved, impress succeeding generations by decorating it. A wealthy generation would expend enormous wealth on a religious relic, a poor lot much less. But for Hester Bateman, that extraordinary silversmith, to add a mystical silver decoration to the work of the other geniuses like Sweet and Tucker, and for that to culminate with the brilliant Russian designer Fabergé . . .

"He was the last," Sarah said sadly. "Before the Great War. The old vicar's father had taken it to Saint Petersburg." I thought, dear God. "Henry had plans for us to put money together and add at least a token piece of art to the Grail. It came to nothing, though. Such a shame."

I questioned her further but got nothing more. The original crystal casket had become the trunk. Different workers had added branches, leaves, jewels for fruit. And inside the priceless tree the battered pewter cup which legend said was the Grail itself.

"James told me the order in which the various additions were made," Sarah explained. "But I can't possibly remember."

"Jesus."

We sat and watched the fire. Sarah's the sort that you never see putting lipstick or powder on. We held hands.

"Er, Sarah. You and Thomas . . . ?"

"Well." That laugh again. "After James died, Thomas asked me. I refused. We were close at one time. I decided to live alone." She glanced across the firelight at me, smiling. "I found the role of a viable widow at least as . . . worthwhile as the wife of a hardworking doctor."

All my suspects were vanishing one by one. And now the commonplace myth was turned into a sober reality. Sanctification by use, Henry had called the process, I thought bitterly. But his precious sanctification had taken place at the hands of several artistic geniuses over some three hundred years at least. The motive for sinking Henry's barge was no longer hidden. It was clearly and utterly greed. I felt ill. How bloody typical of our modern day. Absolutely bloody typical. We can't even be wrong right.

"Are there no more people who might have known?"

"Well . . . no. Not really," she said, hesitating. "Thomas never married. I know for a fact James told no one but myself. Martha's been the same, very much in the dark and reticent. Although . . ."

"Yes?"

"Well, I often wonder about Thomas' nephew."

"Does he live locally?"

"Why yes. Alvin. You know him, though of course he's perfectly trustworthy—"

"Alvin?" I suddenly didn't like this at all.

"Alvin Honkworth. An attractive sort, but—"

And Sarah went on to say how pleasant Honkie was . . . Now I had the missing motive, greed. And now maybe the killer as well. And a splitting headache, because didn't Maslow say that Honkie was the one suspect who had a cast-iron police-documented alibi?

As Sarah was getting ready to leave we arranged for me to report in on my progress. She was putting her hat on in the hall when I opened the cottage door. Betty Marsham's smile faded as she saw past me into the light.

"Good evening, Lovejoy."

"Er, why hello, Mrs. Marsham!" I cried jovially, in an instant panic. "I'm afraid your Regency floral painted butler's tray hasn't arrived. Would tomorrow do?"

"Certainly," Betty said, falling in. "Would you please telephone me without delay?"

"I shall," I promised, and did a clumsy rotten introduction in the doorway.

Betty took one road at the chapel and I ran Sarah down to the railway station.

"I'm sorry about that, Lovejoy." She smiled as I dropped her off. "How *terribly* disappointed Mrs. Marsham was about her Regency serving tray!"

"A serious collector," I lied casually.

"I could see that," Sarah said sweetly. "I'll endeavor to make it up to you. Good night."

I watched her move into the station. She bought a ticket, had it clipped at the barrier and descended the steps. Still in sight, but without turning to look back, she raised a hand in an elegant slow wave while walking on down. I drove off. With idiots like me about, no wonder women are so confident.

That night I was so full of bitterness I hardly slept. Poor Henry's devotion had missed out, founded as it was on mere holiness. The murderer's love of the mysterious little pewter Grail wasn't holy. It was pure greed. I finally dozed. This battle was my kind of war after all.

I may not be much good at holiness. But I'm bloody good at greed. It's my subject.

XV

London has nearly as many street markets as it has streets, but the only ones which matter to me are the antique markets. Naturally, London being London and all, some of the most famous "antique markets" aren't anything of the sort—like Petticoat Lane, which is mostly for new cheap goods. There's another slight difficulty: famous street markets with a name known the world over aren't on the map at all, being called something completely different—also like Petticoat Lane, which is officially Middlesex Street.

In case you ever go, take a tip: ask yourself the all-important question, What am I going *for?* It's pretty vital. Supposing, for example, you are a die-hard collector of antique silver or jewelry. Well, you'd turn off Houndsditch into Exchange Buildings Yard near Cutler Street, the world's grimiest, dingiest and most prolific antique silver market, about eight o'clock on a Sunday morning. And a real collector will be there long before that, when most of the deals are done. If you are only after secondhand modern furnishings, say, you'd go to Cheshire Street, also near Petticoat Lane, and romp there to your heart's content. A regular "trade" dealer in antiques will do better going to Portobello Road—be there at five-thirty on a Saturday morning to get the real flavor of the world's only antiques scrum. If, on the other hand, you've got a reliable alarm clock, breeze into the New Caledonian market in darkest Bermondsey, but five o'clock on a wet and windy Friday morning isn't too early because dealing starts long before that. But the "ordinary" collector (pretending for the moment that there is such a thing) should go to Camden Passage for friendliness and merriment. Go on Saturdays, and arrive midmornings like I do, because it has its own nosh bars—all better than Woody's, you'll be astonished to learn. There are plenty of others.

I've left the Belly last. I'll set the scene first. Time: Saturday about six A.M. and Lovejoy rolling up knackered in his crate after a nightmarish journey through the early London streets wondering if the engine was going to give out from fatigue. Place: Portobello Road, near Ladbroke Grove tube station and already people flocking there. Dealers are always on the site an hour before, but my zoomster wasn't up to it.

By the time I arrived the entire mile-long crush was alive. Seen from the Westway Flyover it looks like a tin of heaving maggots. No antique market's pretty but they're all beautiful, and the Belly's most beautiful of all. There isn't a dealer who won't sweat blood to help anybody selling or buying. It isn't just a street market either. Shops, galleries and antique arcades are there as well, crammed into the entire glorious stretch with alleys and crannies bulging with antiques of all periods—and I do mean all. Care is needed, because for every fixed stall or shop you get maybe ten wandering dealers with things to sell. Like I say, careful. A shop-bound dealer is likely to be reachable next morning, but strolling footloose dealers will tend to be very fleet of foot. Sykes is one of these.

I started at the south end because one's thirst is naturally terrible at the finish, when by sheer coincidence one arrives exhausted at the Duke.

Overcoated hard nuts were about, playing the casing game. You do this by ambling, seeming to pay no real attention to anything except your pals' chat about Newmarket yet actually collecting details of valuable items. You decide which antique dealer has most desirable stuff. Then you simply tell your minions to either (a) do over the particular dealer's home or shop for the money therein or (b) steal the main items and hold them for a ransom price—commonly rumored to be about a quarter to two fifths of their retail price. Who pays the ransom, the trader or an insurance company, is largely irrelevant. Circuses have other endearing mannerisms, but "going on the case" is their commonest trade. It does need a certain number of lackeys however. Sykes has plenty.

I passed a couple of hard lads and dropped word I was cross with Sykie. They knew my name and said he was about, while I went looking for pots.

That delectable puce color on Derby's porcelain is really rare, especially done with inset roses by William Billingsley. You find them with a blue and gilt border, with a landscape in the plate's center by Boreman. I got an option on one, a perfect 1790 piece, all before I'd gone a hundred yards, though genuine chimes belled all around. I was almost in despair after another hundred. No cash, and a perfect "banjo" barometer of West Indian satinwood by Broggi of London about 1787 was sounding sweetly across the crowded pavement. On I went, dropping a word about Sykie and sinking into gloom at the beauty all the way up the Road. Real—*genuine!*—Sheraton wine tables, Hepplewhite elbow chairs, Regency silverware to melt your heart, flintlock weapons by the immortal Nock and Manton, Meissen chocolate pots with the original handles, early blue and white of "Worcester Tonquin Manufacture"—as the original articles of June 1751 termed it—enough apron-fanned serpentine English sideboards to line both pavements, and Islamic and Continental antiques by the boatload.

I was arguing about a piece of Iznik pottery which I craved when the Sykes brothers tapped me on the shoulder.

"Dad wants to see you, Lovejoy."

"Comrades," I said over my shoulder, not letting go of the shallow dish. "You can wait, or we're going to hear the sound of shattered elbows."

I returned the dish, confident that a responsibility problem will always thwart your stomp-happy Piltdowner. Iznik's a curious ware, some of it already very old when the Armada hit the road. I'm never quite sure if I like it, though it's valuable stuff. Occasional designs are pinched from the Chinese, but the Turkish potters weren't half as skilled as their Chinese counterparts. However, Iznik—the ancient Nicaea—did massive exports of the stuff through Genoa and Venice to Europe. The colors are turquoise, blue, purplish, green and "carnation" red on a white ground. Like, in fact, an Imari color scheme in parts. The numbers of the patterns are revealing, mostly a flower eight times on the dish rim, but fives, nines and fours doubled up are common as well.

"Beautiful," I told the dealer, and obediently followed the Sykes brothers. They were my rejects from that time at the pub when I'd picked Lydia. We passed out of the main concourse, walking steadily westward until the hubbub of the market faded. Parked cars lined the roads. I chatted to these boyos about Iznik pottery as we went, quite instructively I thought.

"Can it, Lovejoy," the elder one said sourly.

"I'm giving you free instruction," I complained. "You'll remember that Lane's three-period subdivision relies heavily on stylistic grounds, but insufficient attention has been given to the nineteenth-century imitators from Isfahan and the individual original North Anatolian potters. Luckily," I chuckled, "Deck in Paris, the best copier after Lacheral of Châtillon-sur-Seine, signed his copies during Victoria's reign—"

"We're here, Lovejoy. Shut it."

He meant my mouth, so I did. We three had come a long way from the Belly. We were under a fly-over on one of those sudden desolate spots which modern town planners leave to prove that they too run out of ideas and finally can't be bothered. Sykes was leaning out of his car, casual as you please. No passers-by, no spectators. I noticed with amusement we had gathered three other minions.

"Morning, Lovejoy."

"Hello, Sykie."

He glanced behind me at his younger son, all knuckle-dusters.

"Put them bloody things away, you stupid burke."

"You tell me, Sykie," I said. "Why?"

"How the hell do I know what the aggro is?" he asked, giving me a long quizzical glance. He looked honestly puzzled and sounded peeved. "I thought I was doing you a favor, sending my two lads for teaching the divvie bit. First you sling them out. Then you're here on the Belly smoking cinders."

"Maybe you got narked," I said evenly.

"Course I did." He gazed at the lads so hard I heard them shifting uneasily. "Turned up dolled like a pair of ponces, I heard."

"All rings and hair oil," I agreed, grinning. "Quite pretty, really."

I heard one of them move suddenly forward, but he caught his shin on my heel and took a nasty tumble. It was quite accidental. Worse still his hand got trodden on as I stepped to one side.

"All of you," Sykes boomed. "Stop it." We stopped it. "You two piss off. Get in, Lovejoy."

The inside of his motor was like a small dance hall. He asked me where I'd left my car and drove onto the nearest surfaced road. He told me to cough up.

"A friend of mine got her antique place done over," I said.

"And you thought of me?" He tut-tutted. "Bloody fool. I'd have done you over, not somebody else." He was right. He would have. "And I'd have done it good and proper, not just broken a few pots." He laughed. "Hardly worth the journey."

I should have stopped to think. Or maybe, I wondered as Sykes swung us into Westbourne Grove, there was a serious flaw in my thinking.

"You can drop me at the end, Sykie," I said, thanking him for a nice ride. "I'm talking over an Iznik dish—"

"Not today you're not." He pointed to my crate, still wheezing from its dawn rush. "You're heading for the frigging fens, lad. I don't want you walking about unmarked after the way you thumbed around. My name'd be mud."

"All right." I slammed his door. He didn't drive away.

140

"Here, Lovejoy. My lads. Either of them got it?"

I thought a minute about how they'd marched me down a street full of the most beautiful antiques on earth and never glanced yearningly at a single one. I shook my head.

"Cold as a bloody frog, both of them."

He sighed with weary resignation. "I'll put them out book-making," he decided. "Go safe, Lovejoy."

"Right, Sykie. And thanks."

He drove to the intersection, but I noticed his car stayed there until I'd reversed and turned toward Marble Arch. By the time I'd reached Brentwood reaction set in. I got out quickly and retched and retched on the grass verge. That'll teach me not to use my nut. I'd never been so terrified in my life.

So it wasn't Sykes. Therefore it was another possible contender. I drove on wearily trying to work out who the other contenders actually were.

Lydia was just leaving as I zoomed up.

"Lovejoy!" she lectured. "I've waited two hours."

"Read Lane, A., on *Later Islamic Pottery*," I said.

"What's the matter? You're white as a sheet."

"Travel sick," I said. "It's the speed."

She faced me, suspicion emanating from her eyes. "A child could run faster than that stupid thing."

"You're beautiful when you're angry. Come in." The cottage looked untouched, still suspiciously neat from Lisa's tidying. "Brew up, love."

"You aren't *organized,* Lovejoy." She stepped gingerly toward the kitchen alcove.

"Go home," I said, slumping on the divan. "Or shut up."

"What happened today?" She was standing there when I opened my eyes. I'd told her to go home or shut up and she'd done neither. That's typical too.

"I got frightened." I closed my eyes. "Don't bite your lip like that or I'll tell your mother."

"I'm very cross with you, Lovejoy." I felt her fingers loosen the zip at my throat. "You need putting in some sort of order."

"I'm *in* some sort of order," I told her. You have to stamp this sort of thing out as soon as it raises its treacherous head. "In fact I'm in a very orderly condition, though to the casual observer—"

"What help do you want?" Her weight sank the divan succulently to a tilt. I honestly believe women make this unsettling approach deliberately. You're expected to notice but yet to take no notice, if you know what I mean. It's very subtle. And they're supposed to be moral. I concentrated, safe behind my closed eyelids. Relatively safe, that is.

"A barge blew up, killing a friend of mine."

"I read about it. Go on."

"I believe he was murdered." She got up in the quiet. A tap gushed water. A lid. A click, the switch. The divan tilted. See what I mean, how insidious it all is?

"What had he done? Another woman?"

"No. Maybe for something he had. I don't know."

"And you need help to . . . ?"

"To search the barge." There. It was out. I felt clammy and trembling. I'm not scared of heights or depths or water. And I can swim like a fish, on or under the water. No, honestly. It's just that a deep hull sunk at the bottom of a muddy river's a difficult place to get into, isn't it? And out of. I'm honestly not scared. I told Lydia this about eight times.

"And today?"

I explained my suspicions about Margaret's place and Sykes.

"Yet you were willing to risk thugs—?"

"Antique dealers, not thugs." A silence. Pregnant, as they say.

"You must be very fond of Margaret."

This too was dangerous ground. Still is.

"Well, compassionate," I conceded. "Old acquaintances, mutual help—"

The blessed kettle mercifully did its stuff. The untilt, nearly as seductive as the tilt. The cups, the click, pour, aroma, spoonish tinkle. Seductive tilt again. You have no real defense against all this.

"I dive," Lydia said.

"So can I." But that doesn't mean I want to, especially in deep dark waters where an entombed barge lurks in the murky depths.

"Not *into*. Under. Underwater diving. So does Col."

"Col?"

"You . . . rejected him." Years of criticism came in the verb. "We belong to the same underwater club."

"You? And Col?" I sat up, recovering fast.

"Nothing like that." She was red. I happened to open my eyes. "We swim at the same place, that's all."

"You'll search the barge?" I never look a gift horse and all that.

"Any time you want. Col will come with me."

"An hour?" The untilt.

"I'll phone him." She happened to have his number, not only a stroke of good fortune but an especially interesting one.

"He's delighted," she reported back. "He'll come around."

"Check there's no bloody fishing match," I told her drowsily. "I don't want you nibbling some hairy angler's bait."

"You can just stop that sort of talk, Lovejoy," she said. Her voice sounded smiley. Her shy fingers rubbed my forehead. I never thought fingers could be shy before, but they do funny things to skin. "What are we to look for?"

"A pewter cup. In a miniature crystal and silver tree. Maybe, that is. I'm not really sure."

"I'll tell Col. He's good in the subaqua club. He won last month's prize for . . ."

I dozed, dreaming of a sunken barge with its back broken over a small golden Grail.

Laughter is frighteningly close to terror. Time after time it comes to me that fright and giggling are nearer to each other than they really deserve. I mean, I almost rolled in the aisles seeing Col emerge from his estate car with his aqua gear on—flippers, a mask, eyes goggling and a pole thing pointing heavenward from his mouth. And Lydia hauling a few tons of cylinders and tubes. One glance at the water cooled my merry chuckles. It was deep and black. The barge's front poked ominously up, still tied to the balustrade with one short rope but the steel hawser now trailing onto the grass. The rapidity with which Nature gets its own back scares me. The weeping willow was already encouraging long grass to cover the crescent of hawser glinting about the foot of its trunk. The lawn was still muddied but starting to grass the denuded bits. It's the sides of a sunken thing which unnerve me, going down and down.

I looked toward the house on the opposite bank. No sign of visitors or inhabitants. A fairly warm afternoon but no tea on the lawn today. Maybe no tea on the lawn anymore.

"Okay, team." I sat near on a pile of stuff. Col sank back into the water with a wave. He wore cylinders and had left the black stick with the Ping-Pong ball.

"I wish you wouldn't ogle me so, Lovejoy," Lydia reprimanded, fastening her bathing cap. "Think of Col's signals."

"I can't even see him. How the hell can I see his signals?"

"You just aren't trying."

"Anyway, I was only interested in your, er, valves and things."

"Oh. Really?" She apologized for having misjudged me. I accepted with grace and listened attentively while she told me about air cylinders. Apparently the mouthpiece is sometimes difficult. "There's Col." The hull was being tapped. She stepped gracefully into the water and lowered slowly. For a few seconds she swam about the hull, then dived. Once I glimpsed her orange cap, then nothing.

The bushes along the riverbank had spiders' webs shining in the dull sunlight. It's the moisture glistening which gives you the outline. Scientists call it the Tyndall effect, where oblique light allows you to see particles gleaming against an empty background which therefore remains dark. Like the sawn end of the hawser lying over there on Martha's lawn. The weak sun even picked up the severed end around the willow tree's base. Probably when the firemen cut it they'd had to step back sharpish in case it snapped and flailed across the grass injuring somebody. What a risky job.

Col and Lydia had been gone a minute, maybe two. I walked about a bit, seeing if any spider's web was perfect enough to preserve. That may seem strange if you've never seen one in a junk shop. Mostly people don't look when they come across this double square of glass sealed along the margins and possibly varnished. You may have to clean it free of thick brown copal varnish to see that, faintly refractile between the two small glass panes, glistens the outline of a spider's web. I always feel it's rather a gruesome hobby. They are made by waiting until the day's dried out the web thoroughly and in windless air carefully and *slowly* clapping the web between the glasses. Make certain it's absolutely entire and not eccentrically placed. If it sticks to the glass skewed, give that one up and look elsewhere. You'll never rearrange it in a month of Sundays. For Christ's sake leave the spider to build again. Antique ones are mainly Victorian, about 1840 or so.

I screamed and scrabbled on my bum up the bank like a lunatic because a slimy hand shot out of the swirling water and grasped my ankle. Col was on the wrist end.

"You bloody idiot!" I screeched. My heart was thumping. "You nearly frightened me to frigging death, you stupid—"

"About how big is this cup, Lovejoy?" He stood there like a weeded Neptune.

"How the hell should I know?" I could still feel my face prickling from fear, the moron.

"What's the matter?" Lydia streamed up beside him.

"That's all people ever say to me," I said disgustedly. "Keep on looking. I'm going for a country amble."

I'd told them the general layout of the longboat as far as I could remember, where cupboards were and where Henry and I had sat when tippling that time. Pausing only to rifle Lydia's purse for small change, I hurried down the bank toward the village. It's the little things that worry you, isn't it?

A stone bridge crosses the Stour near the church. Local people are very superstitious about it on account of the legend that King Edmund, martyred by the Danish invaders, was captured after a betrayal when hiding under its single arch after a battle. The Danes then repented and struck their silver coins in memory of the saint, hammered silvers more prized among antique collectors than any except perhaps those of Alfred the Great. There's a telephone kiosk near the tavern. I rang the fire station. The head man was an age coming to the blower.

"Are you the one who gave evidence at Reverend Swan's inquest?" He said yes, cautiously. "My name's Lovejoy."

"I see." He'd obviously been warned by Bloodhound Maslow, but I'd had enough smarm to last a lifetime and cut in.

"Never mind what Maslow said about me, chief," I said in my most pleasant voice. "Why the hell did you make your firemen saw through the barge's mooring hawser?"

"We released the stern rope only," he said after a pause.

"And *then* sawed through that great steel hawser?" I heard a rustle of paper. Somebody had got the file out for him.

"It was already fractured when my men arrived."

"You sure?"

"It's here in the report, Lovejoy. Now, one moment." His voice went sterile again. "State the exact purpose of these questions—"

"Ta." I plonked the receiver down and hurried back along Martha's side of the river.

Bubbles were still rising in the water around the wreck when I climbed onto Martha's wharf. The hawser was thick enough to have moored a cruiser. An explosion tends to rip and fray the toughest steel "rope" and blacken it. But a hacksaw cuts through a steel hawser leaving it shiny, with the serrated marks showing clean and gleaming. Now, why cut? Well, a hacksaw's silent.

I walked down to the balustrade and peered down into the river. The longboat's prow was about ten yards off. I kicked the hawser until Col's head emerged.

"I'm over here. On this side."

He de-goggled, treading water. "What are you doing over there? You gave the wrong signals."

"Is Lydia all right?"

"Certainly."

"Can you look at the front end where this hawser's tied?"

"I think we should finish—"

"No. Right away, Col. Both of you. See if there's a cupboard or a space where something could be hidden at the hawser's join."

I was thinking, now supposing a longboat was securely moored and couldn't move away. Why go to all the trouble of having a huge steel hawser between the bow and a nearby solid tree?

"Hey, Col," I shouted.

"What?" He was climbing up the sloping deck, steadying himself by holding the gunwale.

"When I kick the hawser, what happens underwater?"

"I get the message you tap out. We use a variety—"

"Great. But is it just a vibration or do you actually hear a sound?"

"Both."

"And if it's a rope that somebody taps?"

"No use, Lovejoy. Ropes dissipate the vibration. We'd not hear anything."

Metal carries sound. Ropes do not. I stumbled back up the bank, suddenly breathing hard. It had to be *in* the frigging tree. The reason you have a steel hawser wrapped round a tree is to keep safely locked a hollowed-out space in the trunk. And the slightest touch on the hawser quivered vibes into the world's largest sounding box, Henry's dear old metal-sided barge. *It was all just one big telephone.*

I streaked over to the weeping willow. The hawser had been round the trunk so long that the bark had begun to grow over the outside of the metal, almost as if it was eating into the living wood. Quite high up, though, which explained why nobody had noticed the faint squared mark on the bark once the hawser was cut free. I scrambled up, clung to a low branch and dug my comb into a crack. A square section of bark fell out onto my face. The hollow had been very crudely dug out, maybe big enough to hold a small dinner plate. Empty.

I replaced the square tidily and signaled to Col and Lydia.

"We haven't finished looking underneath the front," Lydia called. "What are you doing to that tree?"

"There'll be nothing there. Dress up and collect me on the bridge."

I waited a few minutes before Col's estate car drew up. Somebody had cut through the hawser to get Henry's precious Grail, which was hidden in the hollowed space in the tree, protected by the steel binding. Henry had been awakened by the vibes. Martha had said he was a light sleeper, always up and down in the night listening on his wires for animal sounds. A convenient covering hobby for somebody with the Holy Grail stuck in a tree.

So somebody had been sawing away, and had been caught by Henry. Maybe even been recognized. Henry was injured after a brief struggle or a sudden blow. He'd been lifted—easy to lift a featherweight like him—into the longboat. Then petrol or oil. A match, and run like hell to where a car was waiting, clutching . . . ? It fitted.

"Look, pals," I said. "We know now what we're looking for. We haven't quite obtained it, but I owe you both a favor."

"What—?" Col began, but I shut him up.

"Only please don't ask for your favor immediately, unless it's desperate. You're in a queue."

"How sweet," Lydia said, smiling.

I wish women wouldn't keep saying that. Col dropped Lydia and me at the cottage. She had a bath while I made some notes on people I'd met recently. Such as Honkworth, Leyde, Dolly, even Martha, Sarah and Thomas. Though sorely tempted I didn't include Maslow. While Lydia trilled a trendy folk song in the bathroom there was a knock at the door.

"Hello, Lovejoy." Jean Evans was smiling there. "I called to make up," she was saying when her smile froze. We listened attentively to splashes and singing. It was one of the Vaughan Williams adaptations of a Wessex melody, if I remember. Jean had a new book in her hand. It had every appearance of a peacemaking gift. "I see," she said witheringly. You can just see a corner of a rumpled divan from the doorway. I'd never realized that before.

I thought I might as well say it, if only for the record. "I can explain, Jean," I said.

"Typical!" she blazed. "Absolutely typical."

She stalked back to her car and roared off. Gravel in Lovejoy's face again.

"Who was that at the door?" Lydia emerged, wrapped voluminously in my dressing gown. It's odd how their shape shows through.

"Only the postgirl," I said. "Tea?"

XVI

The range of possible murderers was getting smaller. I'd have to be more active. I was in town counting suspects by ten.

A word about antique gloves.

Selly's antique shop lies (symbolically enough, I suppose) between the Three Cups tavern and a graveyard. Selly's shop is remarkable in not being Selly's shop at all. He's the underdog of a team of three dealers but, as is often the case with underdogs, he's the only one in the joint that matters. The actual owners are two elegant entrepreneurs called Terence and Christine, who have a great time every single living day. They rise at ten-thirty, like the tramp in the song, have a quick wrestle with Woody's burnt offerings and then make it to the Three Cups in the nick of opening time. They rest in the afternoon, repeating it all over about sixish, and are safely home by midnight after a tiring day. All this takes place within an eighty-yard radius. This middle-aged and wealthy pair live in a town house a stone's throw from the tavern at the back of the Arcade. That's planning for you. The antique game's full of this sort of person, good company but very low productivity. I crossed to Selly's shop because I vaguely remembered seeing a pair of massive Satsuma vases there some weeks back. Maybe they were the same pair that were niggling me.

"Rumor has it," I said, putting my head round Selly's door, "that Christine and Terence once visited here. Correct?"

"Wrong," Selly answered without raising his head. "A mirage."

I've a lot of time for Selly, who's straight out of Dickens. He resembles the elderly benign desk clerk and wears those specs you have to peer over to see anything at all. He has no teeth and is bald as a badger on top with tufts of white hair dangling over each ear. I went in and watched him sort a pile of old gloves. Selly always sits at an old-fashioned counter on a tall Victorian stool in bad lighting. I have a shrewd suspicion it's a set-up, a scenario Selly uses to show how really quaint life can be. It's all bottle-glass windows, stained oak paneling and unsuspected nooks. What amazes me is that I've never yet called at Selly's shop and found him out, or even off his stool.

"Look at this lot, Lovejoy."

He never seems to go out buying. His antiques come by a sort of osmosis. Either that or kindly hob fairies leave them by the fireside.

Ever thought how fascinating gloves are? People tend to forget gloves. Like in those telly serials about Ancient Rome, where posh Romans are shown dressed correctly and sprawling correctly and eating correct grub in correct surroundings, but without gloves. *Very* wrong. They ate in stylish gloves, as did the nobles in Ancient Egypt. Antique gloves are lovely things, but you need to know what's what. Masons wore off-white, the Holy Roman Emperors blood red with jewels, while bishops and warrior knights got gold-embroidered pairs on initiation. Look for especially embellished Tudor pairs, but only at reliable auctions. They'll cost the earth. If you get your hands on—or indeed in—an authentic pair you can often locate the original owner from the insignia embroidered on the dorsum. The chances are it will probably be some important historical figure because gloves were a traditional gift to monarchs. Queen Bess got one measly pair for the cold Christmas of 1562 (when nobody needed to take much notice of her) but over two dozen lavishly jeweled pairs on New Year's Day in 1600 (when everybody bloody well had to).

This heap of gloves on Selly's counter was lovely. Colors are a reliable guide. Typical late nineteenth-century colors are fawns, greens, buffs and creams, depending on what the gloves were for. Good Regency colors are light or sky blues and rose pinks or kid gloves, but please go carefully. Don't assume that the Grecian style required long gloves, or you might pass up the find of a lifetime. Some George III period gloves were wrist-lengths, even with the short sleeves of the period, though most society people thought bare elbows excessively flagrant. Early Victorian ladies wore short white or lavender gloves about the house to remind themselves not to spoil their lovely delicate mitts and to get the gnarled housemaid to lug the coal scuttle instead.

"Any boxes?"

"One." Selly fetched a paste-cardboard box decorated in paneled green with lacquered shells and lavender-backed lettering: "GLOVES."

"Beautiful, Selly." I let him open it, and held my breath. Sure enough, there was a pair of ivory stretchers fastened to the purple satin lining of the lid. Imagine a pair of scissors without finger-holes or sharp blades.

"Flask?"

"Eh?"

That was disappointing, but you can't have everything. Needless to say, even gloves had accessories. You know what the Victorians were like. Buttonhooks are the commonest for pearl or decorative buttons, and folding mother-of-pearl-handled buttonhooks are especially collected nowadays.

"Sometimes they had a wooden flask with a metal plunger for pushing a sprinkle of powder down the fingers," I explained.

Mind you, they're pretty rare. I quickly examined the rest of the gloves. Mainly Victorian outdoor ladies' walking gloves, but the boxed pair were a set of slate-colored four-button "half mourning" short gloves from the London General Mourning Warehouse in 1891. Rare.

"Interested?" Selly asked.

Yes, but broke. "Let me think about it a week or so."

"A day." Selly only looks gentle. We're always like this, tugging for time. I nodded miserably and turned as casually as I could manage to what was niggling.

"Still got those Satsuma vases, Selly?"

"No. Sold them to Liz. Now Jimmo has them." He beamed at me over his rewired specs. "Thank heavens."

"I quite liked them," I lied easily.

"Balls," Selly said. "What are you up to, Lovejoy?"

"Me, Selly? Nothing. See you." And that was that.

Selly's opinion was the same as mine. The vases were the usual run-of-the-mill second period. He knew himself lucky to have got rid of them. I paused in the Three Cups for a gill, thinking what an odd old world it was. And it was becoming decidedly odder.

Mel and Sandy had shouted to me about the Satsumas. I realized how stupid I'd been to offend them by ducking back into the Arcade and not listening. Tinker was in the George, taking on fuel for the day.

"Sandy and Mel?" His expression veered into mischief. "You'll love this."

"Come on, Tinker. Where?" He gets me mad trying to be witty.

"Having their hair done."

"Eh? You mean the barber's?"

"Not likely. Women's poxy hairdresser's. Evelyn's."

"Oh." I thought a second or two. "Er, look, Tinker—"

"Sod off, Lovejoy." He slurped from his glass and wiped his mouth on a stained mitten. "You won't catch me going in one of them fancy places."

I looked at him dispassionately. Tinker was right. An elegant ladies' hairdressing emporium just wasn't him. On the other hand it wasn't me either.

"You're my barker," I told him indignantly. "You're supposed to—"

"I'm supposed to ferret the tickles out, Lovejoy, not ponce
around—"

People who are in the right really irritate me sometimes. I
gave him a bitter mouthful but only left him grinning and cack-
ling into his beer. Friends.

I telephoned Lydia's home and got her mother, she of the
elegant shape and frigid glare.

"Lovejoy." I said. "Where's Lydia, please?"

"She's upstairs, reading about *old chairs.*" She spat the words
out to show whose side she was on.

"Tell her to get down here."

"Don't you use that—"

"At Evelyn's hairdresser's. Forthwith, or she gets sacked, love.
Okay?" I rang off.

I was waiting across the road when Lydia arrived, out of breath
and curious. My face was smiling like a fool's when she came
scampering along the pavement, dropping things and bumping
into people. I hastily changed to a frown. There's no place for
fondness in the game. I keep saying that to myself, for all the
good it does.

"Why old chairs?" I demanded. "I said read up glass, Staffordshire, and Russian ikons."

"Well, Lovejoy." She was instantly downcast. "They aren't at
all interesting. Not like furniture—"

I looked at her dear spectacled face, marveling. I'd have to
accept she was furniture. Yesterday she'd felt the precious Ming
finger jade I'd shown her and asked if it was stone. I'd explained
the chemical tests and the different appearances till I was blue in
the face. "Right, love. But do try not to miss an old master
painting from ignorance."

"Very well, Lovejoy." She looked about. "Why here?" A
smile quirked her mouth. "Are you going to get your hair
done?" Suddenly everybody was a joker.

"Highly humorous," I snapped, but she stayed smiling. She
was less trouble icy. Not so human, but less trouble. "Go and ask
Sandy and Mel—"

"Are they in there?" She was all sudden interest. "Tell them Percy's is cheaper for a shampoo and set—"

I took her shoulders and shook her to silence.

"Lydia, love. Just ask Sandy—" I paused wearily. It was too complicated. "No. Take me in. Just give me the chance of passing a quick word with Sandy."

"I'll pretend to require an appointment. How exciting!" She pushed on the glass door, still smiling at my discomfiture. "Stay close to me and you'll come to no harm."

"Get in."

It was half gloom. A pong of chemicals mixed with perfumes stung my nostrils. There was a row of hoods, rather like beehives, with seated women beneath. Huge mirrors lined the walls. Machines hummed and water trickled. A plush carpet bounced underfoot. Acolytes swished about in shapely uniform. It was a right nightmare.

"There." Lydia indicated a nearby hood. "I'll talk to the appointments girl," she whispered, "but I'll attract his attention first. Is that all right?" She called hello to Sandy as she crossed the carpet. He fluttered his fingers in return.

"Yoo-hoo, Lydia, sweetie pie!" he caroled. I stood by the door, one foot to another. Lydia pointed to me and Sandy screeched in delight. "Why it's Lovejoy, ladies!" he announced. He couldn't turn his head much in the iron bonnet thing. Maybe it was fixed to his head. It should have covered his mouth.

"Wotcher, Sandy," I said, embarrassed, shuffling over.

"Don't pay their prices here, Lovejoy! They're *extortionate*, dear! I'm going to Sweaty Bill's. Mel positively swears by him—"

"Shhh, you noisy burke," I said in an undertone. The women were all smiling, pleased at the diversion. "Those Satsuma vases. What did you and Mel want to tell me?"

"You *hated* our new silver fringe, Lovejoy," he said sulkily. "I could tell. We perspired *blood* doing that car."

"No. It's great," I hissed in a desperate undertone. "Honest. About the vases—"

"Did you really like it?" He smiled at some recollection. "Mel and I had a *terrible* fight—"

"Terrific, Sandy." For Christ's sake, I thought. "The vases—"

"Jimmo took them to Drabhanger."

"Eh?" The words failed to connect. "You saw him?"

A girl was sitting on a cushion by his knees doing his finger-nails. You know, actually filing them like Nero. Sandy snatched his hand away.

"What are you doing, you silly bitch!" he screeched. "Just look! She's marmalized my pinkie! Ooooh!" He broke into the-atrical sobs. "Maniacs. Maniacs on all sides."

"Please, Sandy."

He dropped the hysteria instantly, glancing hard at me. "Ten percent?"

"Anything."

"A poxy slum on the seafront," Sandy explained. "Mel had this idea for a lobster-pot chandelier, but I said to him just think of the *risk* with chiffon curtains—"

"Ta, Sandy."

"Toodle-oo, Lovejoy," he trilled after me. I escaped and stood breathing the fresh East Anglian smog with relief.

A hand gently touched my arm. Lydia, smiling still.

"I'm going to Drabhanger, love." I told her. "Knock around. Suss out whatever you can about Satsuma vases. Tell Tinker what I said."

"Where do I see you next?"

I hesitated. Her mother was tapping her foot and drumming her fingers a few yards away. Lydia saw my glance and flushed.

"I'm so sorry," she said lamely. "I keep telling her . . ."

"Well, the cottage. I've nowhere else."

I waved to her mother and hurried off. Maybe Lydia's parent was becoming keen on antiques, but I didn't think so.

The North Sea coast has strings of small fishing villages. Drab-hanger's small even for one of these. The weather was deteriorat-ing into steady rain as I filled the Ruby with a cupful of petrol and headed toward the sea.

Hal Asprey's Antiques Emporium in Drabhanger was practi-cally on the wharf of the fishing village, sandwiched between an old church and a bakery. I'd never seen a shop so small since my own place went bust. Hal himself was a cheerful unsinister type so calm and chatty I had my doubts within seconds of meeting him. There was hardly anyone about, just a shopper or two bending into the gale. My old crate looked decidedly worried about its future. I could swear its oil lamps were swiveled to keep an anxious eye on the rushing seas. The wharf looked sound enough, though it was already being engulfed by the biggest of the waves at the southern end. The sky had lowered considerably since I'd set out. I stood in the worsening weather with my back to the ugly sea.

"Yes," Hal called from his doorway. "The church tower was used as a lighthouse beacon in the old days. Notice the additional fenestrations?"

I dated it as maybe A.D. 1100 and asked was that about right.

"Not far out," he said, beaming. "Of course the Romans had a beacon light here, but you know what the Saxons were like." We agreed on the Saxons. "Come in out of the rain. I'm just brewing up."

I'd have to watch for the poison-ring bit.

"Thanks. I actually came to see you."

"You did?" He had a little electric kettle and got busy, sounding pleased. "Saw my advert in the local rag, eh? Thought there were only three of us read that thing every week. No, leave it open," he said quickly. I'd shut the door because the wind was driving the rainstorm directly onshore. The sea was rising in a white-flecked swell. I opened the door and perched miserably on a stool near the counter. Well, it was his emporium and not mine, but the bloody weather inside was as bad as that outside on the sea wall. I replaced the cast-iron griffin doorstop, 1846 or so.

"Rough old day," he said, happy as a sandboy, while I looked about. He had a cram of Victorian tableware and household items, including a good linen crimper and an orange peeler of the sort nobody makes anymore, though the orange peeler is today's most wanted kitchen implement. You can get a genuine antique one for a few pennies even now, and it's useful—marvelous to have an orange peeled without getting covered in a sticky spray. The Victorians had their hang-ups, but you can't say they were dumb.

"I'm here about those Satsuma vases."

"That rubbish," he said derisively, grinning.

"You didn't like them," I observed.

"Would you? Fastest few quid I ever made, in fact, so I shouldn't complain, I suppose."

I paused for breath, and it wasn't the gale whistling through onto my back that made my breath funny. He did the tea mystery and gave me a cup.

"Insurance?" he guessed, sitting at the counter. "Mr. Jamestown collected the envelope the same day. I didn't get a receipt for it, but it was all right . . . ?"

"Fine, fine," I reassured him. The poor honest chap seemed so anxious. "And the vases too, I suppose?"

"Yes. That afternoon." A man ran by outside and a car's horn sounded in the distance, faintly submerged in the gathering sea roar. Hal Asprey became inattentive. "It seemed an odd sort of deal, Mr. Jamestown coming back for the Satsumas. I'd assumed he was selling them privately."

"And the envelope arrived here on time?" I had to repeat the question because he was suddenly on edge. A faint plop sounded in a lull of the whining wind. Something was going on outside. Still, it meant that we weren't all alone on this godforsaken coast. Hal was now restless and peering from the window.

"The envelope?" he said, in some secret fret. "Oh, through the letterbox by hand, as Mr. Jamestown said it would. *Dear God.*" He swung round. "Have you a car?"

"Eh?"

"*Have you a car?*" he yelled, suddenly leaping the counter and ripping oilskins from behind the door.

"Er, yes. What's up?" I was scared and on my feet. Three men ran past outside, one shouting toward the shop, but the words were wasted in the gale. A car's horn sounded in short blasts. Hal Asprey had dashed outside into the pouring rain.

"For Christ's sake, *come on,*" he yelled, dragging me after him. "Leave the bloody door, man!"

"But—"

He was already scrambling into the Ruby and trying to drag on his oilskins. I belted over and cranked her into life.

"It's a maroon," he babbled, eyes on the sea. I'd never been so terrified.

"A what?" I screamed. "Where are we going?"

"Follow him. *Fast.*" He reached round and squeezed the bulb in time to the distant car's horn. "Keep doing that," he shouted across the wind.

"Maroon what?" I yelled. "What the bloody hell's going on?"

We hurtled up the road alongside the demented sea. Another car tore by in a fog of spray.

"Put your sodding lights on," Hal howled in my ear.

"Any matches?" I screamed back. He got the point after a quick shuftie at my old lanterns. The torrential rain was driving straight at us and filling the interior round our feet.

As we labored to the top of the rise, an almighty double crack sounded overhead. It was like the end of the world. A brilliant green glow lit the sky. Everything was tinged madly with a green sheen. Even the sheeting rain shone and flashed crazily with the color in scary streaks.

"The maroon," Hal screeched against my ear, pointing down the coast, the bloody nutcase.

"It's green, you daft sod," I howled.

A siren wailed nearby and a dull bell began tolling from behind us in the village.

"Turn off here," he bawled.

I pulled into the flat car park, where people were assembling on the run. Hal was out and racing into a large boathouse even before I'd skittered to a stop. Other cars were arriving. Doors slammed. I was drenched. A woman covered in yellow oilskins flagged me to one side to keep the entrance clear. There was this boathouse on concrete stilts, red and white with railings.

"What is it, for Christ's sake?" I asked her, clambering out and cutting the engine.

"The lifeboat," she called, surprised. "Didn't you see the maroon go up?"

"Green," I said doggedly.

A bell clanged loudly from the boathouse. The vicious swell was cresting and foaming high now in waves against a skeleton ramp which ran straight down from the boathouse into the sea. You could hardly see a hundred yards for the rain and the gloomy sky. The hideous sea and lowering clouds seemed to meet a few yards offshore.

"Stand by, stand by!" Clang, clang. A siren and a bell sounded together, deafening us. There were twenty of us left on the stone apron in the pouring rain when the boat went. She dashed down the ramp, angled crazily under the waves and came up again, the black waters lifting and pouring from her. A blue light bleeped on a stick thing above.

"Is it that little?" I heard my voice say, and the traffic woman told me yes.

The boat blundered and struggled out from the shore, soaring and pushing into the dark storm. I could see faint orange-covered figures for seconds after the boat vanished among the grayness. Within seconds I couldn't focus on anything coherent in this mad amorphous shifting world. The rest of the small crowd seemed prepared to wait. Somebody said a Danish freighter had run aground on the Fasteners. I asked, and a young lad said a group of sandbanks and low rocks a couple of miles offshore. The woman said she was Hal's girlfriend.

I drove sluggishly down to the wharf again. An elderly woman was minding the shop. She'd occupied her time polishing the counter.

"Are you Hal's mother?"

"No. Just passing. I saw the signal."

We chatted a bit while I tried to dry out, sipping the drink she'd made. I didn't need telling this time and propped the door ajar. This old dear proudly told me how she'd collected some money toward a new engine.

"Collected?"

"Oh yes, dear. Boats cost ever such a lot of money nowadays."

There was nothing much to say after that. The old grannie pushed off in an hour or so. I minded the place, selling a small lusterware jug to one miraculous customer for a good price. It wasn't John Hancock, of course, because his stuff is rare—he's the bloke who in 1823 discovered that a certain reddish clay took on a deep glistening luster better than the old Persian lusters. Remember that the process is of considerable antiquity, and some B.C. specimens are known. I was quite pleased with myself. If only it had been a so-called moonlight luster of 1805 Wedgwood type I'd have got Hal a small fortune. A tip: dull pink lusters, universally known as "Sunderland" ware, don't always come from Sunderland. And some of the ones that don't are much more valuable than those that do—Staffordshire, for example.

"Hello." He came in still grinning, the maniac. "Made yourself at home?"

I'd written him a note about the jug and put the money in a tin.

"Yes, thanks. You okay?"

"Not too bad." He put his kettle on, dripping water everywhere. "They called the other lifeboat out from Doon Bay. We got the crew off between us, but the freighter's a write-off."

I cleared my throat. "A write-off? Sunk?"

"All but. It'll stay up another day, then founder. Look," he said, worried. "Was that Satsuma trade okay? I mean, there's no insurance claim or anything, is there? They were in perfect condition when I handed them over—"

"It was great," I told him. "Exactly what I wanted."

"That's a relief. I was worried."

"No need." I rose. "There's no fee for your information, but I'll try to put some antique business your way."

"Who's put new price tickets on all this?" he asked suddenly, seeing his stuff slightly rearranged.

"Me," I admitted. "No good throwing money away, is it?"

"You're no insurance man," he said eventually, looking.

"That's true, Hal," I said. "Cheers."

I splashed over to the Ruby and lit the front lanterns with difficulty, using almost a whole box of matches in the devilish wind. All the while I was thinking how very odd of Mr. Jamestown to bring out his pair of common vases to a dinky trader like Hal stuck on this remote stretch of coast. And receive payment in a big juicy envelope. And then, lo and behold, to collect the same vases he'd already sold.

Hal was still watching when I turned my motor round and came steaming past again toward the road inland. We waved politely, then the village lights faded in the storm's gray wash and I was chugging home. My lonely little cottage would feel like Piccadilly Circus after that lot back there. Mr. Jamestown's nickname's Jimmo, who'd lately been fishing and bought a posh new car. All I had to do now was knock hell out of Jimmo till he told me who he'd been blackmailing. In my innocence I sang happily as I drove. I was still wet through and forty miles from my fireside, but in a sense I was home and dry. Within hours I'd do for the bastard who killed poor old Henry Swan. Downhill all the way. Or so I thought.

A note was on the mat, in a pink and slightly aromatic envelope. "Lovejoy, Esq." Only one person would give me an Esquire on an envelope. It had to be Lydia. I read the letter, a miracle testifying to decent standards and upbringing.

> Dear Mr. Lovejoy,
>   Mr. Dill and I have ascertained that Mr. Cask entered the Satsumas for Mr. Jamestown in the auction. I think it quite possible that the arrangement was for the former to pay the money to the latter in secrecy.
>   With best wishes, I remain
>
> > Yours faithfully,
> > Lydia

I'd never seen so many misters in all my life. Once deciphered, it meant that Jimmo had got Cask to slip the vases into Gimbert's auction anonymously for him. I'd hardly taken my jacket off before the phone was on the go.

"Lovejoy?" No Mister this time, I observed. Something was rankling.

"Thanks for the note, love. You did very well—"

"I visited Lennie and Jessica," she told me icily. "A perfectly horrid woman."

"Er, now, love," I temporized.

"Don't now me," she snapped. "That horrible old vampire . . ."

"Lydia!" I gasped, quite overcome. "How *could* you use such language!"

"Well. It was almost as if you and she were . . . party to some secret, sordid agreement."

"Of course not." I got myself all offended. "Anyway, why are you asking?"

"I'm . . . I'm only expressing a perfectly proper interest in your moral welfare, Lovejoy."

"Thank you, Lydia," I said, moved. "I'll take care."

"Please do." We paused and listened. "Very well," she said at last. "Right, then. Good night, Lovejoy."

"See you, Lydia." What a lot of pauses, I thought.

XVII

I was waiting outside Jessica's house. I'd knocked, but she was probably oiling her face or whatever it is they do.

"Morning, Jessica."

"This *is* an honor, Lovejoy. Sorry to take so long."

I followed the Chinese floral dressing gown into the living room. She has this place overlooking the Colne estuary, with farms and ships and that being boring in the wide window.

"Don't you just adore the view?" She arranged her legs in an armchair opposite. She always has a lot of mascara and that green stuff around her enormous black lashes, and thick layers of lipstick. I gazed admiringly at her. Whatever they say about Jessica, she knows how to use cosmetics right.

"Yes." My voice was thick.

"I *thought* you would. Cigarette?"

I shook my head. All this would have to wait till later.

"I've come for the Satsumas."

"This very minute?"

I nodded. She shrugged, smiling at how the silk gown slipped about her shoulders with the action.

"I do appreciate your . . . gesture, Lovejoy, in this." She was a long time getting up. "It helps Lennie so much. Naturally I will settle your charges." Our eyes still hadn't dawdled on the panoramic view.

"Jessica!" Lennie's drowsy voice called. "Who is it?"

"Lovejoy," she called back, eyes level on mine still. "For his vases. Just going."

"See you, Lennie," I called.

"Lennie's staying a couple of days," Jessica explained casually. "He, er, has a touch of flu and needs looking after."

"Wish him better," I said.

We made it to her dining room, where the two Satsumas stood. I hefted them up, one in each arm. The white embossed overlain outlines on them are so crude, but to keep up the façade I tried to look pleased.

"I'm sure my payments will give you every . . . satisfaction," Jessica said without batting a single yard-long eyelash.

"I can't wait," I told her in the doorway.

"I'll ring to arrange an appointment, shall I?" she suggested, blowing a casual smoke ring.

"Do."

I stopped on the reservoir bridge to get my breath back and inspect the vases. I felt them, touched and stroked. Same old dross. Ah, well. There was nothing for it. I'd just have to go down to the Arcade and strangle Jimmo to within an inch of his life.

I put the Ruby's engine up the hill at a giddy fifteen. Now that everything was inevitable I felt like singing from relief.

Jimmo.

Some people are destined to be failures. Not that there's anything wrong with being a dud, but the tendency is to see them as despicable or misguided, or at least in serious need of rescue when rescue may be the last thing they want. I'll even go so far as to say that converting a dedicated no-hoper can be a grave mistake. To the moralist a last-minute Pearl White rescue at the Crucifixion would have done nobody a favor. What I mean is there's failure and failure. As long as failure doesn't rankle in the actual failer all is okay. It's only when he begins to sulk about failing that trouble flutters in at his window.

Jimmo's a born failure.

I sent word to Margaret and Brad to be on the lookout for Jimmo, but typically it was Tinker found him, ringing and saying Jimmo was collecting some stuff down at the Arcade.

"Keep him there, Tinker," I said urgently. "I'm on my way."

"How the hell can I?" he began, peeved.

"Do as you're told."

"Oh, Gawd. If you're in one of those, Lovejoy, I want nuffink to do—"

I tore into town. It was as if my old crate could sense the excitement and hurtled eagerly forward, clattering and panting like a two-year-old. Even Tinker was surprised to see me so soon. There were very few people about. All but two of the Arcade's shops were shut. I could see the indefatigable Jason hard at it over books and catalogues, and Margaret's always the last to leave anyway. Lydia was probably in there going over the year's local furniture sales. An occasional shopper cut through to the car park. The main street was emptying. Lovely. Hardly a witness in sight.

"Wotcher, Lovejoy." Tinker was relieved to see me walk in. Invention's not his strong suit so he was having a hard time keeping Jimmo there. "Just telling Jimmo here you're wanting a Sutherland table."

"Ta." I gave Tinker a note and the bent eye. He scarpered toward the George, leaving me and Jimmo.

"Could you drop by some other time, Lovejoy?" Jimmo was locking up, but I accidentally nudged the key from his hands. I picked it up helpfully.

"Well, since you ask, Jimmo," I said, smiling, "no."

"Eh?"

I went straight through. Jimmo has one of the smallest places in the Arcade, one room and a nook.

"Right heap of dross you got here, Jimmo." It actually wasn't too bad. There was a perfect Coalbrookdale vase, for instance, but I felt in an offending mood.

"It's not so bad as some."

"Tell me, Jimmo," I said gently. "All of it." A pause, me smiling. "About Satsuma vases. Start with them."

I sometimes think we never really look at people until it's in a battle, and often by then the chance of looking and knowing others as they really are has evaporated. Wasn't it Montgomery who sat hour after hour in a caravan trailer staring at photographs of Rommel? Jimmo's a burly bloke, neater now than ever I remembered him. There was an air of cockiness he had never shown before.

"Your good times are gone, Jimmo. Turned into slush and vanished down the gutters of time."

"You're bleeding barmy." The goon was grinning.

"Satsumas," I said, between him and the door. We'd somehow changed positions.

"Them?" He cackled without an ounce of amusement in it. "I sold them. I charged too little—"

"You know what I think?" I pushed as he tried to go past me.

"I'm in a hurry—"

"I think they're the most crappy, ordinary Satsumas you could ever clap eyes on." His sulks returned. He now looked the same old Jimmo, miserable and down on his luck. You could dress him up like the King and stick him in the Taj Mahal and he'd still look a scrubber. Maybe I was biased.

"Nowt to do with me, Lovejoy."

"Oh, it is." I prodded him, not too hard because there was his Sutherland table nearby. With those curved feet they tend to get kicked enough as it is. "You went fishing on the Stour one dark night. You saw something odd happen on the other bank near the old barge. Like, say, somebody sawing a hawser. And an old bloke coming out and getting done. You put the screws on the murderer, didn't you, Jimmo? To make the handover look legit you said you'd sell him the Satsumas—the biggest, gaudiest things you had. So he's no antique dealer, is he? To save him having to come here you took them to an out-of-the-way dealer down among the fishing villages. Drabhanger."

"This is balls, Lovejoy." He was pale to the gills.

167

"I had a long talk with Hal."

"Hal?" He tried to bluster it out. "He knows sod all."

"The money came in an envelope, Jimmo. Hal passed it on to you."

"It's legal, Lovejoy." He was weighing his chances, glancing more and more at the Arcade outside. Where did he dream he might escape to, for heaven's sake?

"You stupid burke."

"Stupid?" That stung.

"Why did you go back for the bloody vases?" You can't help wondering at people's mentality. "Don't bother. Because you actually began to wonder if they were *really* valuable, wasn't it? A kid of ten could tell you the world's knee-deep in Second Satsumas."

"I didn't want to get robbed." Sulks now, force five.

"Nobody does, Jimmo."

"Anyway, there's no evidence. I sold the vases again." His unpleasing shifty look had returned. It was like seeing a familiar figure reappear from an absurd fancy-dress costume. "Anonymous buyer, Continental. He's got them and only me knows—"

"No, Jimmo." Some people are just wrong every time they open their mouths. "Me."

"Eh?"

"Me. I own them, fingerprints and all. Yours. Hal's. And . . . ?"

His expression cleared into horror as the penny dropped. "You *bastard!*"

It was a yell, sustained and loud. He lunged at me. I just had to take it because my bell had been going since I'd arrived and I saw why the same instant Jimmo moved. The beautiful thing was to my right in a space near a phony oak chest. If I hadn't been so worked up I'd have known instantly. So there I was like a bloody fool partly stunned by a swinger from Jimmo with my teeth rattling in my head. A spray of blood sprung from my mouth as he crashed savagely forward. In the cramped shop the only way I could hit back would have been to kick the gorgeous Cuban mahogany chair aside or leap up onto it to clobber the advancing Jimmo. Naturally, retreating all the time, I had to take three more vicious hooks from the stupid burke before I was in the space near his open door. My right eye got the last blow. By then my mind was clouded and he'd kicked me in the belly, but at least we were clear of the lovely exquisite chair. I surprised him by bringing him forward. That enabled me to hack his kneecap out of place, and while he screamed and doubled I fetched him one under his ear. It's easy in the films, but it hurts knuckles like hell. He fell heavily, still swinging. For a second my heart almost stopped because his foot flailed out and almost scraped the ancient mahogany chair leg. Instinctively I stuck my own leg in the way, which brought me down too. I had to twist to avoid the precious chair. My rib cracked as I fell awkwardly.

Even as Jimmo kicked at me while we tumbled scrappily among the furniture I knew it was a memorable piece. Only the inside of the front legs tapered. Saber-shaped curves would have put it about 1810 instead of its true date of 1785.

Wheezing with the chest pain I got to my knees a second before Jimmo and managed to kick him. There was one almighty crack. For a terrible instant I thought it was the chair, but it was only Jimmo's bone, thank God.

"Lovejoy!" Women are always critical first and sympathetic eighth. I stepped over Jimmo and picked my way back to the chair, wheezing. Beautiful. "What's happening?"

"Happened," I corrected. Lydia was on her knees beside the crumpled Jimmo.

"It's my leg," he whispered. "I heard it go."

"How much for this chair, Jimmo?"

"Lovejoy!" Lydia was up and pulling me round for a lecture, which hurt so much I groaned worse than Jimmo. "Lovejoy! Have you set upon this poor man? How could you! Why—?"

"Give you the Satsumas back for it, Jimmo?"

"Are you hurt?" Lydia was looking at me. "You're a mess."

"Call an ambulance for Jimmo, love. Go *on.*"

She rushed out after a short hesitation. I stood over Jimmo so he could look up and see if I was serious or joky. "Well, Jimmo?"

"For Christ's sake, Lovejoy—"

He screamed because I'd accidentally stood on his leg. It lay turned out in the usual position of a femoral fracture. I thoughtfully turned it inward in case he'd misunderstood. He screamed again.

"Who was it, Jimmo?"

He was sobbing and dribbling saliva. "Who did you see at the barge that night?"

He finally yelled the name out, but it took several seconds to register.

"Honest to God, Lovejoy," he gasped, trying to palm my heel away from his leg. "I took his car number from out in the lane. I only saw it again by luck the next day, or I'd not have found him. Please, Lovejoy. Leave me alone."

"Where's the saw?" I needed evidence badly.

"How the hell should I know?"

"And the thing he took from inside the tree?"

"Some sort of box." His voice rose again to a wail because I'd turned his foot again. "For Christ's sake, Lovejoy. I'm frigging dying—"

"You got it?"

"No! No! Honest to God, Lovejoy—"

"Sell your car, Jimmo. And all other possessions you own. Understand?" I lowered his leg carefully. "Give half to Margaret for her wrecked shop and half to Hal toward a new engine. Understand?"

"Please, Lovejoy—"

He was finally persuaded by the unmistakable logic of my argument. I left him alone, satisfied now.

I examined the lovely chair. Mahogany was a delectable gift —one of many—from the New World to the Old. The story goes that Dr. Gibbons' brother, a sea captain, brought mahogany in as ballast. Their ladies had this strange new wood made into a box, then a bureau, by the famous Wollaston of Long Acre. The Duchess of Buckingham envied the bureau's lovely finish. Naturally, she paid the innocent old doctor a visit and wheedled the remainder of his precious new wood out of his garden, where it lay in thick planks. Master Wollaston was soon busy on a second bureau, this time for the Duchess herself. From then on the days of walnut as the premier wood were numbered. By 1725 mahogany was all the rage, and furniture's never looked back.

The most precious mahogany's Cuban. It's a dark, deep and heavy wood which furniture forgers have only recently learned to imitate with anything like accuracy. If you have the moving and truly emotional experience of handling old Cuban mahogany you'll see it doesn't plane into ordinary wood shavings like, say, pine. It *flakes,* as if you were trying to cut a bar of chocolate with a kitchen knife. Unjointed furniture made of Cuban mahogany over three-foot widths is rarest. Nowadays original Cuban mahogany is almost impossible to get hold of.

This chair was practically black—the shade Cuban mahogany eventually takes up—but its eminences and edges shone brilliantly with a deep hot-toned russet that must be the world's most exquisite color ever seen on any antique. Sheraton preached that brick dust in a linseed-oil base was the way to get that final finish exactly right, and I won't argue.

Jimmo and I agreed to swap the Satsumas for the lovely antique chair, though he moaned a lot. When Lydia returned I was sitting proudly but gently on the beautiful object. I listed a bit, but I'd stopped my face bleeding and made sure my teeth were still in place. My right orbit was bulbous and I couldn't see out of it, but you can't have everything. I tell you it was bloody hard work just sitting.

A worried CID youngster came and took down the details—how I'd been strolling by when I'd seen my friend and colleague Jimmo struggling with two evil bandits, their faces hidden by scarves. Brave me, I'd gone to my friend's rescue and been injured. They'd finally taken flight on the arrival of Lydia from next door. He took it all down.

"She's really a game girl," I praised.

He glanced from me to Lydia and back again. He began to cerebrate. Slowly, but very definitely.

"What is the, er, relationship," he asked carefully, "between yourself and this young lady, sir?"

"Apprentice," I explained. Even the ambulance men paused at that. Jimmo was being put onto the stretcher. The CID man gazed at Lydia, who nodded.

I spelled helpfully, "A . . . P . . . P . . . R—"

"Thank you, sir." He wrote and turned to Lydia. "Can you describe either of these assailants, Miss?"

Decisions are funny things. I could feel Lydia's decision struggle with her training until it rose coherent and immutable. She avoided my eye, still full of conscience.

"In a way, Inspector," she began earnestly. "The tall one wore an old duffel coat and had brown gloves—"

I sank back in a sweat of relief. No use telling Maslow about the killer yet. He'd have us making statements and dithering till the Last Trumpet. I only wanted a bit of justice. And, make no mistake, justice includes reparation, punishment. In my book that doesn't mean two years in clink with ten months off for good behavior. It means that one of us had to get finished when we met up to settle the matter.

I came to with a tired young houseman examining me.

"You're not too bad. We'll sort you out in Casualty," he said. "Come with us."

"No," Lydia said suddenly, and added uncertainly when the doctor looked, "If it's all right I'll bring him. We have a car."

As Lydia drove I watched her face in the early street lights of the encroaching evening. She said nothing and I wasn't up to talking much. Anyway, I was thinking of what to do now I knew. Trust Jimmo. A precious, glowing, delectable antique throbbing and singing in his own back yard, and there's him trying to compete with an educated clever murderer like Dr. Thomas Haverro. Don't people get on your nerves?

XVIII

That night Lydia made my divan bed up and went to fetch a hot meal in from town. We had it before the fire, by which time I'd made up my mind. You can't muck about with killers.

"Greed undid it, Lydia." I told her what Sarah had said about the Grail. "Only an antique pewter cup. A reputation as a local religious relic. Sarah's husband was loyal to the idea of preserving it by having generations of silversmiths add to it. Old Henry protected it, too. Wires to the bedroom and everything."

"It must have been a terrible temptation," Lydia said. "Almost as if it was a genuine Chippendale." Her eyes glowed with relish.

"Er, quite." I tried to distract her from furniture. "Thomas Haverro just couldn't restrain himself. When he realized Henry was consulting a divvie—"

"You."

"—it was too much. Maybe he worried about Henry selling it on the quiet." I had to smile ruefully at the very idea of Lovejoy Antiques, Inc., offering enough to get it photographed, let alone buy it.

"Shouldn't we tell that nasty inspector?"

"Yes." But I'd hesitated.

"I suppose that means you're not going to."

"Yes."

She slammed the dishes down and marched across to face me. "Then you're wrong, you stupid man."

"Am I?" I tried to speak gently, without rancor or anger, but only succeeded in sounding tired.

"Have him arrested. They'll put him in prison."

"For a week or two—"

"Life." She walked about holding her elbows, the picture of any woman wanting a serious issue avoided whatever the cost.

"If convicted, Lydia. Any lawyer will make our evidence look fraudulent. And the Grail. Think of that."

"It won't vanish. It'll still be . . . well, *somewhere* around."

"In the hands of Dr. Thomas Haverro. He'll be out in a couple of years at most, and pick it up from where he's put it. And then?"

"Don't, Lovejoy. Please."

"I want the Grail Tree off him."

"Lovejoy." She sat with me and almost made as if to take my hand for an instant. "Don't. I know what you want to happen."

"I don't want to kill anybody," I said. "Honest."

"Then tell Maslow."

"No."

It was almost midnight when I phoned Haverro. He sounded as if I'd got him out of bed.

"Lovejoy here."

"Oh, hello! How—"

"Cut it, Thomas, you bastard." I let the hatred sink into his ear long enough. "You killed Henry."

"Killed—? Don't be absurd! What an extraordinary—"

"The Satsumas were cover to pay Jimmo, Thomas. To keep him quiet. He saw you." I added a bit more, about Hal in Drabhanger and the Grail Tree, to show him it was all up.

"A . . . a mad tale you crooked antique dealers have cooked up, Lovejoy."

"I knew you'd say that, Thomas. It's not a bad defense."

"So why ring me?"

"Because I want the Grail Tree."

A pause. "I haven't got it."

"Liar. You want me to call Maslow?"

"Very well," he said, cool as you please.

"Okay, Thomas." I was as smooth as he. "And when Maslow gets a search warrant to see if you've anything hidden anywhere . . ." We waited some more. "This is killing my phone bill, Thomas."

"Tomorrow, then." He sounded strangled. "We can leave it till tomorrow."

"Tinker's already watching your place with three others," I lied confidently. "We don't want you sneaking off to hide it, do we?" A long, long think.

"What do you suggest, Lovejoy?"

"Give it to me, Thomas. Sarah told me about it in detail. It's too precious for the likes of you."

"So Sarah's sided with you. The stupid bitch."

It took another five minutes, round and round the same sentences. The threat of Tinker's mythical arrival at the nick to tell Maslow finally did it. He agreed.

"Call Tinker off, Lovejoy."

"No. Just in case."

He wouldn't dare taking any risks, in case I actually had Tinker's mob scattered in his bushes. I swear I heard his thoughts. Actually heard them, felt their very substance. He would agree to meet me, but it wouldn't be to give me any precious antique. He had a different intention in mind.

"I'll meet you, Lovejoy. Your cottage?"

"Not likely," I said cockily. "Too lonely out here, Thomas."

"Then . . . in town?"

I'd already thought it out ahead of him. "The Castle Park. Tomorrow. And no funny stuff. I'll have a bird for witness." I was meeting Lisa there. My personal witness.

"You're off your head, Lovejoy. The fireworks. There'll be thousands there."

"Not *in* the castle there won't."

"Inside? But the attendants—"

"At dusk, Thomas."

"It'll be shut."

"Try just the same," I said cheerfully. "There's only one way in. Across the old drawbridge to the main keep door."

"Will it be guarded?"

I sighed with relief. He was beaten and I had him. In the palm of my hand. Him, and the Grail Tree.

"Let's hope, shall we?" I put the receiver down gently. "Lydia, love. Call a taxi. Go and tell Martha Cookson all about it. That'll be one less person on our side to worry about."

Needless to say Lydia's mother rang just after Lydia left. I put on my voice to say of course I wouldn't detain Lydia at the cottage on her own so late. I pleased myself by getting in a hint that anyway I preferred slightly older women. Only I said mature, not old. For once we parted friends.

Then, tired as hell, I turned in. It was going to be a hard day in the morning.

XIX

Fire Day dawned clear and blue. I sang as I shaved, keyed up and wheezing from my scrap, but confident.

The castle is not quite a ruin. It's a square, now covered in by a flat roof of ugly tarred concrete and lovely red pantiles capping the four corner towers. To save electricity they've put a central glass roof over the main bit. The stone is flint, like so much East Anglian building of medieval and Early English, with a crude mortar welding the stones. You can't help admiring the surface, which has a curious texture, made up of the blacks and grays of severed flintstones and the fawns of the interstices. The Normans who were the builders of the keep—all that's really left of the original castle—were fairly useless architects. Most of what they did was cadged or done by proxy. So the castle keep has a decorative air about it. Bishop Odo (a nasty piece of work who got his just deserts at the hands of Rufus) built it on the ruins of the Roman temple to Jupiter and made his builders pinch Roman tiles and bricks for corners and reinforce the walls in clumsy lines. These flashes and columns of deep mandarin red give a warmth and character to what would otherwise be a formidable and excessively grisly keep. It's a museum nowadays, with a main door reached by a fixed wooden bridge from a paved terrace mound constructed as a pleasant walk between rose gardens and flower beds. The Mithras temple is covered in under a grass bowling green nearby. The rest of the ruins—Roman, Norman, practically everybody else you can think of—outcrops like a sea-washed cliff among the grass. Part is converted to decorative flower beds, but the rest is left alone. Children and pigeons occasionally play there among the stone mounds, which pleases me. I'm absolutely certain that the Emperor Claudius and Rufus would approve.

Every year our town has a huge fireworks festival. Nowadays we call it a "gala" day, or seek some local or national jubilee to justify it. Last year it was the Anniversary Fireworks Festival, but after weeks of arguing none of us was quite sure which anniversary we were commemorating. Not that it matters. The fire festival goes on. This year it was called River Remembrance Day, as if we were all in danger of forgetting the river which runs in clear view from the castle mounds. The point is that, like the rest of Merrie Olde England's festivals, it's entirely pagan and likely to remain so no matter what we pretend.

The Castle Park stretches down to the river and beyond—and I do mean down, down steeply from the terraced walks along the moat mounds on the north side to a small plain, about ten or so acres. Lovely and flat there, in the river's elbow, and a copse of trees here and there. On a fine evening you can sit on stones carved by Roman masons and watch the regimental bands parade glittering on the green plain below, looking close enough to touch. The Fire Night, as our locals call it, starts with a parade of torches and Morris dancers into the plain at dusk. There we build a great pile of wood and rubbish. The dancers and marchers as they arrive in turn sling their torches onto the heap, creating a massive bonfire which I've known burn for three days sometimes. Anybody can make a torch and simply join the procession, which makes a lovely sight winding from across the river or down the slopes to whirl in a slow circle round the bonfire. Once the fire's lit fireworks begin. By then we're all gathered on the castle keep's huge soaring mound, sitting on the grass and watching the exploding colors and gushing fire fountains marvelously reflected in the river's blackness. It's a major spectacle, as you can imagine. I hate to wonder how it all began, back in the dark autumnal days before civilizations began to iron us all out and send primitive urges to hide deeper down in our fabric.

It's more pretty than sinister now, of course. A little illuminated fairground brings roundabouts and catch-a-penny stalls near the bowling greens, which adds to the general gaiety and allows parents to come with the legitimate excuse that they're only taking the children to the festivities. Needless to say Fire Night is always crowded. The town turns out en masse. Villages empty into Castle Park from as far as the Norfolk borders and the bigger fishing ports. Today they could have it all, from start to finish. I was only interested in one spectator. And he and I would have our own personal fireworks.

I have this system each morning. Up, radio to see who we're at war with, switch it off for sanity, bath, get mad because socks have gone missing again, breakfast from horrible powders and gruesome packets, and cut up some cheese for the robin. He's a tough nut, waiting by my unfinished wall scattering competitors. I feed him on my arm because I'm interested in how he manages to make so much noise. It's a really lovely sound, a thick mellow flutey singing made without any effort. I mean, he never seems to breathe in or anything like that. Sounds just keep coming.

"The benign Dr. Thomas Haverro," I explained to his beady eye. "He'll try to do for me tonight."

He gave me a tilted stare and bounced up and down my arm to keep a couple of intrusive sparrows off. You never expect their feet to be so cold.

"The question is how. I'm younger than Haverro is, Rob. And fitter. And tougher." He patrolled my arm, singing. "He can't bring a howitzer and blow me to blazes, or good old Maslow will come sniffing. So what will he do? There'll be people everywhere. Picnics on the grass. And I've got to get into the castle before he comes. Easy enough." I'd done that before to weigh and do specific gravity tests on various Bronze Age artifacts in the Prehistory Gallery. Our curator had said no, but true love will find a way. "It's got to be an accident, Rob," I explained. "He could push me off a gallery. There's a Roman mosaic in the central area. I wouldn't bounce much. Maybe an old club or a sword from a display case." But that would be useless. I'd hear him take it out, and then I'd be warned and could arm myself. He was stout, obviously slow. I could make rings round him. "None of the bows is in working order. No strings in the crossbows. The flintlocks are all in the barred case and can't be lifted out even if you break the glass." It seemed just him and me. I said this to the robin, but he seemed unconvinced.

"Anyway, the Grail Tree will be worth it, whatever he has planned." The point was, I told myself eagerly, he couldn't leave fingerprints or other sorts of evidence that he'd attacked me with some weapon from the display case because Maslow would trace him. Then Haverro would have lost just the same. Guns were out, because you can trace any modern gun by ballistics easy as that. And powder burns on bodies. And minute flecks of powder on clothes and skin. Every kid who watches television knows these elementary facts.

"Rob." I interrupted its effortless windless song. "What weapons do we know which are neither prehistoric, Roman, Early English, medieval, Conquest, Renaissance, post-Elizabethan or modern?" To help him I added, "It can't be a bow and arrow, crossbow, modern pistol, rifle, club, mace, lance, flintlock, et cetera. But it must finish me and let Dr. Haverro get away unscathed and unrecognized. Well? Any offers?"

He flew onto the grass to do battle with encroaching thrushes. An omen, I thought, pleased. Doing battle with only what he has. Like me and Thomas. A contest with just ourselves. Still, I was certain I knew every inch of the museum. And Haverro didn't. That was my main asset. But I knew he was going to try to finish me. And I already knew he was capable of trying very, very hard.

Brenda was helping to shuffle the crowds into indescribable disorder when I arrived at the park about two o'clock. Children

ran about hoping to get themselves lost and dramatically re-
found. Ice cream sellers sounded their bells. The town's main
streets were one gigantic concourse of people drifting toward the
colors and sounds of bands from the show grounds. Teams of
Morris dancers tinkled to and fro or sprawled on the grass for
a quick ale before the great procession.

"Still as big a shambles as ever," I said.

"I don't want any criticism from you, Lovejoy." She laughed,
not a little distraught.

I paused. She looked attractive even in that grottie traffic warden's outfit. Why don't they pension these uniform designers
off? It would do us all a favor. "Is there anything you do want
though?"

"Look. Don't bother me right now." She waved out a small
decorated lorry which was trying to enter the main gates. A
jubilant group of dancers cheered and whistled, booing as their
vehicle rumbled off down a side street toward North Hill.
Brenda looked over her shoulder as I moved on. "See you at the
plinth, soon after dark, Lovejoy," she said, smiling. "Maybe."

"I'll be there, beautiful," I said. "Maybe." And got away
onto the moat walk as she was stung to a half-laughing retort
I didn't quite catch. The plinth is on the opposite side of the
castle to the entrance, a small monument where two dubious
heroes were executed by Cromwell's men. It's something of a
lovers' trysting place, lying as it does deep in the moated hollow. Her bloke would be around somewhere. I wondered
who he was.

The castle has this system of closing in the afternoon on week-
days. I checked on the wooden notice. There it was, three o'clock
close. My heart was banging. I had an hour. I drifted casually into
the castle among a horde of children and their parents. The
eagle-eyed museum guardian sits in a small booth placed back
from the entrance. He was safely nodding off as usual, which
meant my unlikely prepared story about having to go back in at
closing time for a lost niece need never be tested.

The main central area was crowded. A Queen Anne coach
stands to one side of a massive fireplace you could drive into, and

a waxwork tableau had been arranged on the other side. It depicted the visit of Queen Bess to the town and showed how merrily she'd been received at the castle on the selfsame spot. You have to smile. Not one of the notices mentioned the complaints Bess had made about how the castle's primitive latrines stank to high heaven.

One of the children had ducked under the restraining rope and was trying to set the Galileo pendulum swinging. He got a cuff for his pains from the old uniformed attendant who creaked after him and returned him squawking to his indignant parents.

"You've no right—" they started up angrily.

"Yes he has," I intervened, pushing among the throng. "I'm Inspector Maslow, CID. Kindly keep your brat from damaging the exhibits." I turned grandly to pat the old sweat on the shoulder. "Well done, my man," I said. "Keep it up." He looked bemused, because he knew I was Lovejoy Antiques, Inc. Wise in the sudden moods of the public, he said nothing but gave me a creaky salute. "Carry on, Smith," I said, hoping on statistical grounds the name wasn't far out. He'd remember I was in. With luck, he'd even be able to swear blind I left with all the others when closing time came.

I strolled on upstairs to the Roman Galleries and thought I'd have a look along the Georgian displays. Maybe they'd done something about them since my irate letter of complaint last month. The plan was to follow the main mob at closing time, ambling in stops and starts toward the main door where the attendants gather to check you out. They use a technique so as not to lose anyone. Rather like sheepdogs on the high fells, they move in crescents to and fro round the back of the crowd, sweeping us all toward the funnel which leads to the exit. If anyone shows a tendency to wait at an exhibit one attendant just stays politely by his side until he moves back into the crowd. That way you can't lose anyone and the entire crowd gets winkled from the honeycomb galleries and poured outside. It's a well-tried, almost foolproof system.

But.

There's one serious flaw in it. Think of the sheepdog. The one lamb he loses and has to go back for after lights-out is invariably the one which is too scared to move. For some reason it stays put. Maybe it has a foot trapped or something. Anyhow, it's immobile when it should be on the hoof. So the herd technique only works with those of the herd *who are moving.* Stay still and you're free. Next time you're in an art gallery or museum pay attention when the attendants call, "Time, ladies and gentlemen. Please proceed toward the exit!" *All* visitors will at least turn a head, take a step, glance at a watch, look about for a coat or reach for a child's hand prior to making their way. Get it? Movement. It's what the attendants look for. After all, the rest of the things in a museum are pretty well static, aren't they?

The Temple of Jupiter lies under the main area. An entrance, made into a descending spiral staircase of lovely Georgian wrought iron, is situated to one side of the main area's bookstall. I'd chosen this because it's well lit and because most of the foundation arches of the underground temple are visible from the main level. Some five or six dungeons are down there, constructed for William Penn and similar subversives in early Quaker days. I've seen the attendants do their check a hundred times. They switch on all the lights, clatter down the iron staircase, glance along the arches and open the one—first—dungeon door which is unlocked. They lean in, holding the grille-and-stud door, and peer about for strays, then come out and step upward onto the main level. The one who does this stays there until the main door closes. Inference: nobody can get down again unnoticed once the ancient temple has been declared empty. But a cunning Lovejoy can hide behind an arch, casually stock still so as not to create any moving shadows which could hint at an interloper getting himself left behind for possibly nefarious purposes.

I wandered around the main tier of galleries where the Roman and pre-Roman exhibits were on show. Glass cases lined the ancient walls, and in alcoves statues of Roman funeral statuary alternated with cased models of scenes—the wharves, galleys, household interiors, industries, clothes and military displays—constructed by local historical societies. I popped in to see my display of model Roman furniture for old time's sake. That was from the time when I actually made things to give away, which only goes to show how much sense I had. No change to the crummy Civil War section, I noticed in annoyance. The same two heaps of saltpeter and sulfur, the same single unmounted cannon and the dusty armor hanging askew. A breastplate had been added now, lodged unerringly on an old clock movement fixed to the wall. A bloody disgrace. I told an apologetic attendant so, but they haven't a clue and you might as well talk to the wall.

By the time three o'clock was approaching I'd made an estimate of the number of attendants the curator had put on duty this festival day. Eight. I hadn't forgotten to include the old lady at the bookstall, who was doing a roaring trade in reproductions and postcards. There was always a nighttime caretaker, but he was lodged in a little office in the large house at the edge of the park gardens, which the castle had taken over as an art gallery and additional museum for household items of post-Georgian times. After an hour or so's concealment I reckoned I'd be safe.

The Civil War gallery is on the second tier. As the castle keep is basically rectangular in shape each gallery is identical in area and has more or less the same margins and alcoves as all the rest. Four galleries to each of the two tiers, one gallery to a side. I only wished you couldn't see all the way across the central space. Still, I consoled myself, even Tarzan couldn't leap across a gap that size. I peered over into the central area below. The drop from the square glass ceiling to the floor I guessed about a hundred feet. Without pacing it out the galleries seemed maybe half as long again. A staircase split into symmetrical runs up to the first tier, too showy but essential for so many people. My mouth was already drying when I noticed the castle attendants beginning to signal across the space that time was getting on. My big moment.

Apart from the background blare of the distant bands and the murmur of the crowds the chatter in the museum was deafening. That's the best of museums where antiques are placed in their original settings—the atmosphere, the antiques themselves, the customers, everything becomes so much more relaxed. In those brand-new mausolea the antiques know they're entombed for all

184

eternity in unloved glass coffins made without a thought as to what a precious object, lived with for centuries and loved as it deserves, actually needs. It beats me why councils believe that a plate-glass cube glaringly badly lit is exactly right for displaying a Viking shield, a jeweled casket of Saxon design, Victorian spectacles, Georgian enameled or gold toilet sets, and an array of Queen Anne ladies' shoes. They ought to remember that a glass box may look very swish and efficient and modern, but it's the only permanent home a precious antique will ever have once it gets stuck in there for us to gawp at.

The crowd was thinning noticeably as I reached the bookstall and bought a couple of postcards.

"Have you a postcard of Bishop Odo?" I asked Mrs. Tyler across the counter. I'd seen the rack empty.

"All gone, Lovejoy," she apologized, tut-tutting. "You're the third that's asked." That was no good to me. I needed remembering, not to say remembrance, I thought uneasily.

"Er, then I'll have a reproduction galley, love."

"I'm so sorry. They've all gone too. We expected some more—"

"Er, then a copy of *History of the Local Bay Industry,* please." I drove my demand home with a breezy grin.

"I'm out of those, too, dear," she said helplessly.

"Pull your socks up, cock," I remonstrated. "Nil out of three."

"Well—"

I pulled her leg some more till she was smiling and scolding, then said I'd see her in the car park if her husband wasn't around and melted swiftly back into the drifting tide of humanity certain she would remember my departure. I strolled around the postcard racks until I was near the spiral stairwell. A casual look about told me no attendant was in sight. I crouched down, quite offhand but seeming interested despite myself, to feel the surface of the Mithraic figuré in the mosaic by the opening. One more casual glance and without rising I slipped my leg onto the lowest iron stair tread I could reach, drew in the other leg and slowly strolled down the narrow iron staircase with as little speed as my nerves would allow.

The lights in the underground temple were still on, naked bulbs placed every few feet to hang from the arches just above head height. The first dungeon's door was ajar. Nobody around. I trod the sloping sandy floor along the row of sealed dungeon doors, almost giving myself a heart attack when I peered in through the grille of one and came face to face with a terrified wax image of a dummy prisoner stuck at the bars, evidently rotting away in punishment for very little. My cry of alarm echoed along the subterranean vaults. Mercifully there was nobody there. I let my heart slow down as long as I could, but had to start searching about for a place long before it had stopped thumping.

I'd cut it fine. They were calling closing just as I settled behind the arch's pillar second from the end. The very farthest would have been a mistake. A light came back behind the pillar there, reflected somewhat from the whitewashed wall through a vertical fenestration in the recess. Probably one of the deities had been honored by a place there for its effigy. I was near the Mithraic altar at this end. One of our societies said the whole place had been used as a grain store throughout early medieval and Norman days on account of its dryness. It was cold, but I drew myself flat against the upright and checked the ground and walls for revealing shadows cast back to show my silhouette. None.

The calls on the main floor above were becoming more frequent. Families added to the racket. Children were being assembled and last-minute purchases made. Keys rattled as the single wooden bars were locked in place along the sections of each gallery. The attendants' calls and pleadings approached the head of the spiral stairs. If one came down and walked conscientiously along the length of the temple I was done for. I'd a notebook and a black drawing stick with me just in case. My pose would be of an absent-minded artist drawing the altar if I got found out. Earlier, though from memory, I had drawn a rough sketch, partly completed, to lend more conviction.

"Thank you," a voice called, too near. "The museum is closing now." A boot sounded on the iron stair. Steps and the same call.

"Three o'clock closing, please." A pause. Scuffling steps on the floor. A door, chains going. My heart lurched again. Please God there wasn't an iron manhole cover or anything to go over the stairwell, was there? I'd be entombed in this bloody place. I almost cried out in fear but held myself back. Surely if there was I'd have noticed it on my way in. I told myself this a few times for encouragement and was bathed in a sweat of relief when finally the steps sounded receding up the staircase with no further sinister rattlings. I was clear. Still scared, I stayed rigidly behind the pillar until the main castle door slammed with a dull booming echo overhead. Clear. And safe. A few boot-shod feet clashed on the paving above, but my confidence returned. Naturally the attendants would make one last check for stray infants. They'd set alarms at the windows, switch on the central alarm. Then the round of the glass cases. Then the lights off in the crypts, the temple, the dungeons, the alcoves. Then the signatures to say they'd done the security check. Then the bookstall to be locked after signing the ledger. Then the phone call to the caretaker at the distant house.

Then, blissful silence as they departed and locked the main door with an utterly final boom. The echoes hummed and throbbed gently, and silence. I almost yelled with delight. I'd done it. The entire castle was mine, the entire keep crammed with precious antiques for which you could only feel reverence. The silence waited all about me, obedient and attentive.

XX

The trouble is there's silence and silence.

For the first couple of hours it was great. True to my original plan I waited behind the pillar in the semigloom until the stiffness in my legs threatened to fix me irrevocably to the spot. My back, bum, knees, even my shoulders were cold. It was about half an hour. Down in the temple the temperature was much below normal, a factor I had reckoned with. I'd thoughtfully put on a pullover and some socks Margaret once knitted for me, so I was frozen but moveable.

In case I'd misheard the attendants' calls on the main level, when I eventually began to move I did so stealthily, working first one leg up and down, then the other. Arms, knee bends, rotations at the hips and touching my toes. I was scared at the coming attempt on my life, but not so stupid I would confront even a geriatric killer when I was stiff in every limb.

Sunshine was streaming obliquely from the windows, quite resembling the interior of a still, kindly cathedral, when I climbed at last from the vaults onto the main central floor. Curious what a sense of power being alone in a building gives you.

When that building is a genuine castle's main keep and you are the only person on earth inside, the boost your ego gets is breathtaking. Nobody can come in unless you say so. We tend to forget these elementary but obvious points when reading history. No wonder the knights and their women wanted possession of these places. Once you're in there's no doubt who's boss.

The bands outside were still at it. I could hear the roundabouts and the organs piping away. Crowds were arriving yet, pouring past in the late afternoon sunshine. Twice teams of Morris men danced jingling by, fiddle and drums going. A Northumbrian bagpipe played its sad melancholy refrains near the drawbridge for a few minutes, maybe a stray Morris man halting for a glass of ale before the main events. I listened pressed wistfully against the main door, thinking how valuable such lovely instruments are. They've shot up in price, especially any dating before 1900, though they don't really count as antiques. Another team came by and he joined them. I danced whatever steps I could remember, skipping and trying to do the foot-waggle along with them, but it's never quite good enough without the bells on your legs and trailing hankies. The Queen Anne coach stopped me dead. The sounds, fife and drums, the delighted screams of the passing children as the team's Fool chased them with his painted bladder, the faint crash-crash of the bells and the cracks of sticks all receded.

Then I noticed the hubbub was beginning to lessen. It was still considerable. The music, the fairground. It was all there, including the giant deep murmur of the crowd nearby, but not as nearby as all that. The silence inside had changed in character somewhat. Whereas before it was large and friendly, a personal sort of silence very much *belonging* to me, so to speak, now it seemed . . . well, not unfriendly. Definitely not unfriendly, but with wider dimensions it never had before. While I was waiting underneath in the temple's vaults it was protective, an extension of me somehow. I knew its edges, where they began and ended. I could control the silence, clap my hands, and it would disappear obediently. A moment ago I coughed gently to clear my throat after dancing. The silence never went at all. It stayed there, retired a step back and then shuffled back around me. Still protective. Of course it was still that, but not so much my own personal silence as it had been before, if you know what I mean. My control of it had gone, been lifted and folded away. Nothing sinister, but a bit disturbing because it went without asking.

After the crowd's all in they close the Castle Park gates so that folk can't wander out into the main street when it's dark and traffic becomes careless. In a way it's a good idea because wandering children can't suffer road accidents this way. I began to wish they weren't so careful. The castle where I waited is situated close to the park gates. Maybe, I hoped, they'd left somebody on duty there.

I climbed the stairs to the first, then the second tier of galleries. A recess near the riverside corner, once used as a prison for religious offenders, leads to a few steps and a door set in the wall. It was easy to go around switching off all the peripheral alarms because there was a map of them by the bookstall in the porter's glass booth. The central one was just as easy. And by the recess door the key was hanging on a nail. Tut-tutting and shaking my head at their useless security I unlocked the door and stepped out onto the roof.

For some reason this action brought considerable relief. It wasn't that I was really very scared or anything, being alone in the castle, because that would have been stupid. A grown man isn't that daft or that easily swayed. I'd checked every corner of the place as soon as I'd got going, and unlike the attendants I'd done it properly, inch by inch, until I became certain nobody else was inside but me. I'd even inspected the waxwork figures, palpating their arms and wagging a hand in front of their eyes. They were wax all right. I'd swung around a million times to surprise anybody tiptoeing along behind. Nobody. But the roof was pleasant. Slanting sunshine, birds, crowds below the ramparts and a perfect view to the north where the hills sloped up from the river and houses could be seen quite clearly—full of lovely normal people. The river plain below was ornamented by imitation decorated castle walls and scaffolding. Tiny figures moved along the pantomime ornaments, probably workmen responsible for the fireworks. They had a tableau for the big finish, as always. I could see the royal coat of arms in outline on the poles and an immense crown and flags.

To one side the fairground glinted. From this enormous height it seemed near enough to reach over and pick up the roundabouts by their pennants. A Morris dragon danced in and out of the tiny colored tents followed by a crowd of dancers, but they were too far away for me to hear the music. Maybe fifty thousand people on the castle mount's slope were facing the field. It was a lovely, cheering sight. Every one of them faced away, looking intently down into the plain. Every back was turned away from me. Well, they didn't want to stare at an empty castle, did they? And it would all happen down below. Marching regiments, bands, dances and then the bonfire. Fireworks. By contrast nothing was going on inside an old museum, so where's the point looking? I walked around the roof, carefully avoiding the central square, glassed over. The park gates were closed, as I'd suspected. Clinging tight to the rampart railing I peered over as far as I dared, but nobody was on duty. Brenda had gone, the selfish woman. She could have stayed. Only she didn't know where I was. She'd assumed I was among the rest waiting for the spectacle to begin. Anyway, if any bobby was on duty at the gate he'd gone for a quiet smoke to one side among the trees. This sort of thing makes me bloody angry. I mean to say, no devotion to duty these days.

I went back inside. Stood there, thought a second, then locked the parapet door and replaced the key. How long had I been outside? I never carry a watch because they always stop, so I unlocked the door again and went out to look for the town hall clock. Five-thirty. How long till dark? I'd distinctly told him dusk, and I'd said *in* the castle keep. There could be no mistake.

Back inside. What time is dusk, actually? Absolute pitch black is too late for what people can call dusk, and late afternoon like now is too early. But there's no proper accepted definition of dusk, is there? The more I worried about it the more it seemed to me that people call any old time of day dusk. Loose thinking. Anyhow, I'd told Lisa to see me at dusk as well. She'd be my witness. And I'd said on the drawbridge by the main door. Lisa's the sort who's never late. She'd be on time.

The interior really did seem dark now. It had somehow gathered up a dusk of its own while I'd consoled myself on the roof with the sight of so many thousands of people nearby. My steps echoed slightly, yet with a muffled echo I found distinctly unpleasing. The silence was developing an unnerving solidity I hadn't bargained for. It was just not mine any more. From being in possession I was now a mere visitor. If not an actual intruder. The feeling was hard to shake off.

Keep busy. That's the thing, people always say when you have an attack of nerves. I moved briskly about, putting up with the disturbing muffle my footsteps had developed. Inspection time again. It took me the best part of forty minutes to examine the entire museum again, inch by inch. I switched on the alarm circuits and descended to the temple, braving that ghastly wax prisoner's face at his dungeon door again, but determined not to be overawed, and even more obsessed with the idea of not getting spooked by the place. The temple vaults were still empty. Nobody doing a Lovejoy behind the arch's pillars. Nobody in the Queen Anne coach. Nobody except wax dummies in the clothes of Bess and her entourage. Nobody in the Egyptian mummy's case there shouldn't have been, and nobody in any of the huge earthenware granary pots lodged in the alcoves along the walls. Nobody behind the Roman funereal statues, and, humming noisily, I poked the figures themselves to make doubly sure.

To make trebly sure I went downstairs and crossed the main central area to look again into the huge fireplace. Nobody. I peered upward. The flue ascended, narrowing to about a third of its starting width to open in the wall near the roof. The light was faint but convincing. When I turned in again the sudden contrast between the pale sky's reflected sunset inside the chimney flue and the darkening interior of the museum made me momentarily myopic. I walked back across the central mosaic straight into the Galileo pendulum, almost knocking myself silly. I picked myself up, staggering slightly. My nose was bleeding.

No hankie, naturally. I dabbed my nose on my jacket sleeve, cursing inwardly at my stupidity. You'd think I'd have known about the pendulum. It's only been there a couple of centuries. I held the lead weight until it stopped swinging. The less movement the better when some bloke was coming to make an attempt on my life. At last I moved off, wondering what to do next.

Attempt on my life. The words have a final ring to them. Attempt's not so bad, but life is a finite and terribly temporary thing. I sat on the stairs leading to the first gallery and thought what I would do if I were Thomas. Of course he had some advantages over me. A doctor. Educated. Therefore poison was a natural weapon, I supposed, and you could stretch a point by assuming that you could make a sinister kind of arrow from syringes. And a surgeon's instruments start off pretty sharp and lethal. But somehow all of these seemed unlikely. When the chips were down and he stole the Grail Tree from old Henry it had been with a crude and utterly devastating vulgarity. A saw for the hawser. Petrol for the barge. Physical assault for poor Henry. That was it. The message seemed to be that Thomas, faced with the necessity of killing a fellow human being, spurned anything which hinted of his profession. I didn't like that word necessity, so tried desirability instead, which was as bad. Wanting. He *wanted* to kill me. That was more like it.

So it would be direct. Sudden. I glanced around the museum. That bloody pendulum was swinging, almost imperceptibly it was true, but definitely swinging. Maybe half an inch, side to side. I made myself smile. Try to stop it. A chunk of lead on a string hung from the ceiling's center will carry on swinging however small its amplitude. Every small breath sets it going. School kids are forever chucking toffee papers at it to move it. Anyway, I had better things to do than stand holding a plumb line. Count the weapons, for example.

I set about searching on the first tier. Maybe I was stupid not bringing at least a bread knife. A Great War French bayonet would have made me a lot more cheerful, and I had one of those back in the cottage. Like a fool I'd been too confident. Anyhow, I knew what I was up against. No matter how uneasy

I was becoming, Thomas was still only one man, and a lot older than me. And I'd already worked out how little he could do, how restricted his choice of weapons was. So there was no reason to start worrying unduly ahead of the doctor's arrival. It would be straightforward. No matter what mood I talked myself into, I'd have to keep my head and remember that. Thomas Haverro was only one bloke, unarmed. I was the same. We stood at least even, and I had the edge because he couldn't come in until he knocked and I let him in. There was only the one door. I'd checked its one key on the inside a million times. I switched the main electric off so we'd have to fight without lights. Better for Haverro to come into darkness from the lighter outside than to arrive in an electric glare. I wasn't scared of him, but I was going to make sure any advantages going spare came to me.

The sun was slanted lower now, and fading. Across the central area the shadow of the Galileo pendulum had moved from the far corner, crept imperceptibly along the wall and now was fading with the shadows by the staircase. Soon it would be gone. Anyhow, even without an electric torch there would be light from the big bonfire to illumine the night air. And fireworks. And the park gates were surmounted by large spherical lamps, so there would be a background glow. And however keen Haverro was on the museum and its lovely antiques, I was damned sure he couldn't know it anything like as well as I. After all, ever since I'd come to live in the area I had been in twice or three times a week. I've helped with the ancient coins, Celtic finds, tableaux, and paid several visits to help the curator's special exhibitions of weapons because he's not so strong in that specialty. And a doctor doesn't have all that much recreation. Every way you looked at it, I was a head start.

The Roman weapons were virtually crumbling. Best preserved were arrowheads and the blades from spears. Other than those there wasn't much, apart from a pair of hefty models of Roman siege implements, and I couldn't even lift the stones placed to show the size of the missiles used in the real thing.

Good news, therefore. If I couldn't lift the bloody things, neither could Thomas.

Along on the other gallery were household items, pottery, querns used to grind wheat, even surgical instruments. Again it seemed to me you were either tough enough to lift them and chuck them at an adversary or you fought barehanded. And the probes, scissors and lancets of the long-dead Roman doctor were too small and neat to be much use. For quite a while I tried working out whether any of them could be stuck into a stick for use as an arrow, or put into a blowpipe, but gave it up. There wasn't a usable bow in the museum, and the crossbows were too fragile on the cross to use without putting your own eye out, though their stocks were fine. Most were stone, incidentally, and still available as fairly cheap collectors' items, in full working order. The spear held by the Roman waxwork in the gallery's corner was, I knew, balsawood and easily snapped by a finger.

The Egyptian lot were useless. Two spears from the Ancient British were solid enough—firm and nasty sharp flints knapped in Suffolk by ancient hands in the prehistoric Grimes Graves. These two were set in roughly hewn modern ash staves and looked pretty menacing, though they were drilled in the shaft and held in the case by a slender chain. I cheered up again. I'd hear the glass break, and while Thomas struggled to break the chain and get the spears out . . . The clubs were under lock and key, and the glass looked tougher than was used to make the rest of the cases. Good news again.

On the ground floor a few waxworks, the coach, sundry small cased models. Nothing. The Civil War gallery was worth another visit, maybe. As I trudged upstairs to the second tier I began wishing I'd had the wit to come properly equipped. Sandals or strong nonslip slippers to pad about unheard. That's what I needed. And, I realized, pausing at the top of the second flight, an electric torch. If the doctor brought one I'd be less well off by a hell of a long chalk. For some reason I was becoming uneasy, more so as the minutes ticked on. I set off along the gallery, glancing down toward the main door, in case. But in case what?

The swine would have to knock and do as I said before I'd let him in. I could even search him at the door.

For a brief second I stopped to stare. I could no longer see the door. It was hidden in shadow. I peered across and failed to make out the shadow of the plumb line. That too was merged with the shadows on the far wall. And the shadows were shadows no longer. The whole museum was now not a pattern of sunshine and shadows, but was submerged in gloom. One faint gleam lit the glass ceiling, but even as I looked at it the shine died and the interior chilled further. The day had emptied from the castle. I knew the sun would be rolling beyond Friday Woods like a penny off the edge, tumbling as I'd seen it go so many times from my unfinished wall in the garden while feeding the robin and pouring pobs into the hedgehog's saucer.

Come *on,* Lovejoy, I told myself. Dogs shake themselves, so I shook as best I could like I'd seen terriers do coming out of the Blackwater onto the sands. It did me good, for a second. At least it got me moving again.

If you examine a museum there isn't a great deal of weaponry usable any more. Suits of armor: valuable in money but useless because a bullet or arrow can pierce almost any antique armor that can be worn. Shields: ditto. Swords: well, a couple of Civil War swords were in good nick—one an Ironside's Cromwellian basket sword, the other, with fine impartiality, a Cavalier's cross-hilted heavy sword taken at Marston Moor. Both were open for inspection but chained, mercifully. There were three or four flintlock pistols but none had a flint in, so even if they were in working order they'd be useless and couldn't be fired. The cannon looked in good order, but of this date, 1645, they were still merely thick iron tubes without shells and working firing parts, so I could rule it out. The local historians had obtained some cannon balls, probably wooden casts. Cromwell had to resort to round stones as often as not to keep going. I felt safer still.

Along the now dark furniture section in Gallery Six was my notorious piece. No weapons there. That left me back at the recess which led to the roof door, and now I was in accelerating gloom. In fact you had to really start thinking of it as dusk, if not actual darkness.

A bang startled me, and a series of pops sounded overhead. The fireworks had begun. Successive whirrs and fizzes created light for me now. Cheers came in wafts, probably the breeze from the estuary carrying the sounds toward the town. A faint glow was established constantly as a kind of background. The processions were starting. There was my light, so I was back with all my advantages again. My heart was bumping and I could feel an ugly dampness trying hard to cool my forehead. Still, up here I could dimly see most of the central area as far as the fireplace and at least across to the opposite gallery, admittedly in outline. Well, better than nothing. And if I couldn't see the details of the main door I could make out the faint black limits of the entrance porchway leading into the museum's center.

Red glows succeeded blues. Whites and greens and yellows came and faded. It was wiser to stay inside, I decided, because Thomas might try to struggle if I met him on the roof. And it was a long way down to the dry stony spaces which once were the castle's moats.

One thing was worrying me sick. *Why* was I cringing in a recess in a second-tier gallery, when the only way in Thomas possibly had was that single bloody main doorway down below on the ground floor? Why was I so scared? In fact, I was prickling all over. I could scent my own fear, wrinkling my skin and lifting hairs from my ankles up my legs to my scalp. I found I'd crouched down, stupidly believing that would help. Come on, Lovejoy, I lectured myself firmly. You are alone here. Be quiet, okay, but behave resolutely and with deliberation. I forced myself erect and, with the next swish of colored glow from the ceiling, nonchalantly read the emergency notices hanging on a threaded card on the back of the roof door.

And there, in a wash of violet light crackling above me, I read the name Thomas Haverro, M.D. It puzzled me at first, like a simple arithmetic sum written down obviously wrong which you can't immediately decipher. With lunatic patience I waited for the next skyburst. It was a cluster of vivid screaming gold snakes exploded from a rocket salvo. The name was still there, on curling paper, among many others on a list. "Contact in the event of an emergency," it said in typed capitals. Still I stood there. Dr. Thomas Haverro. It was his name and address all right. So what? So he was the doctor on call for the museum, for anybody taken suddenly ill. And a doctor needs access.

Like a key?

Suddenly I was prickling and sweating clammily down in the balcony recess. *The bastard could get in.* Last night I'd been too confident. Sure of myself, I'd agreed with his suggestion of the castle. I had talked myself into believing it was my idea, whereas he had gently and cleverly nudged me into agreement. The bastard *meant* us to finish up here alone. He'd known I would come innocently to the slaughter. And as soon as dusk fell he would let himself in with his passkey. Of *course* there were other keys. Now that it was too late I realized the obvious—no attendant leaving a museum *could* lock the door from the inside *and* leave himself outside to go home, could he? And I'd not realized the significance of that single key behind the main door. If it had been the only key, then how the hell could the bloody attendants get back in tomorrow morning? Stupid, stupid sod. I moaned to myself and crouched lower, face tight with sudden fear.

Haverro could let himself in. *Had?* Already? I tried swallowing. Whatever state I'd landed myself in, I had to use my loaf. If he was here he'd come armed in some way. His cleverness in persuading me into this mess told me he wouldn't know if I would be armed or not, so he'd have to go carefully at first. That is until he realized. Then he'd walk up to me and . . . I tried swallowing again, failed again. Too dry.

And from now on I'd act as if he were here. Inside. With me. My legs were quivering uncomfortably in the confined space of the recess. At least the swine couldn't come through the roof door, could he? Not without a hang glider or a lunar capsule. So he was inside, having come through the main entrance. I smeared my hair down over my forehead and peered over the ledge toward where the door was on the ground floor. The next bang lit the skies red and gold. No red glare from outside through the arched gloom down below. Therefore he had locked the door behind himself. And, careful as ever, he would have taken the resident key for good measure. He wasn't the sort to forget details like that. It was only the accidental presence of Jimmo, silently fishing in the dark of a riverbank, which had caught him out before.

Ducking back, movement caught my eye. I froze, frightened to ice and unable to breathe. The next glare was green, coming downward in hideous washes which made gargoyles of every object in the long galleries. It was the pendulum, swinging gently. Well, I'd started that. My nose still throbbed. But hadn't I guessed its movement after stilling it to be minute, maybe less than an inch? Now it swung several gentle inches from the vertical, slowly to and fro. Somebody had moved it. A solid figure had brushed against the lead weight, gently nudging it into action.

I could get out onto the roof through the doorway behind me, maybe shout for help. But the distant bands, the Morris music, the crowds' oohs and aahs at the fireworks and the fairground were creating a constant row. Who would hear me? Brenda *might* be immediately below, waiting for a quick snog by the martyrs' plinth. Immediately below. But Haverro would see the pale rectangle of the opened door. He'd been sickeningly confident so far. He wouldn't chuck it all away now.

My one hope was to get out or get help. My heart jumped suddenly. Lisa! She'd be waiting outside the main door this very second! Lisa! I stood up, practically lifted by elation, into the bathing light of a rocket salvo exploding white and gold directly above the glass roof.

"Lovejoy!"

A gunshot cracked below. Stone clattered on my face and I fell, stunned by the sudden action. I hadn't seen him, but it was Haverro's voice.

"Stay where you are, Thomas!" I yelled in despair. "I have a gun too, you bastard."

"Liar!" The pig was deriding me. I gave a quick peer over the margin, but hadn't the nerve to stay looking until the next firework lit us up for each other.

"Try coming up, then," I shouted.

"You're not that stupid, Lovejoy," he called up. "A gun can be traced."

"So can yours, you frigging killer."

"Mine?" He actually laughed. "Have a look at the bullet."

I fumbled and found the crushed lead sphere. The bastard was using a percussion muzzle loader. You fire, not an elongated bullet, but a round lead one. No marks are ever left save those of the impact. Therefore they are utterly untraceable. Black gunpowder down the muzzle and a lead sphere. A box of percussion caps for a few pence, and you can murder with a hell of a lot of noise but nothing traceable back to you, no matter how clever the CID's ballistics lads become. I found myself on my feet screaming fear and hatred down into the main rectangle.

"Bastard! Murderer! And you call yourself a doctor, you—"

A pop overhead. In the scarlet glare I saw him lean out from behind the rear wheel of the coach, long arm raised and glinting. I flung myself backward as he fired and felt the wind slice my arm along its length from wrist to shoulder before the wall snickered a shower of dusty spicules onto my upturned face.

Almost gibbering with pain from my arm and terror I scrabbled back into the alcove. He was across the way. On the ground, two galleries below. I tore off my jacket as best I could, lying on my back and ripping at the stupid thing. Underneath I had this woolen pullover but couldn't find a loose thread with my quivering fingers. When you want your clothes to stay mended they unravel and perforate in all directions. When you want one to fall to bits they're like chain bloody mail. I could hear the bastard scuffling below, probably loading as fast as he could. I was almost sobbing with fear. I hauled off a sock instead and bit the top end with my teeth. I caught a woolen end and began hauling, unraveling the useless malicious wool like a maniac.

"Lovejoy?"

"What?" I made my voice as even and confident as I could while yanking and jerking the sock into its original thread in terror, cursing and blaspheming under my breath.

"Lovejoy." His voice sounded modulated, carefully not needing to shout any more now that we both knew. "I don't believe you have a gun at all."

"No?"

"No."

"Why not risk it then? Come on up, you murdering bastard."

"Don't go on about Henry, Lovejoy." He sounded full of reproach. "I feel bad enough as it is."

"You have no sympathy from me, pig." I'd got a mound of wool unraveled beside me. The Pythagorean theorem. What the hell was it? The square of the hypotenuse of a right-sided triangle was equal to some bloody thing. Why don't teachers take more care with our education, the useless buggers? I was sobbing, bleeding from my shoulder, pulling like a maniac at the wool until there was nothing left of the sock and thinking that if the maniac killed me it was my old teacher's fault for not drumming his idiotic algebra into my thick skull hard enough. He'd been a lazy old swine.

"I'm coming up, Lovejoy."

"I'll shoot you, Haverro. I'm warning you."

"If you have a gun why didn't you shoot earlier?"

"Trying to give you a chance."

"Liar."

"Anyway, you've muffed it. I'll fire if you move an inch."

I'd lost the sodding frigging bullets, found them after a lunatic grovel in the dark recess. I reached up and jerked the type-list card down and bit its string through. My arm was stiffening, the useless rotten thing. Just when you need a limb it goes and gets itself shot to blazes.

The bullets were heavy and deformed. Easy to tie the cord from the cardboard notice around each until they dangled like battered cherries from a single pliant string stalk. It was about a foot long. Small, but it would have to do.

"Then you'd better be ready, Lovejoy."

"Take one step, Haverro, that's all."

I tied one end of my wool to the middle point of the cord and desperately passed the wool's entire length through my hands. The bastard was coming.

"Very well. Ready?"

In a glow, a mad spurt of oranges and crimsons, I saw him step swiftly from concealment and then dart back.

"No shot, Lovejoy?" he chuckled. "Too fast for you?"

"A little, Haverro. Do it slower and you'll regret it."

I'd reached the wool's limit. Surely to God it was long enough to reach the pendulum's wire. It felt like miles, but my hands were wet with sweat and shaking. Maybe I'd overestimated. Anyhow, there wasn't any more. A sustained glow came, silver and blues this time. He ducked out, back, then emerged finally to stand erect by the coach's rear wheel. The glow faded. A few seconds till the next fireworks salvo lit the sky.

I tied the free end of the wool to my ankle and swung the homemade bolus. As long as I kept out of the way of the wool cord as it followed the bolus in its flight—I threw. A pause. The bullets clattered on the mosaic. Missed. A sky flash came. Haverro had darted back again. I hauled on the wool to recover the bullets on their string. They cracked glass, scraped exhibits, but I kept on hauling dementedly until I had them in my hand again.

"Who's there?" Haverro said.

"Some friends," I said in a hoarse quaver. I'd fixed the position of the pendulum's metal flex and threw again. No clatter. I pulled slowly on the wool. For Christ's sake it hadn't to break. Not now that the bullets on their cord had wrapped themselves around the pendulum wire.

"Who?"

"Police," I lied. Maybe he'd believe me.

"Liar, Lovejoy. They were the bullets I fired." He laughed and I heard him step confidently out. I gave way to fear, pulling on the wool feverishly until the pendulum bob crashed a glass stand over on the gallery beneath. "Panicking now, Lovejoy?" he purred, enjoying himself. "No place to run to, I'm afraid. So sorry."

I reached out, felt the swing and grasped the lovely life-saving metal cord of the Galileo pendulum in my hand.

"Okay, Thomas," I said. "Stay there. I give in."

"Come down here." He was suspicious.

"Let me go."

"Not a chance, Lovejoy."

"You can have the Grail Tree."

"I've already got it." He sighed, sounding like they do when telling you the needle won't really hurt. But then they're always on the blunt end. "Come on. Here or there."

I had the wire. The lead weight was hanging somewhere below. Please, God. It couldn't be caught on anything, could it? Not after all this. I bit through the wool and waited.

"I'll come, Thomas. To talk." He'd never believe I'd surrender so near the thing we both coveted.

"Very well. To talk." He sounded full of smiles.

"Promise?"

"I promise, Lovejoy."

His footsteps sounded clearly on the mosaic. He was crossing the central area.

"Coming then. Stay there." With a prayer I let go and stood up. The wire jerked away and outward under the weight of the hanging lead. I took as long as I could, noisily stamping and cursing. What if he wasn't in the center? The pendulum would miss him every swing. Please make him stand there, just where the lead would hit him. At least knock him over, daze him maybe. Give me a chance. "You shot my arm, Haverro."

"I was always quite good, but of course I'm more used to a modern shotgun." His voice changed. "Hurry up, Lovejoy."

"Coming."

I started down the stairs. The pendulum would swing and return, swing and return. If he moved there was still a chance, one faint chance for each swing. As long as the fireworks didn't light it up at the wrong moment. Please, fireworks, I prayed. Don't light up the macabre scene in time for him to get out of the way.

"Jimmo's next, Lovejoy," he was saying as I reached the top of the lowest flight. "It's a bit hard on him, of course. Naturally, I'm sorrier—"

The sudden thud coincided with a burst of violet sky and the skittering sound of aerial snakes from several rockets. By the time I'd reached ground level the light had died and I couldn't see a thing. I crouched behind the staircase waiting for the next glare. If he was still on his feet and it was some trick I'd just have to try rushing him, even though it would be hopeless because he would be expecting it. Anyway, I only had one arm that was any use. There was no sound from him, no footsteps. Had I heard a clatter, a gun falling? I couldn't focus my mind any more.

The glare came and I screamed. Haverro's head was inches from mine on the ground, only his was crushed to a bloodied mess. I retched onto my own feet, quivering and heaving. Sweat dripped from my chin. I leaned back, sitting under the staircase. I'd done it. Now all I had to do was find the Grail Tree and keep out of the way of that bloody lethal pendulum.

The next burst showed me the case, lying near Haverro's body. I lifted it reverently, feeling its beautiful weight. Even in my ruinous condition the chimes it emitted shook me to my marrow. Whatever it was, it sang and pulsed inside its case stronger and with more exquisite peals than anything I'd ever met before.

I crossed to the main door, carefully walking around the edges of the rectangular mosaic for safety and carrying the case. He'd left the key in the lock after turning it—a wise move. Then nobody from outside could possibly enter, key or not. I wished I'd thought of that.

I turned the key. "Come in, Lisa, love," I called, and in came Lydia, pushing and scolding.

"Lovejoy!" she cried furiously. "Exactly what have you been up to? I've been knocking for over an hour—"

I looked beyond her into the reddish haze. Nobody.

"Where's Lisa? I told Lisa—"

"She's gone."

We went inside. I was still carrying the case. Lydia saw it. We could see each other's face in the rose red sky sheen. Distant cheers sounded. They'd lit the bonfire. Soon the big finale with the fireworks tableau. Sparks would be tumbling into the night sky. The procession would be circling, chucking torches into the flames. Some would show their bravado by dashing tangentially at the fire and throwing from close to so as to show singed eyelashes for bragging at the drinking in another hour.

Lydia left me recovering at the bookstall and went to where I pointed. "Mind the pendulum." That is, she didn't go all the way. Merely paused halfway over to the huddled mess, took one further courageous step and halted.

"Is it . . . ? Is it . . . dead?"

"Thomas. Yes."

She returned, spectacles glinting redly like a menacing figure's eyes on a Frazetta oil.

"The police."

"No."

"Whatever you say I shall phone them." She looked about. "There's a caretaker's phone along the furniture gallery." And by God there is. I'd forgotten. That explained why Thomas had come in so quietly. Despite all his confidence he couldn't afford to trap me on Gallery Six. Clever old sod. Lydia had gone. It was easy to see in the firelight. I trailed after her as fast as possible though I was badly shaken. My arm was leaking and dripping drops alongside all the way up the stairs to where Lydia was scolding the telephone for lack of cooperation. There were printed instructions but hard to read.

"No, love." I put my hand over the buttons.

"We *must*, Lovejoy."

It was precisely then that I knew we were going to die after all. A dull boom echoed through the museum. I signaled frantically for her not to speak.

"It's only the fireworks." I'd have crippled her if she hadn't whispered. "What's the matter?"

"Shhh." I listened. Somebody had entered the castle. Somebody who had no key, but who had followed Haverro or Lydia. And who now was here. They'd locked the door, because murderers always do. I heard the squeak and that horrible rumble of the ancient lock. Fireworks crack, zoosh, fazz and pop. They never, never boom. It takes a castle door to boom. Or a gun. Jesus, the gun.

"Stay here." My fright had spread to her. "Shhh!" I pointed

to her necklace which gave a soft rattle with every movement she made. Of all things it was Whitby jet, a lovely old 1830s carved effort. Why the hell did she come dressed up like that? To a fireworks outing in a park it was bloody ridiculous, high heels and stylish suit. "Stop that frigging racket," I hissed. She nodded, frightened now. Lydia held my hand, but I shook her off angrily and crept along the gallery to the Civil War section where you can see over.

A figure was crouching over Haverro. Hair glistening, shoes gleaming and watch sparkling. Two rings flashed against dull gold. I crawled away from the edge just as he glanced up and around, but maybe he had seen me. I rolled over on my side to see where Lydia was and why the hell she was creaking and rustling so much. She'd got one of her stiletto heels stuck in the bloody planks of the gallery floor.

"For Christ's *sake!*" I mouthed at her, and mimed taking a foot out and leaving the stupid shoe where it was. While she was at it I pulled her down and clawed the other shoe off as well. If she fell about when balanced on two she'd be uncontrollable wobbling on one. We crept on hands and knees into the Civil War gallery as far as we could go. That meant under the ancient silent clock and its lopsided breastplate. Lydia's jet necklace ticked a series of low rattles against the Cromwellian cannon, making me grab her and stuff the absurd beads into her clothes in a frightened rage.

A creak from below. A second while we stayed rigid. Breathless. He was coming upstairs. A third. Then a pause, with a faint tock of metal on metal. He was loading the muzzle loader. A sudden loud rattle and a roll. He'd dropped one of the spherical bullets. It had rolled down the steps and across the floor a short distance, but from the silence he wasn't worried. Therefore he had plenty. Thomas had come really well equipped and here came the evil geltie to reap the rewards.

I caught a faint glisten on the ceiling of the vaulted gallery. Lydia's ring, picking up a gleam from a last single rocket burst. I clutched her hand. She clutched me back gratefully, but I twisted away and dragged the ring.

"Diamond?" I mouthed. She gazed modestly down.

"Yes." She pulled my ear close. "From Preston's in the High Street—"

I don't believe it, I thought, marveling. She'd tell me where you get spuds on discount next. That's women, and me terrified by maniacal killers everywhere I bloody well go. I crawled one-handed to the flintlock case. No flints, but the ingredients were there, almost. I put the diamond down the glass in a horrid screaming squeak loud enough to wake the dead. A creak again. He was on the first tier now, looking stealthily along the galleries and listening for the next giveaway sound. What the hell. I rocked the diamond ring down the window again and a third time, leaned hard with my useless hand and kneed it through into the case. Too much noise now to worry. I reached and got the two little beakers. Sulfur in one, saltpeter under the bell jar because it gets sticky from collecting air moisture. No time to check they were still chemically okay. I mixed them swiftly in the inverted bell jar, stirring the powders with a finger.

"Gunpowder," I whispered in Lydia's ear. "Sulfur, charcoal and saltpeter." I had only guessed the proportions roughly when helping to arrange the display, but fat chance of weighing anything at this stage.

"Charcoal?"

"Carbon," I whispered, pleased at my one stroke of luck, the artist's charcoal drawing stick I'd brought as cover in case I got caught in the temple crypts. "I've got some," and felt in my jacket pocket. Only I'd no jacket pocket, because I'd ripped my jacket off when I'd tried to unravel my pullover. And no jacket pocket meant no artist's stick of lovely charcoal. "I've no fucking charcoal!" I screamed in an insane whisper into her aghast hot face. *"We've no frigging charcoal!"* Gunpowder won't go off without it, not properly. You only get a faint hiss and smoke everywhere. Friar Bacon knew that centuries back.

I grabbed Lydia, thinking maybe to make a run for it, but paused. Her necklace was under my hand. Beads. And jet. Jet burns, being fossilized carbon. Light and lovely precious jet.

"Gimme a nail file."

"I beg your—"

"Nail file. Quick!" I heard her fumble in her handbag. It only took a few months while those horrible creaks went on one by one. The second-level railings were creaking now under his weight. The cold nail file. I rummaged under Lydia's clothes and yanked at the necklace.

"*Lovejoy!* This is certainly no time to—"

"Shhh!"

"We should go down and discuss—"

Women. I snapped the string and began filing madly at the jet, working crazily to get it shredded into one of the beakers. He was near our level, with maybe a few steps to go. No more time. I groped for a flat stone place and crushed five or six of the larger beads under my heel, scraped the crushings into the beaker with the finer filings and poured the lot into the bell jar. I stirred the nail file frantically, even trying to hold the finished gunpowder up to the practically nonexistent light to see its color like a fool.

"Hold this. Upright. For Christ's sake, don't drop it."

I pulled on the cannon. It rumbled round. Twice I darted in front of it to check the alignment. With those old cannons, which nowadays always look absurdly small, the elevation's always a problem. I'd just have to guess. The closer he came the better, but I didn't like the thoughts of that. I snatched the bell jar and tipped it clumsily down the barrel. If the thing was spiked or blocked in some way we'd had it. The ramrod was no problem. You can chain a gun but not a ramrod, so I had scores of the bloody things, all too thin by a mile. Still it had to do. I tapped and tapped until that solid feel came. Then the ball. The fifth one fitted, but with too much windage. Anyhow, it hadn't far to go. I ripped a piece of Lydia's blouse. Another squeak, but a piece of flimsy cloth to go down the barrel on top of the ball. I rammed the lot in, breaking the thin ramrod in the process, swearing and abusing everything in sight, demented.

The last sprinkle of gunpowder I'd kept for the touchhole. I made sure the hole was clear with the tip of the nail file and poured it in.

"Match." I held out my hand.

"I beg your—"

"A frigging match," I screeched in a mad whisper. "I want a frigging match!"

"I'm afraid I don't carry—"

"*Lighter,*" I hissed.

"I'm so sorry. I don't smoke—"

"Oooh." The moan came from my very soul. Now that I could blow the castle to blazes we had no matches. The nearby flint-locks had no flints. Furniture? We were near the furniture gallery. Adjacent to my forged piece was a Sutherland table. On it was a tinder lighter, a small gadget resembling a pistol but acting exactly like a modern flint lighter. A wheel and a flint. I was up and rushing before I knew what I was doing. I snatched up an attendant's chair and smashed it through the window case. God knows what damage it did to my lovely piece, but to break fragments over the genuine stuff would have been criminal. I grabbed for the tinder lighter. A blessed flint. I raced back, ducking low. A flash and a spatter. The swine shot at me. Lydia screamed.

"There's two of us, Leyde," I howled as I ran. "We'll get you." A second shot. Glass fractured all around.

Over the landing I flung myself down beside Lydia, ripped at her blouse again and threw it away. I wanted the string bunched up.

"The necklace string!" I thought for a second I'd lost it, but she had it. I just don't believe women sometimes. Lydia was passing the gentle hours by rethreading the remains of her neck-lace on its original cord. Screaming again as quietly as I knew how I scattered the beads with a grab and folded the string.

"Dear me," Lydia whispered. I screamed silent abuse and hatred at her to keep out of the way.

Three clicks to adjust the flint and I was off, clicking sparks onto a folded piece of Lydia's blouse. He'd have to reload. My hands were trembling so much I was practically useless. Clicks shed sparks, but it seemed an age before the lovely aroma of smoldering cloth rose. I put the cord in, still clicking sparks down.

It caught. There was a red erosion starting in the cloth. I held the string to the spreading spark and blew and blew. That pure delicious scent of smoldering string came and I subsided in ecstasy. I had it all together, the touch match, the cannon and now the time. For that split second I didn't care. Not a damn. Even if Leyde finished ahead, I felt overjoyed I'd created a weapon from nothing under impossible circumstances. I looked up to see Lydia thoughtfully spreading the smoldering remains of her torn blouse on the cannon's barrel to beat it out. That restored me again to sheer screeching abuse from terror.

"You'll explode the frigging thing!" I hissed, pulling it away and flinging it aside.

"But it was a present from—"

I pulled her to me by the throat and thrust my face furiously at hers.

"Lydia. One more fucking word from you. That's all."

"Well, really!"

"Shut up!"

My rage gave way to terror. The paces were loud and uncontrolled now. There was plenty of gloom about, and we had most of what there was. But the fire glow was constant. Even the alcoves caught reflections. You could see the statues and the cases lit from the sky's dull red light. He couldn't miss seeing us.

"Stay over there. When the bang sounds, run."

"Where?" she whispered.

"How the hell do I know where?" I said. "If I knew that I'd already be there, you stupid— *Any* sodding where. Just run."

"I only want to do the right thing, Lovejoy," she whispered, offended. "There's no need to—"

"Shhh."

We crouched on either side of the cannon, immobile. I'd scraped the spare grains into the touchhole by feel and had the string concealed in my hand. I reached over and squeezed Lydia's shoulder hard to say stay put. A few more paces. The gallery darkened even more. He was there. He'd come.

The double-barreled muzzle loader was at the slant. Probably a Greener, or maybe a later retailed Birmingham-proved Forsyth. Certainly it was a high-quality antique. At least there was that. He loomed in the arch leading into our gallery, waiting for his eyes to adjust. One pace more. I needed one step forward. I reached across to Lydia and pushed. She fell from her crouching position with a cry of alarm. He heard, turned slightly, saw, stepped forward. My string dipped into the hole. I fidgeted it round and round. Nothing. He raised his gun as the cannon cracked a deafening double sound. My leg was smashed between it and the wall. I was screaming now and openly as loud as I could go. Lydia was tugging feverishly at the cannon, of course the wrong way, but we finally got it off me. She looked a mess, but I suppose I was worse.

It had caught the fleshy part of my calf, miraculously leaving the bone alone. The skin was ripped in five or six places under the trouser leg.

I leaned back against the wall. There was no point in looking for Bill Leyde. I didn't even give the space where he'd last stood a single glance.

It was Lydia who rescued it all from the jaws of Maslow. She got us both reassembled, found my jacket and note pad, and incidentals like a million miles of wool. And her shoes, nail file and bits of blouse. There was no point in rubbing fingerprints off anything. I'd been putting them all over the museum for years, at the request of the curator.

We were outside in the lovely air before I spoke.

"I'm going down to the fireworks, Lydia," I told her. "I have to stand there and let Maslow see me. Can you find him, or bring at least one of his merry men?"

"Bring him to the fireworks?"

"Where they set them off. Soon as you can. Say I have some news for him."

"Will you be all right?"

She helped me across the bridge on the terrace walk. We'd left the castle door ajar after a lot of careful thought.

"Yes. We can't be seen together, you helping me along like a bloody walking wounded. Tell him I've an urgent message, that Jimmo's a witness to old Henry's killing by Dr. Haverro."

"I understand."

"And don't say anything about being in the castle. We've not been anywhere near, see?"

"Will you wait there for me?"

"Yes." I saw her look long and hard. "Promise, love," I said, which seemed to satisfy her honest little innocent soul. "One thing, Lydia. You *did* explain to Martha?"

"Exactly as you said." She glowed in the firelight with pride of a job well done. "This morning."

"And only to Martha?"

"Yes. Her niece, Dolly, was *so* interested—"

"Dolly was there too?"

"Oh, yes. We had such a lovely chat . . ." Her voice faded. "Was that all right?" she asked anxiously.

Which explained how Bill Leyde had learned. It wasn't thick stupid old Honkworth who was monitoring the search for the Grail Tree. It was the geltie, clever, quiet and self-effacing. With Dolly to collect the essential details.

I looked into Lydia's face. After all, I'd ruined her lovely necklace. And I just hadn't the heart.

"Yes. You did fine, love. Exactly right."

"I *knew* you'd be pleased," she said brightly. "Have you change for the phone, please?"

"Press the emergency button," I said brokenly.

"Oh, how exciting! I've never done that before!"

I drew breath. "Look, Lydia," I got it out. "Sorry about losing my temper in there so much. It's just that . . . well, I don't really see the need of dying."

"I quite understand, darling."

"Eh?"

She checked me over once more and trotted eagerly off. I watched her go, marveling.

That's what I like, I thought bitterly. Help. I limped down toward the huge crowd and the fireworks. I needed to get round the back of the tableau where the reserve firework cases would be stored.

The Fire Night's big finish was marred only by an accident in which one of the many helpers at the fireworks lit the trailing blue fuse prematurely. It was reported that this caused a series of explosions in which the miscreant, one Lovejoy—a well-known local antique dealer of Lovejoy Antiques, Inc.—received injuries inflicted as a result of standing too near the main fireworks tableau. Reports were profuse and critical. Injuries sustained, the reporters said, were to his left arm and right leg, cuts in several places and some facial injuries. He was allowed home after emergency treatment in the casualty department of the County Hospital. Doctors said no permanent defects were anticipated. Lovejoy has since apologized, a festival spokesman informed reporters, to the display organizers and especially to the Silver Band who were not in position in time to play the required music appropriate for the final tableau which took place five minutes ahead of schedule. Lovejoy had inadvertently caused the tableau and six reserve cases of fireworks to ignite without adequate supervision.

The miscreant when apologizing admitted his folly, but explained it had been the result of an overenthusiastic desire to help. Lovejoy Antiques, Inc., has, it was reported, promised a donation to next year's fireworks festival. Festival organizers were preparing a report on existing safety precautions in the vicinity of the bonfire site. A report by the fire services was in preparation.

Nice touch that, I thought, being driven home by Lydia from the hospital, telling the reporters I'd see Lovejoy Antiques, Inc., would make a donation, though where the money would come from . . . I was covered in traces of fireworks powder which would nullify any sinister forensic investigation of my clothes for traces of gunpowder. My injuries accounted for, I waved to Maslow glowering at the hospital gates, but only to show him my bandages. He didn't wave back, the heartless slob. That's the modern copper for you, always losing sight of justice.

Fair's fair after all. It may not be legal and it may be miles away from proper justice, but fair's very definitely and unmistakably fair. That's not too bad, as the antiques game goes.

XXI

Dawn was coming as we arrived at the cottage. I staggered out of the car and turned to thank Lydia, but she'd descended too.

"Er, well, Lydia . . ." I began.

"Inside," she said. I stared. She had my key. Somehow she'd nicked it from my coat. She scooped a letter from the doormat. No stamp, I noticed.

"If you'll just leave the case," I suggested, limping after her.

"Sit there." She dialed, leaving the door ajar so I could hear into the hall. "Hello, Mother?" Pause. "Yes. Cynthia and Mirabelle are here. Yes. Flight Five Nine." Pause. "Oh, I expect a couple of hours. They haven't announced yet." Pause. "Of *course* I'll write. Don't fuss. Bye." Click. Burr.

She came in and started taking my shoes off.

"Er, look, Lydia . . ."

"I'm going to the Channel Isles," she said happily.

"Oh, good. Er, have a good holiday—"

"*Stupid,*" she said scathingly. "I'm not *really* going. That was only a . . . front for Mother's sake."

215

"You're not?"

"I'm staying here."

She felt for hot water in the alcove, complaining in a mutter when everything ran cold.

"Er, Lydia."

"Yes."

"What happened to Lisa?"

Without turning Lydia pointed. The unstamped letter lay on the divan. I opened it with one hand and my teeth. From Lisa, saying ah well maybe some other time but good luck and ending with three kisses. Somebody had given her the push. I wondered who that somebody could be, watching Lydia boil some water. The situation wore all the signs that Lovejoy Antiques, Inc., was going to be washed and darned to within an inch of his life. Amid the preparations I tottered to the clamoring phone for an unpleasant conversation.

"Lovejoy? Lydia's mother. Sorry to ring so early."

"Oh. Look—" My anxious explanation was cut short.

"No need to account for Lydia's absence, Lovejoy," she purred. "Last evening she explained everything. I ought to say I've seriously misjudged you, Lovejoy. You were so *right* to suggest Lydia take a holiday with her old schoolfriends, to give her time to . . . well, adjust to a new occupation." I quickly realized I was being praised.

"Not at all," I said, gently kicking the door to. "I began to perceive signs of a certain . . . attachment, shall we say. It seemed wise to—"

"I do agree. So wise," she breathed. I grew reckless, remembering my previous score with her.

"Anyway," I cruised on. "I find that maturity is something far too lacking these days—"

"I'm *so* pleased to hear you say that, Lovejoy. Youth is all very well, but—"

"Well," I said happily. "I'd better get on. Thank you for ringing."

"Not at all." She didn't ring off. "I . . . I may be out your way later. Today or tomorrow. Only passing through to see a friend for coffee, that sort of thing. I may call in and thank you personally." Then she rang off.

I watched the receiver in my hand, but it just looked blank.

"Who was it?" Lydia asked, fetching a bowl to the table. "Put your hands to soak in that. I'm going to wash your face and comb your thatch."

"Er, Tinker," I said. "He's found an early penny-farthing bicycle for sale."

"How nice." She put my hands in the water. "Stay like that till I say take them out. I'm going to unpack." I soaked as she instructed.

"Unpack?" I thought a bit. "Clothes?"

"Of course, you silly," she said briskly. "Does it get very cold in the cottage at night? I've brought an extra blanket for us, till I get used to it."

"Er, look, Lydia—"

"No." She sat with me. That seductive lurch again. I was getting to know it. *"You* look for once, Lovejoy." She faced me, serious and determined. "I don't pretend to be Cleopatra. But lately I have been examining my, well, appearance. I have come to the conclusion that my figure is really quite presentable, even attractive. It pleases you to watch me. I've already observed that. Of course there's a problem."

"Which is?"

"In experience," she said gravely. "I can't pretend my experience in . . . in *carnal* matters is very profound. But my willingness will, I anticipate, be equaled by your patience."

"It will?" My head was spinning.

"Let's hope so, Lovejoy." She rose. I pulled her back with a wet hand.

"Hang on. I usually have . . . other visitors."

I'd been thinking of Jean Evans, if ever she cooled down. And Betty, who didn't need any cooling at all. And Lydia's mother, who wanted to call for reasons as yet unspecified. And Jessica, who was keen to balance our respective books. And Sarah, who I liked now I'd got used to all that high breeding. And . . . and Lydia had a scrap on her hands if she stayed. I sighed. Some days things are just too much. Lydia was smiling.

"I'm quite looking forward to those confrontations," she informed me earnestly. "In any arrangements between kindred souls, disputations appear an inevitable characteristic. Under your influence, Lovejoy, I am persuaded that attraction is inseparable from conflict—"

There was more of this junk.

"No," I said finally. "No, Lydia. I couldn't stand the aggro. You're lovely, but—"

"Oh, but you can," she said, all smiles. "I'm going to be good for you, Lovejoy. In every way. You can't send me away. Or else." I thought about that, but she had no cards left to play.

"Or else what?"

She was smiling, absolutely confident.

I suddenly stood up, yelping at the pain. It had gone. "The case." The little box carrying the Grail Tree. I'd kept hold of it until I was taken into Casualty. Then I'd given it to Lydia for safety. "Where is it?" I screamed. "What have you done with it?"

"Safe, darling." She put her arms around me happily. "Perfectly safe. I'm keeping it for you."

"Where is it?" I sank, groaning. "Oh, hell fire." See what I mean about women?

"In a month you'll be convinced of my . . . attributes, darling," Lydia said calmly. "If I haven't persuaded you that I am exactly what you need, Lovejoy, I will fully deserve to be banished. A month is a perfectly fair trial period. Do you agree, darling?"

I thought and thought while Lydia waited, smiling compassionately. There was no other way.

"And then you'll give it me, no matter what?"

"I promise," she said seriously, placing her hand on her heart. I watched her hand and her heart. She did have a lovely heart. I swallowed. "Agreed, Lovejoy?"

I managed to say it third go. "Agreed, Lydia."

"Lydia, *darling,*" she corrected.

"Lydia, darling," I said at last. She clapped her hands delightedly. "There's only one thing, love," I asked. "Will you, er, answer the door when people call? I don't feel up to many visitors just yet.''

Trapped, I listened helplessly to her singing as she brewed up, honestly not knowing whether to hate or admire her. You can't beat a woman for trickery.

I don't think they'll ever learn to be honest and fair-minded, like me.

FOR THE BEST IN PAPERBACKS, LOOK FOR THE

In every corner of the world, on every subject under the sun, Penguin represents quality and variety—the very best in publishing today.

For complete information about books available from Penguin—including Pelicans, Puffins, Peregrines, and Penguin Classics—and how to order them, write to us at the appropriate address below. Please note that for copyright reasons the selection of books varies from country to country.

In the United Kingdom: For a complete list of books available from Penguin in the U.K., please write to *Dept E.P., Penguin Books Ltd, Harmondsworth, Middlesex, UB7 0DA.*

In the United States: For a complete list of books available from Penguin in the U.S., please write to *Consumer Sales, Penguin USA, P.O. Box 999— Dept. 17109, Bergenfield, New Jersey 07621-0120.* Visa and MasterCard holders call 1-800-253-6476 to order all Penguin titles.

In Canada: For a complete list of books available from Penguin in Canada, please write to *Penguin Books Canada Ltd, 10 Alcorn Avenue, Suite 300, Toronto, Ontario, Canada M4V 3B2.*

In Australia: For a complete list of books available from Penguin in Australia, please write to the *Marketing Department, Penguin Books Ltd, P.O. Box 257, Ringwood, Victoria 3134.*

In New Zealand: For a complete list of books available from Penguin in New Zealand, please write to the *Marketing Department, Penguin Books (NZ) Ltd, Private Bag, Takapuna, Auckland 9.*

In India: For a complete list of books available from Penguin, please write to *Penguin Overseas Ltd, 706 Eros Apartments, 56 Nehru Place, New Delhi, 110019.*

In Holland: For a complete list of books available from Penguin in Holland, please write to *Penguin Books Nederland B.V., Postbus 195, NL-1380AD Weesp, Netherlands.*

In Germany: For a complete list of books available from Penguin, please write to *Penguin Books Ltd, Friedrichstrasse 10-12, D-6000 Frankfurt Main 1, Federal Republic of Germany.*

In Spain: For a complete list of books available from Penguin in Spain, please write to *Longman, Penguin España, Calle San Nicolas 15, E-28013 Madrid, Spain.*

In Japan: For a complete list of books available from Penguin in Japan, please write to *Longman Penguin Japan Co Ltd, Yamaguchi Building, 2-12-9 Kanda Jimbocho, Chiyoda-Ku, Tokyo 101, Japan.*